Death Dreams Deluxe
The Complete Works
of Chris Robertson

Death Dreams Deluxe

© 2015

ISBN-13: 978-0-9861114-5-7

<u>Contents</u>

1. The Thing in the Cage

It was not at first, an unusual Friday afternoon in any regard. Dan had already mentally departed from work, envisioning himself shutting down his computer and leaving it all far behind for the duration of a weekend. When five o'clock did come Dan wasted no time in leaving, casting a quick wave and a smile as he strode silently out to his car. He had no weekend plans, but this was the very definition of freedom. "One is not truly free," he reasoned, "Until he has reached a state of blissful boredom."

Later while he drove a plan came to him, as a sudden flash of perception within his mind. It was the peaceful euphoria of solitude that he desired most. Without hesitation he determined that he would remove himself from the masses of people, for a night of solitary comfort within the woodlands north of town.

In less than an hour he had packed (for he kept all camping supplies and foodstuffs readily at hand), dressed for the weather, and packed all of this along with his tent into the car. Some of his neighbors were still arriving home as he backed out of his driveway. He offered a few half-hearted acknowledgments to any of them who looked in his direction.

"Yes, yes," he thought, feeling the burdens of modern life begin to seep away as the houses became fewer and fewer, and each of the roads he turned upon more desolate.

And then there it was; the dirt lot off to the side of the road. Behind it was the trailhead and nothing but glorious trees for mile after mile. There were four other vehicles, one of them having recently arrived, as the owners still busied with unpacking. He parked as far away from them as the lot would allow and turned his back upon them as he unloaded. Within moments he was carrying all of his gear and leaving the other campers behind as he departed.

"Glorious, glorious," he thought as the enormous old growth trees surrounded him, and he trekked determinedly toward his goal; the point where he could depart from the worn trail and step through the wall of thick brush and into the spacious pines that grew beyond.

He passed no one on the main trail and was soon at the point where he could break away; stepping from the well-worn dirt path and into the growth beyond. He smiled broadly as the thick branches enveloped him. Their pliable girth first resisted him and then gave way, before swinging back to their original posture and leaving no trace that he had passed to the beyond.

From that point onward the journey in Dan's mind was perceptibly altered. It was as though the wall of thick brush he had passed through was a literal barrier to the now distant world that contained his problems. The knot in his guts untwisted a bit and he knew that soon he would be free of discomfort altogether.

Dan looked toward the sun and it still showed early evening. Yes, he could feel it now distinctly as he walked on; the knot was beginning to melt away. His legs were strong and his wind fair, and he did not anticipate any problems.

He kept the arc of the setting sun roughly aligned with his left shoulder so that his direction remained northward. But roughly is a relative measurement, and he did not ponder this as a point of concern. His mind was too full of the pleasantries of solitude and agreeable sensations.

And so it was when darkness was only an hour into the future that Dan came to a seemingly older growth section of the forest. It was not especially remarkable, except to say that the trees had changed to old and gnarled conifers and the undergrowth had all but disappeared. And it was darker as less light penetrated the canopy overhead. Soon Dan walked beneath the twisted limbs, upon brown pine needles which had accumulated over the seasons of many years. This new area of the forest brought with it an even more profound tranquility because he sensed inherently that human footsteps had not passed over these grounds for many years.

It was with this generally blank frame of mind that Dan followed the openness along the trunks of the massive trees until he emerged quite some distance later into an area abruptly void of vegetation. The openness of the place shocked him as strongly as a sudden slap upon his face. Man had been here after all, or so it now seemed apparent.

The space was perfectly rectangular, and within the space was a metallic cage encompassing a peculiar design. It was like no cage which Dan had seen previously, with thick uneven bars which appeared welded at random on a formation which lacked precision and symmetry.

"The work certainly of an old-world blacksmith," he pondered, "but why here in this distant forest and what purpose could it possibly serve?"

It was with these questions in mind that he stood transfixed and pondering, when he first saw the shape that was occupying the space within a far corner. To Dan's brain it seemed immediately similar to the irregular structure of the cage. That is to say, peculiar and purposefully elusive. Appearing simply as a mass of hair and leather-like tissue upon the welded floor, perhaps asleep or now long dead, he could not at present say.

"An orangutan certainly," he thought as his brain wanted badly to believe this conclusion, because it would have provided the first bits of comprehension to such a surreal finding here in the woods. But no, he realized quickly, that simply was not an orangutan, despite his desire for it to be so.

And then some limb of the animal-mass showed movement, as some appendage perhaps sniffed at the air. Yes, it could not be denied, for the thing now smelled him and began to rouse itself as such into some unique version of a wakeful state. He could only watch in frozen horror, with his camping gear now long forgotten upon his back, as the hairy mass began to rise. He felt certain that it arose for the sole purpose of investigating the new scent which had stumbled into its domain.

The odor of the thing could not be denied any more than the sheer ugliness of its form. For as it rose and uncurled from the heap in which it had lain (perhaps for years?) and the limbs extended one after the other, the air was filled with a stretch to which the degree of foulness was as yet unmatched by Dan's memory.

The thing at last arose fully and displayed its true shape. It was some hair covered bipedal ape-like creature whose head appeared to be missing. Yes, it could not be denied, as the thing stepped toward the edge of the cage wall beyond which Dan stood transfixed: it was a walking ape without a perceptible cranial appendage.

When it reached the cage wall they stood facing one another (if the thing did in fact possess a face) and it neither grabbed the bars nor attempted to reach for him.

Dan's fear did not subside, but he did gather himself enough to step backward slightly into the path at the base of the pine trees which had so randomly drawn him to the peculiar location.

This new vantage point gave a new perspective, and he now saw that the limbs of the surrounding trees grew to within arm's length of the beast at all sides of the cage. The plant life had been picked away by the horrid mass of hair with appendages, reasoned Dan. But then it occurred to him that perhaps the growth of the trees was somehow naturally repelled by the awful stench of the beast.

The creature stood there looking upon Dan (if a creature with no visible head or face can in fact look), and a new sensation began within his being. It was a new form of tranquility, somehow intermingled with new desire. It was the strong urge for *friendship* with this abominable thing that resided within the cage. Or perhaps put more accurately, it was an allure that pulled upon him, urging him to acquiesce to a subliminal request that somehow originated from the creature's being.

The desire pulled quite strongly. Yes, and it was benevolent Dan now felt certain, and so he began to extend a hand toward the thing behind the bars. The creature remained upright, moving only to push its chest closer toward the bars until it rested against them and then *squished* somewhat through. This patch upon the upper torso of the thing began to moisten and glisten, emitting some sort of nectar that removed all memories of the other, abhorrent odor, and beckoned Dan closer still. His nostrils and mind were filled with the wonderful new scent of this thing, elated even, as he took another step toward the bars.

"I simply must befriend this lonely creature," he thought, and as his arm was nearly within reach of the beast, a bird flew suddenly from the thicket, its trajectory apparently predetermined as it literally crashed into the oozing chest of the thing.

The hairy beast then snapped into motion and clutched the bars in ecstasy, its chest churning and writhing like a wave filled ocean as the bird now seemingly aware of its fatal mistake shrieked and cawed. The death cries of the poor bird were for naught, as it remained momentarily stuck like a fly upon paper before the oozing flesh waves enveloped it fully, and it disappeared into the cavity within the beast's torso.

This was the horror that Dan witnessed, made all the more vile due to the certainty that he had been inches away from a similar fate. He cowered backward into the safety of the trail beneath the ancient confers, all the while staring at the awfulness standing heedlessly in the cage.

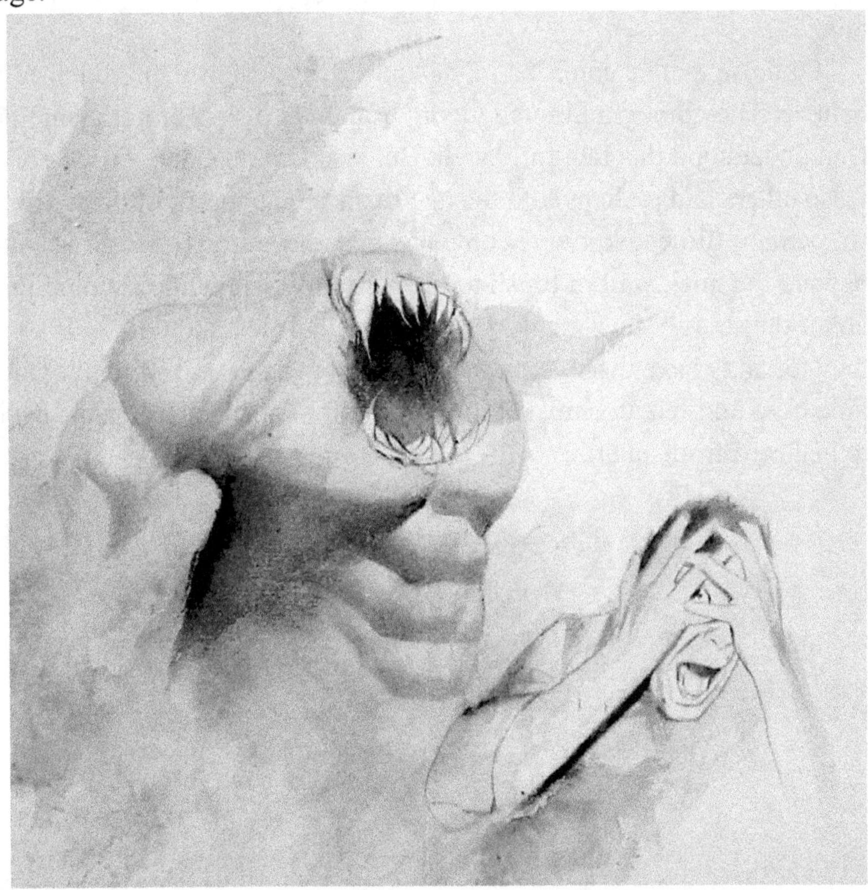

No further answers presented themselves; not the origin of the creature or how it had become permanently entrapped in the peculiar welded structure. Nor the age of the thing, or the people that had found this to be the final solution to the problem which the beast had presented. And so, without any answers to these questions apparently forthcoming, Dan retreated hastily in his state of confusion back from whence he had come. Darkness was almost total when at last he found his way back to the thick wall of brush that allowed him to emerge once again onto the main path from which he had fled.

The knot of tension had returned to his belly. It was now however, a form of tension quite like that which he had initially left behind. This tension would not soon depart. Not during the first weeks as he tried to forget the thing within the cage in silence, and then thereafter as he attempted to release himself of the burden by relaying the story to others.

Of those that he confided in, he knew that most of them did not believe. They thought him the victim of mental illness or hallucination. Dan understood this fact fully well. But also Dan wondered if one of these others had perhaps told the tale to an acquaintance of their own. If so, perhaps these unknown people had become curious enough to walk beyond the thick wall of brush to the north of town, while keeping the arc of the setting sun roughly aligned with their left shoulder… If so they too may have discovered the peculiar open space beyond the old pine trees and felt an empathetic yearning for friendship, perhaps never to be heard from again….

2. Dr. Baetki and the Nirvana Device

Dr. Baetki looked at his invention, and then out of the pseudo window of his minus-third floor laboratory. During the first year after installation, he had complained about the falseness of the pseudo windows. During the next two years he had then tolerated them. Now he found their illusion oddly comforting.

"Will they say the same of this device?" Dr. Baetki wondered as he returned his gaze toward it, setting there on the table. He had not had natural sleep for fifteen days, but he felt remarkably rested. The device certainly did the job that it was intended to.

He looked at the phone upon the table, next to the device, indecisively.

"No, I fear that they will curse the day they first heard of it, and equate the name "Baetki" with the utmost disdain." He missed the taste of coffee.

The pseudo window showed a bit of lightning off in the distance. It was a mirror image of the true weather three floors above. "It's only a matter of time," he reasoned. "It's either me now or someone else in the near future. Why shouldn't it be me and the shareholders of Salatech, Inc. that get rich from it?"

He thought again of the absent coffee taste, then stood to make the call that would notify his employers of the completion of the device. "May God help them…"

***

"Carlton please join us in the conference room," said the department manager. Thomas Carlton set down his soda near the keyboard and arose to join the others.

"Another motivational speech, or another motivational book for us to read?" scoffed colleague Bretowski quietly to Thomas before they entered.

Inside the room all of Finance was already there, and most of Customer Service. Thomas saw a series of small machines covering the table. The others continued to file in. And there was one face unknown to him standing against the wall near the corner. Thomas determined that the unknown man's countenance was one of observation.

"This is a big day for Tacklesmith, Incorporated" said the manager when both departments were in. "No doubt you've heard these past two weeks of the Nirvana device invention. We have gathered to announce that the Tacklesmith board of directors, and the core management lead team, have approved the largest capital expenditure request in the corporation's fifty-six year history. All of the Finance Department and the Customer Service Department have been selected from our location to receive the devices."

Thomas looked around nervously as cheers and applause filled the packed room. "*It makes them feel special,*" realized Thomas. "*I suppose everyone wants to be on a winning team.*"

"With this investment it is hoped by upper management that all employees will be able to perform at the peak of their ability, at all times," said the manager. "Each employee will be responsible for their assigned Nirvana, just as those of you with laptops are currently for those assets."

"So it will help us with our sleep?" asked Martha the blond from Customer Service. "From what I've heard about it, the machine will help us with our sleep, right?"

"That's right," said the department manager with utmost assurance. "It will make the sleep you get even more beneficial to your mind and body. For instance if you sleep for six hours while enacting the device, you might feel as though you've slept for nine hours instead of six. You can feel fully refreshed each day, and give each day your very best working performance. You can even use them during your lunch break if you like."

Thomas observed that awkward confusion had spread across the faces of the room.

"Pardon me sir," said Angela from Customer Service, "but how could we use a sleeping aid during a thirty minute lunch break?"

The department manager seemed to lose momentarily his composure, and then regained it quickly as he began to speak. Thomas observed that the unknown man in the suit against the wall seemed to be watching silently with vehement interest.

"That's a great question Angela," said the department manager. "We will be converting the vacant cubicle area upstairs, and some of the file storage area, into short term sleeping quarters." He paused to let the announcement sink in. To his left, against the wall, the unknown man stood motionless.

"The space will be occupied by single occupancy cubicle-type rooms, equipped with sofa-type cots, and a table for personal effects and the Nirvana devices."

"What if we over sleep?" asked Martha as she shuffled her index finger from one side of her mouth to the other.

"Oh, that can't happen," said the department manager, "the device has alarm type capability. But lunch use is completely optional – but it will be an option. The majority of your use of the device will be at home. Essentially it's a time-saving invention. It simply accelerates the chemical, molecular effect of natural sleep. It is medication free and includes no side effects or health detriments whatsoever. Formerly about one-third of all of our lives were spent sleeping. Now that non-value added time will be greatly reduced."

After the meeting Bretowski approached Thomas in his cubicle within the Finance department. There was some apprehension on his face.

"So why would the corporation invest its largest capital expenditure of all time into devices that help us sleep better?" said Bretowski.

"The answer is the same as it always is," answered Thomas quietly. "Efficiencies."

The next day was a hailstorm of activity. The Nirvana devices were each given asset tags, and the asset numbers were recorded into the fixed asset register to begin depreciation of the capitalized purchases. The asset numbers were then cross referenced to each associate by name and recorded by the Human Resources department, at which time they were distributed to the workforce.

As Thomas walked from the conference room with his device under his arm, he noticed some outside contractors installing large monitors at the center of the Customer Service department. They were facing opposite directions so that one would be visible at all times.

"What is the purpose of those?" asked Thomas to the blond Martha quietly.

"They'll display the length of time we're processing orders or on the phone helping a customer, or something," she answered with seeming indifference.

"The changes just keep on coming," said Thomas.

"Oh that's not all of it," said Martha. "They're also adjusting our start times. They're going to be more staggered or something, so we can use the Nirvanas during our lunch breaks if we choose to. And we're allowed to work longer than eight hours if it is approved by management."

Thomas nodded his head and walked away with his device. Back in the Finance department things were a bit more like a usual day. Month-end was upon them and there wasn't time to focus on anything except working to close the month.

That night at home, Thomas sat silently and ate his dinner across from his fiancé. She was quite a good cook, and had made a new skirt steak recipe, garnished with green onions and soy sauce. Stabbing the green onions first, and then pieces of steak, seemed to help dissolve his thoughts of work.

"I think it's good," said his fiancé Linda of the meal.

"Yes, it's very good," answered Thomas.

"Is the month-end close particularly hard?" she asked.

"Oh, no," he replied, "It's fine. It's just these new changes at work. The Nirvana devices they've issued, new time monitoring devices, and extended shifts in the Customer Service…"

"But it doesn't affect you," said Linda. "You don't have to… *sleep with* one of those machines…" She gave a bit of a giggle as she spoke the words.

"Well… I didn't think I'd be given one, but I have."

"Oh," she said, "When do you get it?"

"I already have it. It's in the trunk of my car. I'd be content to leave it there but I should probably…"

A text came through then on his phone, sounding the chime. Thomas walked to the mounted ledge where he kept his phone and wallet and read the message.

"It's from Davis, the Finance Manager. It reads... *'We're going to try something new this month. Going to try and reduce the 7 day accounting close to only 5 – all regions affected not just us. Email to be sent with time schedule. Mandatory to read tonight.'*"

Thomas felt as though he had been punched in the stomach by an invisible antagonist. It must have showed upon his face he judged, per the response given to him by his fiancé.

"Well at least we didn't have anything planned tonight," she said comfortingly.

"I don't think it would have mattered if we did." He set the phone down and then took his seat to continue eating.

After a few moments Linda spoke. "So are they working through the night?"

"Maybe. The email will explain it. I'll logon when we're done."

"So they intend to have you sleep with the machine this evening, before the work begins?" This time she did not giggle at the wording.

"I would imagine. Me and everyone else in the department. Maybe not the clerks… but maybe them too." And then after a few moments of silence, "It is a good recipe Linda."

After the meal he hesitated a moment before removing the laptop computer from the carrying bag. The time was 6:45. Soon after he had logged in, he heard the texting chime of his cellphone. It was Bretowski stating, *"Seriously???? Hockey playoffs start tonight!"*

Thomas thought for a second and then replied "Haven't read the email – logging on now."

The email wasn't difficult to decipher, but the message was peculiar. It read, "We're continuing work again on month-end close tonight at 10:00 p.m. Eastern. Recommended to use your Nirvana sleeping device for at least one hour between now and then. We plan to work until 2:00 a.m., resuming work as normal at the office tomorrow at normal time. Recommended to use your Nirvana devices after work is concluded at

2:00 a.m. This new schedule to continue until month-end Accounting close is completed."

Thomas sat silently in disbelief. It was small consolation that he had seen this coming from the very beginning. He, unlike the others, had not been fooled.

"Looks like I'll be working a lot of hours for a couple of days," he called to Linda. "And I'd better try that damned device and catch a nap."

Not long after he and Linda sat side by side on their bed after having read the device's instructions. "It seems straightforward," said Linda. "It should guide you to sleep using electromagnetic waves….*harmlessly.*"

"Harmlessly," scoffed Thomas. "Yes, no downside at all…whatsoever."

"It says that you'll awake feeling refreshed right at the programmed time." Her voice had a tone of consolation. "Close will be done in a few days. If this device works, it could be a good thing I suppose."

Thomas did not share his suspicions of worse to come. Instead he acquiesced and lay down, pulling the attachment device over his forehead. He and Linda had already set the time for waking.

"Don't forget the Go button," said Linda.

"You push it," said Thomas. She did so and then turned out the light.

***

There was a mild annoyance when the waking chimes began roughly one hour later. Thomas felt the peacefulness of the sleep recede and then disintegrate. He blinked awake and removed the device from his forehead. By the time his feet touched the floor all of the haziness had faded. Thomas looked at the clock with disbelief. It read 8:36. Logically he knew that it was the same evening in which he had recently lain down, but the restfulness of his mind and cognitive sharpness seemed to dispute this.

When he stepped into the living room he saw Linda sitting before the television winding down from her long day. She looked beautiful, and tired.

"She's going to love being engaged to a professional with a corporate-sponsored Nirvana device!" he thought.

***

Eight weeks later Thomas walked past Bretowski's empty cubicle en route to his own. Thomas caught his reflection in the spotless glass of the conference room and liked what he saw. He had upgraded his wardrobe and now always found time to press his slacks and shirts. No more business casual. He was going to look as flawlessly as he felt.

Taking on Bretowski's work was a burden, but it was now easily managed. The twenty percent pay increase he had received was practically free money, now that there was no reason he couldn't be at his best each and every working hour.

Later that morning a business matter took him out of the Finance department and over to Customer Service. Martha the blond was gone now too. Thomas looked up at the monitors and saw that there were two available Customer Service representatives awaiting a call or other business function. *"That's two employees too many,"* he thought, and knew that it was only a matter of time until the staff would be right-sized.

When the "office" portion of the workday concluded at 5:30 p.m. Thomas drove home to prepare for his evening M.B.A. classes. *"No reason not to attain an M.B.A. now,"* he thought. *"Heck, maybe even a Doctorate..."*

***

Dr. Baetki sat inside of his research laboratory as the pseudo window displayed what nature was doing just thirty feet above. His corporate award and letter of nomination for the Nobel Prize lay amidst the other documents on his desk.

He had been watching the television financial market report. It seemed that the stock markets were at record highs, but so was the level of new unemployment. *"Wait until consumer spending decreases from all of the unemployment,"* thought Dr. Baetki with melancholy. *"These idiots are smiling about the stock prices now, but in just six months they'll understand..."*

3. The Sickness

The sky had darkened greatly from the brilliant blue of their departure the previous morning. Jonathon attributed the change to an increase in altitude, as the carriage slowly climbed the ever rising northbound road. He shared this reasoning with his fiancée Melinda, thinking that surely it was the gloominess of the sky that had caused her mood to have fallen. Melinda politely agreed, and then returned to sitting in silence.

Jonathon drew back the curtain of the carriage window to view the changing landscape. Outside, the fog of the hills had grown dense around them, and now encapsulated the carriage as it rolled onward. He looked to Melinda to see if she had seen it also, but she had not turned her head.

Then, as though they were made to withdraw from a peaceful dream, the fog rapidly dissipated and the carriage emerged into the cleared air. Jonathon saw the shape of a small village through the tiny window, and then opened the portal to address the driver.

"Query the first man you see," he shouted through the tilted glass.

"Aye," yelled the driver, who had intended this action already. "Pardon sir," the driver called out minutes later, when the horses had come to a halt. "How far to the manor of Baron Edmonson?"

The man of the village looked at them in silence a moment, and then turned his gaze from the driver, into the open carriage door from which Jonathon peered. The eyes, it seemed to Jonathon, looked beyond him to beautiful Melinda.

"Ten miles," said the man, as he gazed back upon the driver and pointed onward down the road. The carriage driver offered no thanks, but sent the horses trotting onward immediately, straight through the village as the man had directed.

Jonathon delayed closing the door so as to watch the stranger until they had passed. He saw the man's eyes upon his own as the carriage rolled by, and thought he saw in them perhaps a message left unspoken.

"Perhaps my uncle is not well liked amongst the commoners," he said to Melinda when the door was again closed. To this remark she sullenly shrugged an agreement.

The terrain was now dominated by stone, and was seemingly unfit for farming. The road wound around the masses of rock and soon small peaks could be seen at either side. "It's the beginning of the mountain ranges of the north country," said Jonathon cheerily, still attempting to lift Melinda from her mood.

The castle of his uncle's residence appeared suddenly as they emerged from a channel within the bedrock. The castle appeared to Jonathon as more magnificent than he had imagined. The dwelling differed little from the surrounding peaks, from which the stone had been quarried for its construction long ago.

Light was visible within the windows, and this seemed to Jonathon a wonderful sight after the weariness of the prolonged travel.

"We arrive," he said to Melinda, with the excitement of his relative youth revealing itself in his tone. She leaned over him to peer for herself, through the window upon his side.

"It is different than I pictured," she replied, and then looked onward further in silence.

The carriage came to rest upon the cobbled stones that led directly to the castle door. Melinda stepped out as Jonathon guided her, and saw a servant who had emerged from within. He was a man of dark complexion, mature but not elderly, and a countenance bearing no warmth. He wore a collarless black shirt and displayed despite his manual employment, an appearance of acute cleanliness.

Melinda made all of these observations in a mere instant and had then quickly looked away. The servant's eyes produced within her an uneasiness, and so she looked instead to the familiar face of her loved one.

Melinda noticed the chill of the air, and this dark place seemed to her as being very cold. Never before had she been surrounded by such multitudes of stone. Likewise, she realized also, the complete absence of anything green.

Jonathon finished his duties with the driver who then departed without a word. The young couple stood upon the cold granite stones looking at the servant who observed them in silence.

The strange dark man took the pieces of luggage from the ground and turned to reenter the dwelling. Jonathon and Melinda looked to each other, and then followed him through the large entryway door.

The room before them was impressive, although not extravagant be any means. A large fire blazed invitingly in a hearth across the room. Most appealing, it seemed to Melinda, was the pale marble which covered the floor, illuminated by the soft light of the oil lamps. The pale flooring provided the large room with a much needed deviation from the gray of the stone walls.

"Welcome nephew Jonathon," spoke a warm voice from the height of the stairway, as they turned to meet the sound. There stood, somewhat above them, a short man in a perfectly tailored brown jacket. He wore a slender mustache that seemed to improve the appearance of droopiness around his eyes. Perhaps it was the earthy color of his jacket, but he seemed to Melinda like the pale marble floor, a pleasant distraction from a dreary scene.

"I have looked very forward to your arrival ever since receiving your acceptance to my invitation," said the Baron, who began to descend the stairway with a quick stride, while retaining the initial elegance displayed. Jonathon saw that the Baron held a strong resemblance to his own deceased father, although their statures were not the same.

"Hello Uncle," said Jonathon with affection and joy that he could not hide. Both of his parents had died of illness years ago, and he had been since effectively without family.

The gaze of the Baron returned a similar affection and a clear lightening of the heart. When the Baron stood upon the floor before them, he outstretched his arm and shook the firm hand of his brother's son. "Ah yes, but I am being rude," said the Baron after a few moments had passed between them. "Surely this young lady is your beautiful fiancée. Hello madam."

"This is Melinda," said Jonathon.

"I am pleased to meet you sir," she said. His charm did put her at ease.

"Come," the Baron said, "Let us acquaint ourselves properly over dinner, after you have had time to freshen up from your travels. I apologize, but it has become my custom to eat nightly at this extremely late hour." The Baron led them up the stairway to separate but adjacent bedrooms. "Please take as much time as you would like," he instructed, "I'll await you down at the hearth."

Melinda finished her preparations quickly, and then sat in an ornate chair amidst the hall near Jonathon's door. It was not long before Jonathon emerged also, and both rejoined the Baron below. He led them promptly through an archway to the dining room, after checking his pocket watch for the time.

The dark servant reappeared and seated them at a dark wooden table of enormous size. The Baron sat at the end, and the couple near him at each of his sides.

"That is my humble servant Alawald," said the Baron, after they had been served plates of roasted quail, and the servant had withdrawn from the room. "His wife Lucinda serves here also. I have instructed her to be available to you, my dear, as you may need," said the Baron to Melinda.

"We are not as isolated here as you might believe," spoke the Baron again after a moment of pleasant silence. "This quail comes from the village folk, whom Alawald visits once per week. The northern side of our location holds many more villages than you passed on the south."

"Do you still engage in export to Europe, Uncle?" asked Jonathon.

"Ah, no," the Baron answered, "Those years have long since passed. I did not wish to continue after a…dispute with my partner and friend. The days of greatest profit had already passed also, and I did not have the desire to continue." A bit of the charm seemed to have left the Baron's demeanor when he spoke of these years past. "I hope that you have found the accommodations to be of comfort?" he then said to Melinda, as he withdrew his watch again from the pocket of his jacket.

"Yes, my room is very nice," she answered, "As is the entire castle."

"Splendid," said the Baron, and then stood suddenly from the table. "Please excuse me," he announced, "there is a task I must attend to. Alawald will show you to the library when you have finished your meal. I'll rejoin you in a short while." The Baron then departed in his dignified manner, leaving a half eaten meal, through a plain door at the far side of the room.

"Your uncle is a very kind man," said Melinda.

"Yes," Jonathon answered as he looked at the distant plain door, and then toward the entryway to the kitchen to see if Alawald stood in attendance. "Did you notice that there were downward stairs beyond that door?" he asked quietly as he leaned in toward her.

"No," she replied.

"Yes. He went downward. I can't imagine what task my uncle would have below living quarters," said Jonathon. But it seemed to Melinda to be a trivial matter, and she moved their conversation onward.

"Would you like to wait in the library?" asked Alawald, immediately after he had cleared the plates. There was no offering of tea, and it seemed to both Melinda and Jonathon, as though dinner's completion had been hurried.

But as Alawald opened the door to the library, both became occupied fully with the beauty of the room, and set to browsing around. This room was the most charming yet, of which they had seen within the castle. The appearance of the dark stone floors was warmed somewhat by a large luxurious rug with a deep, golden color. It matched very well, it seemed to Melinda, the leather bindings upon most of the hundreds of books upon the shelves. An abundance of oil lamps were hung about the room, providing a perfect atmosphere for reading.

"Beautiful," said Melinda as she strolled leisurely upon the rug, enjoying the ambiance of the room.

"Yes," said Jonathon as he browsed more closely around the book cases, "And such a fine odor… like aged leather complimented superbly with the sweet mustiness of old paper. My father was a reader also, although we had nothing as grand as this." After a few minutes he withdrew a book from one of the shelves and sat in one of the leather chairs at the center.

Melinda soon began to yawn and looked at her fiancé with an apologetic look. "I'm sorry dear, but I must get some rest," she said. Jonathon closed his book and set it upon the table, stating that he would see her to her room. The door opened just as he had risen, displaying the well dressed form of his uncle. Behind him the servant woman entered also, halting once inside the room.

"I hope you have been fairly entertained," said the Baron as he strode to stand at their side.

"Indeed sir," answered Melinda, "It is a wonderfully beautiful room."

"Yes, but Melinda is ready for bed, I think," said Jonathon, "I'll be back just as soon as I've walked her to her door."

"Allow Lucinda, my servant," said the Baron, "It will enable you to tell her anything that you might need." With this elegant imposition the Baron raised his hand, at which the servant Lucinda held open the door.

"Goodnight," said Jonathon," to which Melinda did not reply, though certainly due only to awkwardness. Instead she looked to the Baron and wished him goodnight before departing. Both men watched her beautiful young figure as she exited the room.

"It is pleasing to me, to have the health of youth in my home again," said the Baron when they were alone and comfortably seated.

"Forgive me uncle," said Jonathon, "But I know very little about your life here. My father rarely spoke of you. I know only that you and he had a falling out."

"Yes," said the Baron, "It was about money, as are most family squabbles. The details are not important now, but I did keep abreast of his goings on, as the years progressed. That is how I knew of you, dear boy, although I must apologize for not acquainting with you sooner."

"That is no matter now, uncle," said Jonathon. "We were very happy to receive your invitation."

"Yes, but you see," said the Baron, "I do have an ulterior motive. For when my wife died three years ago, I spent much of my time in a drunken stupor. I thought many times of ending my life, until I at last found again my faith. I reconnected with God stronger than I had ever done so as a younger man. And so, recently I thought of my dead brother and wished greatly for reconciliation. But alas, he had already passed, and so I must erase my mistakes through his son, and his wife to be. Do you understand, dear boy?"

"I do," said Jonathon earnestly.

"This is why I have inquired about you, and invited the both of you here when I learned you soon would marry. And now as a devout man of God I am obligated, to ensure that your marriage begins as a holy union, free of the sins of lascivious youth." The Baron looked into the face of his nephew with a face as stoic as the cold granite walls around them.

"I see uncle," said Jonathon with his prior earnestness, although with a bit more reservation. "We are both devout Catholics ourselves, that is to say, both Melinda and I. Perhaps I have given you the wrong impression, having traveled here with her as my fiancée. But you see I am without any family as you know, and Melinda was raised and schooled at a convent after her parents died. It is for these reasons that we have not yet married, and the ever present lack of money."

"There is a priest in the village to the north," said the Baron immediately, "I can send for him if it would be easier for the both of you, but I insist that you both confess your carnal sins. If you do so, with utmost truth, I will give you the funding to begin your virtuous lives."

"Uncle," stammered young Jonathon, "truly you are a generous man. But I tell you truthfully…"

"And Melinda?" interrupted the Baron, "Surely a young woman so beautiful..."

"Uncle I implore you!" snapped Jonathon, "I tell you now, she left the convent only two weeks ago, after which she took a room from an elderly aunt."

The Baron looked at his nephew with ferocious determination. "I shall give you the monetary gift regardless, my dear boy, I simply request that you honor my beliefs and confess to the priest. No one shall be any the wiser."

"I swear uncle," said Jonathon with an uncomfortable smile, to this man whom he had met only hours ago.

"Very well," said the Baron as he ran a finger over his neat mustache, and his charming attributes did return. "Very well, I believe you nephew," he said. "But I do hope that you will remain a few days before returning south for your wedding."

"Indeed we shall uncle," said Jonathon, although his thoughts had turned to wariness, and the money that he had been promised. He assumed that it would be given just before they were to depart.

Upstairs in her room Melinda sat somewhat uncomfortably upon a plush chair, before a mirror larger than any she had ever seen. Gently, the servant Lucinda stood behind her and combed her long dark hair. The servant had somewhat insisted, and Melinda not wishing to offend, had been quite unable to refuse. It had not seemed right to her to deny the middle aged servant woman this polite request. The servant's eyes looked only downward, and so Melinda was able to stare into the mirror's vast reflection and drift off into meditation.

"I have never seen such a beautiful mirror," confessed Melinda aloud. "They were not allowed in the private quarters of the convent were I was schooled."

"It is good that you have a Catholic education," said Lucinda as she continued running the ivory comb through her locks. "I was not a virgin when I married my husband," the servant said after a few silent moments. "I speak of it only because I know that you will soon marry. My greatest regret is that I failed to confess this before I took my vows. The result has been the scorn of God and the punishment of a childless marriage."

"Forgive me," said Melinda timidly, "But surely such things can be forgiven."

"Only when confessed before the sacrament is taken," said the servant firmly. The hardness of the ivory comb scraped more firmly against her scalp. "It would be a very quick and discrete matter, for me to take you tomorrow to the chapel of the north village. I travel there nearly daily. You could say that you wished to assist me at the market."

"Thank you," said Melinda uncomfortably, "But I have never given myself to a man, I…"

"Even your fiancé?" inquired Lucinda firmly, as the comb snapped free of an entanglement.

"Not even him," she answered meekly, "I have only kissed him. Oh, you must think badly of me for traveling here at his side unmarried…" Melinda leaned forward in her chair and ran her own hands through her hair, so as to reclaim it.

"I do not judge you," said the servant woman as she stood upright behind the chair, "But I ask only that you allow me to help you from making a terrible mistake. The priest in the village is very discrete…"

"I have told you the truth," said Melinda, "I have gone to confession last week and I will do so again when we are again home. But I do not have such large sins to confess, and have never had."

Behind her the servant woman stood silently and then placed her worn hands upon Melinda's shoulders. "Very well, my dear, I did not mean to be so presumptuous. I believe you, and I shall never mention such things again. Goodnight." Lucinda removed her hands promptly from her shoulders and quickly excited the room.

"Yes, my days of exporting have come to an end, although I do miss the excitement" said the Baron as both he and Jonathon ascended the stairway to the bedroom quarters. "I now pass my days reading, and with the hunting of small game and fowl. In fact, it is this activity which I have planned for the morning. Do you shoot?"

"Yes, I am a fair shot," said Jonathon through his exhaustion. He was also succumbing to the expenditure of the day.

Lucinda stepped into the hallway just as the men reached the top of the staircase. As they approached each other there were no spoken words. Jonathon yearned only now, for his bed, and enjoyed the silence. As the servant woman approached, she passed to the Baron perhaps a slight nod, although Jonathon through his weariness could not say for certain.

"Ah, I cannot tell you how happy I am that you have come!" said the Baron when the servant had passed, at the decibel of a near yell. "And to think of the perfect timing, certainly the love of God still shines upon this clan! Goodnight, my boy," said the Baron when they had reached the door of Jonathon's room. "Tomorrow we shall hunt pheasant."

"Goodnight uncle," said Jonathon, but the aged man was already off and departing merrily.

He opened his door and lit the nearest lamp, and then desired greatly to wish Melinda goodnight. He thought that perhaps he would even tell her of the monetary promise which had been made. He reopened the door and stepped out into the hallway, where he saw that Alawald had come to stand. The servant stood near the peak of the staircase, holding sentry in his own uncomfortable way.

Jonathon was confounded with surprise, and simply nodded to the man before returning to his room and closing the door. Tomorrow would come soon enough he reasoned, and passed soon thereafter into sleep.

In the morning they were roused for an elegant breakfast of poached eggs and lingberry jam, served with biscuits and tea. All the while they were entertained by the ceaseless conversation of the Baron. He had adorned a deep green hunting jacket and matching hat, which he politely removed for the meal. Afterwards the men went directly to the Baron's favorite field of wild wheat, which grew sporadically from the rocky terrain.

The Baron and Jonathon shot two of the best shotguns in the Baron's collection, while Alawald and the Baron's dogs, retrieved the birds as they fell to the ground. Behind them at a fair distance, Melinda sat elegantly upon a chair as Lucinda stood nearby. Occasionally Jonathon looked back upon his beloved young woman, and anticipated conversing with her alone.

But this alone time did not seem to come, even at lunch when they had returned. One of the servants seemed always to be present, even when the Baron excused himself for minutes at a time.

At last, just before dinner, Jonathon excused both of them for a walk in the garden. His uncle agreed with his usual charm, and then advised them not to stray. For wolves had been hunting the fields lately, he stated, and some of the villagers had been killed. Jonathon happily agreed to this condition, and they were shown to a rear doorway which led them out of the castle.

"It is a bit overwhelming," said Melinda when at last they were free from listening ears.

"A bit smothering more likely," said Jonathon, "Perhaps my dear uncle could even chaperon our marriage holiday." To this mock suggestion Melinda laughed and all seemed right between them. He told her of the vague promise of money, and she could not help but feel overjoyed.

"We will invite him to our wedding," she said, "although I suspect that he will not come. He seems…stranded here somehow." She looked to Jonathon to see if he agreed.

"I do not pretend to know him thoroughly," answered Jonathon, "But he is the only family that I have. We will thank him extensively at dinner, and then tell him that we shall leave in the morning. Surely Alawald can fetch a local driver."

"And you will invite him to our wedding," she reminded.

"Yes, of course," he replied, before enjoying a few more minutes of solitude with the woman he loved.

The path of their reentry took them near the kitchen quarters. Melinda, who had assisted with the meals of her convent, could not resist a spying look as she passed. Prepared for the oven, she saw distinctly, were all three pheasants from the sport of the morning. This seemed to her as excessive, and she wondered why one had not been given to the Baron's dogs. But this soon passed from her mind as they rejoined the Baron in the front room beside his massive hearth.

"We shall eat early tonight," said the Baron, after greetings of their rejoining had been exchanged.

The dinner bell came within ninety minutes, nearly three hours earlier than the night prior. Neither Jonathon nor Melinda remarked about this, but rather thought of how exactly, they would break the news of their hastened departure.

"The brandy here of the north country is nearly the best in world," said the Baron, who had been sipping it since they had rejoined him after the garden. "Nephew, you must try it, for I must prove to you my boastful claim."

"Certainly uncle," agreed Jonathon, and a filled brandy glass was placed by Alawald on the table just before him. He sipped it and then remarked that it held a remarkable flavor.

"Yes, it is due to the fine grapes and cherries which arrive at the northern ports," said the Baron whose drunkenness had begun to show. The alcohol in his veins seemed to wash from him the elegance and sophisticated charm. Melinda looked at him and felt a resurgence of the unease which had set upon her when first they had arrived.

"Splendid," said Jonathon cheerily after he had sipped again, and then prepared to broach the topic of their impending morning departure. "Uncle," he began, "We would like very much for you to travel south to attend our wedding. As you know, there is only Melinda's elderly aunt, and it would mean to us a great deal if you could come." Jonathon became aware of a discomfort within his throat and took a larger sip from the brandy to clear the source of his pain.

"Travel south?" said the Baron. "I had not thought of making such a trip. Oh, it has been a very long time since I have been to the south lands…"

Jonathon's eyes began to water as the discomfort moved into his belly and a sensation of nausea began to form. He took a larger drink from his brandy and tried to blink away the tears in his eyes.

"Thank you, I shall have to think about that," said the Baron. "I am getting very old now to travel so far."

As these words rolled off of the Baron's tongue Jonathon moaned and slumped suddenly forward, into unconsciousness from the tainted drink. Melinda who had watched in silent horror called out to him and then rushed toward his side. Her loved one did not respond but drew breath visibly. She loudly implored that the Baron and Alawald help lay him upon the floor.

"The hour draws near," said the Baron coldly from his seat, and all fallacious good will had left his eyes. As though within a nightmare Melinda watched as Alawald descended upon her and clasped her with the strength of his gangly arms. She was helpless and could only scream, as he carried her away to the far door of the downward stairs.

Jonathon emerged from nightmarish dreams that were filled with unspeakable horrors. Even before the veil of sleep had fully departed, he became aware of the dreadful aching within his throbbing head.

"He stirs," came a voice into Jonathon's ears, which urged him to awaken further. He blinked repeatedly as his eyes adjusted to the dim oil lighting of the stone chamber. He saw first the face of the servants who stood stiffly against the wall. They made no motion to assist him, and only stared down upon him with stoic coldness in their eyes.

Jonathon became aware that he was lying upon the hardness of the cold stone floor. He was able to stand with great difficulty, although his sight again failed him and a sickly blackness filled his eyes. He felt also a clanking heaviness upon his foot, but did not yet realize that his left leg had been chained to an iron ring mounted into the stone.

"Melinda…" he called out weakly as his vision began to take hold. The blurred shapes before him began to condense, and soon he viewed the great horror to which he had awoken.

His beloved Melinda had been stripped of her clothing, and her arms were pulled taught with chains that held her upright against the wall. Her nude form was illuminated by oil lamps placed at either side, and the whiteness of her innocent and beautiful flesh cried out to be covered from leering eyes. Her eyes were alert and fell upon Jonathon pleadingly, although no sound escaped her mouth. It had been bound with a tightly wound dark cloth which muffled her frightened cries.

"I take no pleasure in this nephew," said the Baron dryly, from his seat upon a chair across from helpless Melinda. "But a father must do all that is within his power to save his only son."

"Uncle!" cried out Jonathon, who pulled with great strength upon his chain and the iron that penetrated the granite. "What is this madness? Release her, I demand it!"

"Ah yes, you demand it!" said the Baron angrily, "Now you sound more like the brother whom I despised. And it is he that I do blame, for the curse that has beset this house. For it was your father who betrayed me so many years ago, and accused me of greed and immoral trade! The very same man who then cursed the wrath of God upon me when I seized from him the partnership, and ho, God's wrath did find me at last! For it is my son who now holds the demon sickness, and it is he who is punished for my sins. Look upon the deterioration of his form and tell me if I speak lies!" With this remark the Baron cast out his right hand, toward a cage at the farthest end of the room.

Inside of the iron bars upon a bed lay the sickened form of a man. The age could not be readily determined, for the face shown red with the color of exposed muscle where the skin had been eaten away. Upon the man's scalp, red and brown sores lay amidst the patches of remaining hair. The condition of the bodily flesh was equally repulsive, and only small areas of skin remained. All areas of his ravaged form dripped the puss of festering wounds, the ooze of which ran down the sides of the sickened body and soiled the sheet upon which he lay.

"He is my son, Alexander, the inheritor of my fortune and the resolve of my life's work," shrieked the Baron. "And now he is infected with the Devil's disease which plagues the whole of his body."

"You see," said the Baron without pause, "It is not like the diseases of man. It is rather, both illness, and the infestation of a satanic entity. Ah, madness, I hear you thinking, but I assure you this is the truth. For the sickness was passed to Alexander from a woman, who came upon him within the first hour after dark. Her dark beauty seduced my son, and thus, a demonic infestation passed into his body, formerly virginal and pure. I learned these facts as he confided in me, days after his moment of weakness, when the signs of the sickness began to appear."

"You see, only one person can hold the sickness, at any given time. That dark woman who came during that night cured herself with the act of coitus with my virginal son. Alexander himself knew this to be true, as the sickness began to attack his mind. It showed him the faces of all the others it had taken as host, since the beginning of man and sin. This knowledge of the sickness became inherent to my son, and he learned that the only cure to his ailment would be the flesh of a virgin woman. And so, after sunset he began to search for a pure mate, during the first hour of darkness when his sick flesh would regenerate. But an innocent girl he had not encountered, for the host must be of sufficient age to bear a child, but not yet guilty of carnal desire. Now his flesh no longer heals in the hour after sunset and this window of opportunity has passed."

"Uncle I implore you…" cried Jonathon when he saw the terror in the eyes of his beloved. Tears flowed freely from her eyes, induced by the vile words of the Baron, rolling from her beautiful chin and landing softly upon her nude bosom.

"Silence!" the Baron shrieked. "The hour when he is most human comes upon us! Look, he begins to stir! Lucinda, prepare his meal. He shall need nourishment after he is cured!"

The female servant hastily departed as the sickened form of the young man began to pulse and shudder. An arm first was raised, spilling the fluid of infection as the tendon exposed hand braced the body to arise. The visible muscles of the torso flexed as it swung its legs to the floor. The sheet which had covered the genitals of the Baron's son fell in a soiled pile upon the stone.

Melinda saw then the festering portion of flesh which would enter her, and fainted limply against the wall. Jonathon cried out and tore mightily upon the chain that tethered him to the wall. But the Baron no longer listened, and strode to unlock the cell door which separated all of the others from his son. It swung open with a creak and crashed loudly against the bars.

The sickened form of the man-child stepped slowly upon the stone floor, as though a corpse ambled across the room. As each foot lifted it left the mark of blood and infected flesh upon the ground. When it beheld the naked form of Melinda, it paused and stared upon the voluptuous curves of her body. She would never in the future hold any more beauty, than that which she possessed at this age. Her shape was the culmination of youth and sexual maturity, a gift which she had intended only for her beloved Jonathon.

The Baron's son stood a moment as though entranced, looking upon her magnificent beauty. His sickened form then turned slowly about and faced the searing gaze of his father. "Alexander, she is yours," spoke the Baron lovingly as madness blazed in his eyes. "She will be your salvation!"

The Baron's son then reached out his hands, and seemed to study their repulsiveness a moment, before lunging toward his father. The son spoke no words as he moved for the first time with the speed and strength of youth, forcing the head of his father backwards and slamming it violently against the wall of stone. The Baron's head cracked with a sickening thud and his body fell limply upon the floor.

Alawald ran to his master's aid, throwing his gangly arms over the boy's bleeding body, trying to force him into submission. Then, perhaps with the strength of the parasitic demon, the arms of the son lifted the servant mightily above his head, and threw him heavily upon the floor. Alawald emitted a shriek as his bones fractured, and then pulled himself weakly into the corner. The repulsive form of the boy lunged upon the pleading servant and squeezed the remainder of life from his gurgling throat.

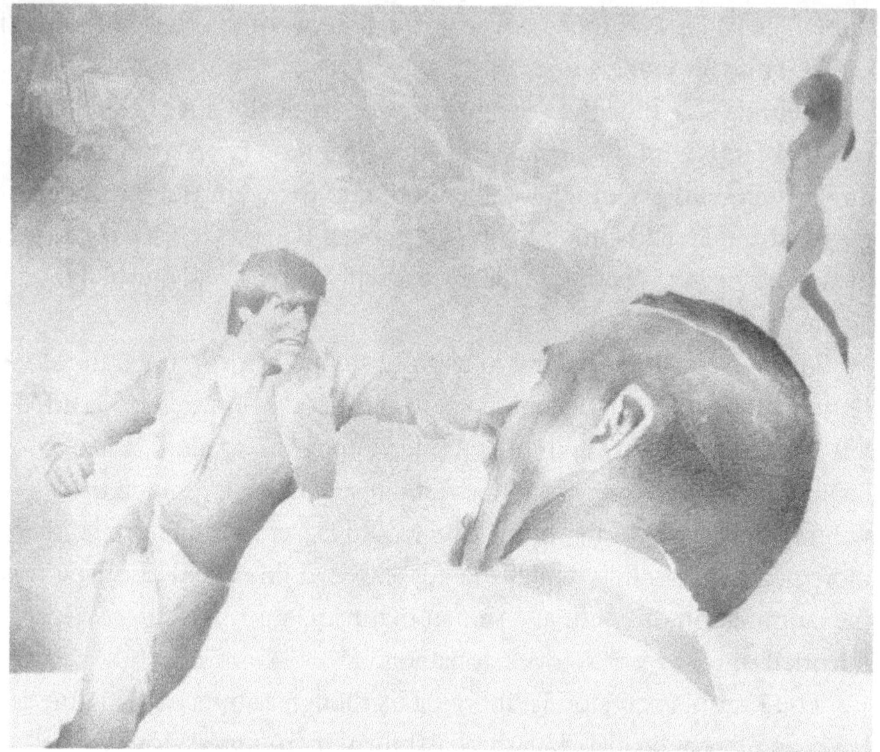

The iron ring that held Jonathon's chain at last broke free of its mount from within the stone. He charged forward to attack the terrible figure who now shed blood from every pore. But instead of violence, the Baron's son rose and stood peacefully, as a look of acceptance appeared in his eyes. His sickened hand then pointed slowly downward, to a sheathed dagger in the belt of his father. Jonathon seized it and stood confusedly, as the Baron's son pointed imploring toward his own heart. Jonathon obliged this brave request of the boy, and drove the dagger deep into his chest cavity, killing what remained of the poor cousin who stood before him.

Jonathon did not watch the body as it crumpled to the floor, but rather took the keys from where the Baron formerly was seated and released the chains that bound the beautiful form of Melinda.

4. The Fear Puzzle

"I'd like to hear it from the beginning," said Doctor Reed, who was unquestionably one of the best psychiatrists in the state. The dullness of his profession had long since set in, but for this interview, he had earnestly awaited. The facts of the case as he knew them promised something far removed from the ordinary patient's drivel.

"Please Calvin," the doctor began again, "I have no direct affiliation with the police. I've no obligation to tell them anything. I am simply here for you."

Calvin sat in the patient's chair, wishing only for a night's sleep that was free from the torment of his dreams. "It was all so random," said Calvin, and his tone made it apparent that the ordeal still burdened his cognition. He had spent hours relaying the story to various police detectives, and he did not wish to speak of the events again.

"Just start with the facts," said the doctor, "We can dig into their meaning in the days to come."

Calvin shifted his eyes downward to the doctor's desk, where there lay an iron paperweight shaped like a fly. He found it easier to tell the macabre tale while not looking at his interrogator directly.

"I suppose it started when my friend Collin picked us up in his van. You see, it would have been a three hour drive, if we had made it…"

***

Collin, the driver, was greatly annoyed by his friend's request, but he did at last stop and allow Jake to relieve his bladder. Collin had been the first to spot the small roadside building, which was the first structure they had seen for miles.

The van came to a halt within the small dirt lot, and was notably the only vehicle present. All four of the young men stepped out to relieve themselves or stretch the stiffness from their muscles.

"I thought this was a store," said Collin, the most athletic of the group, as he stretched and looked about. The place had the appearance of desolation, but the wooden sign still displayed the words *Food & Supplies*.

"There's another building back there," said David, the fourth and final member of the travelers. He pointed his hand to the rear of the lot, toward a large aluminum structure set back by the trees. It held the appearance of a large shed, although its roof was oddly low.

"We'd better be off when Jake is done pissing," said Calvin, "This is private property I think." Jake stepped out from the trees still pulling on his zipper. There did not seem to be any reason to prolong their stay.

"Private indeed," came an unknown voice from the porch of the wooden building nearest the road. All four young men turned to see a man approximately the age of their fathers. The man stood observing them, with a posture that displayed no sign of malice. He wore workman's clothes like those of a mechanic, their color a darkened gray.

"Hello sir," called out Collin, who would have been impervious to intimidation regardless, if any had been presented. "We saw the sign for the store. Is it open?"

The man walked and stood nearer to them, and Calvin observed that his eyes shown a radiant blue. They were the only bit of color upon him, contrasting with the darkly grayed hair and weathered clothes. "No, it's not a store any longer," said the man. "Not since I've acquired it."

"We apologize for coming onto your land," said Calvin, "We're on our way through to Billings."

The man looked at him thoughtfully for a moment, and then spoke before the silence passed into discomfort. "No harm…," said the man slowly, "…Perhaps though you boys could help me move a few things before you go."

The three others waited for Collin to speak, knowing fully well that he was their leader. Calvin continued to look at the face of the gray man, and perceived that it held the imitation of a smile.

"We can certainly spare a few minutes, if the job is nearby," said Collin.

Slowly the gray man turned and walked toward the other, peculiar structure that sat hidden away from the road. The gray man began to speak as they walked along, his gate not outwardly displaying any sign of age or disability.

"You see," the gray man said, "I've always been intrigued by…the choices we make as human beings… as we utilize our God given free will. You see these decisions are based upon values. And values vary from man to man of course, to a degree as severely as their faces. But these variances lie normally hidden, as we all go about the business of our daily lives."

The structure grew close now and the men approached the door. Calvin glanced over the faces of his friends, but none of them seemed to be even moderately concerned.

"Psychology," spoke Calvin to break the silence, for it seemed more desirable to engage in awkward conversation, than the awkwardness of the dead air. The gray man walked more quickly now, ahead of them, and unlatched the door once he had reached it. It seemed to Calvin that the gray man looked at them with conjecture, as though he anticipated some secret pleasure.

"Yes psychology," answered the gray man. "It seems to me, the final frontier of exploration. And I aim to be its Magellan. That is to say…my methods will certainly be seen as radical. But now I am rambling. You boys certainly wish to get back upon the road."

The gray man clicked on the lighting of the interior structure by pressing a button near the outside of the door. He waved them inward with a loosened hand as he maintained his place on the exterior. "You see my back isn't what it used to be," said the man as Collin walked inward. "Again I thank you boys, for my work has been forced to sit idle and a bit of youthful assistance is just what is needed. In fact, it is precisely the answer to my prayers."

Jake and David followed Collin, as was their habit, laughing a bit under their breath at the peculiarity of this strange old man which they had so randomly encountered. Only Calvin had misgivings, and he looked back to the gray man as soon as the walls were around him. Calvin saw only the bright blue eyes and a victorious smile, before the door had closed and the daylight disappeared.

"Hey!" shouted Calvin, as he heard a latch being put in place, followed by the sound of another and then another. He ran to the door and pushed upon it, but it did not seem to budge. Frantically he searched for a release lever, but the inside of the door was completely smooth. In fact, once closed, there was no sign of a door at all.

"Where is he?" asked David who had come up to stand where the entryway had been.

"Don't tell me that door is locked," said Collin. "Here move." Calvin stepped out of the way and Collin began his examination of the door. When it did not open he stood upright and assumed a rigid pose. "Sir, your door has locked. What is it that you need for us to do?" His voice portraying forced calmness. No answer from the gray man was returned. "Sir, we do not have time to waste here. Please open the door and help us finish the task you asked us to do." The four of them stood in silence as the seconds ticked away amid silence. "Sir, I'm going to break down this door unless you reply."

The others knew that Collin had not voiced a bluff, and they stood back to give him room. He set his feet in a staggered position and threw a mighty kick upon the door. The room filled with a massive echo that was repeated with each blow. The door gave not a hint of breaking.

"God damn it!" yelled Collin as he stumbled backward heaving for breath.

Deeper inside the room Calvin had begun to exam their surroundings. The lighting shone brightly from the ceiling through small holes cut into the aluminum panels. And the ceiling looked as durable as the walls. He guessed that the dimensions of the room were fifteen feet by ten. It was, in his determination, a securely constructed cell.

"Sir!" screamed Collin when he had recovered most of his breath.

"Enough," said Jake. "He's clearly an old fool. This is just a joke brought on by his madness."

"I don't know about that," said Calvin, "Look at the design of this room. The lighting shines down through those small holes of the ceiling so that even the wiring doesn't enter the room space. And the floor is solid with aluminum, and it seems as solid as the door. And I've been looking at the walls also. I can't find even a single screw."

"So what is the point?" barked Collin.

"I think we are in a carefully constructed prison cell," answered Calvin.

"But what about this?" called David from where he stood behind all of them. He pointed with a hand outstretched toward a little rectangular panel upon the wall, across from the entry door.

"This looks like it might open."

Collin pushed his way over and began running his hands over the rectangular shape three feet above the floor. It was an anomaly that contrasted with the rest of the room. Collin pushed firmly upon its middle, and it swung outward with a mechanical sound.

"Ah, it opens!" Collin shouted, as a passage was revealed. Its width was no larger than the tiny panel. "I think I see, yes, it's another door at the other side." He reached an arm inward and there came another mechanical sound. Instantly the tiny passage filled with the light of a second room.

"What do you see there?" asked Jake, as his voice betraying hints of fear.

Collin stooped and looked silently inward, with his hands upon the edges. "It appears to be more of the same. Stand back, I'm going through." He thrust his arms in before him, followed by his muscular shoulders. The passage was nearly too small for the young athletic man to wriggle through. The other three watched as their leader's feet were pulled into the shaft. On the other side Collin tumbled loudly onto the floor as the others awaited his report.

"What do you see?" yelled David through the tiny aluminum tunnel.

"It's another room," said Collin as his face appeared to them from the other side. It's like the first one, but set three feet deeper into the ground. And perhaps a bit smaller I think. I think I see another panel in the farthest wall."

"And where does that lead?" said David with frustration, "To still another room just like this? Come on back through there and let's take turns breaking down the door!"

"It won't break," said Collin decisively with his face still peering back at them. It seemed as though he implied that the door was impenetrable because he himself had failed to break through. Collin again turned to peer at the new room at his back, and then returned his gaze through the tunnel toward his friends.

"I'll not go any deeper into this place," said David. "Don't you see how calculated this is? Surely we're meant to venture through there for some purpose in this sick game. Come on back through, please…"

"Alright, a vote then," said Collin. "What do you two think we should do?"

"I'm coming through," said Jake as he pushed inward and began to shimmy onward.

"Well we can always return," said Calvin to David, who seemed now to be the most concerned. David did not answer this but rather stood in frustrated silence. Jake emerged from the other side, and Collin pulled him out.

Calvin shrugged his shoulders to David, before pushing himself also into the hole. The others before him each took one of his arms and heaved him from the tunnel. Once on his feet within the new chamber, Calvin stooped and peered back through. The first panel then snapped forcefully closed and David's face disappeared before his eyes.

"Hey!" came David's voice as it carried through the wall.

"David, open the panel again," shouted Calvin back into the darkened tunnel.

"It won't budge!" David shouted. "How did it open the first time? I didn't see…"

"Push the center," called out Collin, but their friend did not reply. Each of them called to their friend but no sounds were returned. Finally Collin pushed himself headfirst back into the tunnel, and then both beat upon and pushed at the now firmly secured panel. When at last he had removed himself again, both Calvin and Jake had grown weary of calling to their friend.

"Maybe the front door opened and he got out," said Jake. It was the first bit of hope that they had felt.

"Perhaps," said Calvin stoically, as Collin stomped around behind them with frustration covering his face.

Collin soon walked to the new panel of this second room, upon the now most-inward wall of the chamber. It opened easily when he pressed upon its center, just as the former had.

"So that man can lock them and unlock them at will," said Calvin. "And why is this room set lower? If that third chamber does the same, we'll soon be fully underground." A silence fell over the three friends, for this thought added a new source of dread. They were indeed captive, but the thought of being buried alive was worse yet still.

"David!" yelled Jake one last time but the result did not change. All three of them then began a thorough investigation of the room, for they knew a hasty decision must not be made. Collin and Jake repeatedly kicked and slammed into the walls, before giving up and taking rest.

Calvin meanwhile ran his hands over the walls, trying to calm his mind with their smooth coldness. The walls were made of aluminum sections not dissimilar from planks of wood. Each ran from ceiling to floor and held a width of about two feet. It seemed clear to him that the planks were secured from the other side.

Soon the three of them were back at the new tunnel, having given up on the rest of the room. This second tunnel contained a far side panel like the first, which opened into a third lighted room. The men spoke only intermittently until at last they fell into a silence.

"I'll wring that crazy fool's neck when I get out of here," stated Collin after much time had gone by.

"He's watching." said Calvin quietly. "Remember that crazy talk about psychology and people making choices? This madness is his hobby."

"I don't care about any of that," said Jake, who had now lost his previous nonchalance. "The question now is whether or not we squeeze into that third room. And do we all go through? And can we keep that panel from snapping closed?"

Now Collin spoke. "I don't know about each of you, but I'll not be the one left behind." Each of them realized now that someone would have to be last, just as David had been prior. "I'm going into the next chamber," said Collin.

"Wait," said Calvin, "We'll each have to hold the panels to ensure they don't snap closed. I'll go second, and the moment your feet are past, I'll hold the first panel open with both hands until I can get my head inside. And Jake, you'll do the same when my feet get past the edge."

The three of them were in agreement, and Collin took the lead. His broad shoulders squeezed against each side as he moved through the tunnel. Calvin followed his own instructions and held the panel outward with the strength of his arms and his body. But it did not attempt to close on him and soon he was passing through.

It was not intentional, but Collin broke the pact. Instead of holding the second panel open, he pulled Calvin's shoulders as he emerged. Then with the same dreadful mechanical sound, the second panel snapped firmly closed as soon as Calvin's feet had fallen to the floor.

"The lights!" screamed Jake from the other side with terror, "The lights have gone out! I can't see…" Then Jake's screaming stopped as quickly as it had begun, and the two of them stood waiting within the third chamber.

"Jake!" cried out Collin.

"Quiet!" shot back Calvin, then said softly, "I want to hear!" He pressed his ear first to the closed panel and then to the wall just beside.

In this pose he stood for several moments. "I heard something. I don't know what exactly - movement of some kind…"

"Well if it isn't Jake, then it's the old man," said Collin. "There's another way into each room. Maybe some of these wall sections are concealed doors that open inward."

"Perhaps," said Calvin as he looked around with great dismay, and a realization set upon him. "This room is much smaller. And it does indeed drop another three feet into the ground." The two of them looked about and saw with horror that it was true. This third room was easily one-third smaller than the first. Each of the walls, ceiling, and floor seemed to close inward upon them. This coupled with the certainty of the depth caused both of their stomachs to churn.

"It's like a coffin, sweet Christ!" snapped Collin. "We are buried alive! We should have stayed in that first room and knocked through that door. Jesus, God, David was right!"

"Collin… look…" said Calvin as his eyes stared at the floor. Collin looked downward and saw a small puddle of blood, with droplets that ran away from it. The redness shone brightly amidst the colorless gray of the room.

"It leads…to the wall," said Collin. He walked over and peered down at the droplets, and then put his hand against the side. With only slight pressure from his hand, the wall panel sprung open like a door. Collin took hold of it, swinging it open into the room.

Inside lay David's crumpled body. About his throat, there was fastened a wire garrote that showed clearly that he was dead. Blood had run from a puncture in his hand, which Collin and Calvin struggled to understand.

The two of them stood together absorbing the reality of the situation that was upon them. They felt terror, but also calmness, for they now knew the seriousness of the game.

"We were meant to find him," said Calvin. "I think that blood on the ground was intentional, from the puncture on his hand."

"Then there are ways in and out of here," said Collin, "We are not simply buried in a tomb. The overpowering claustrophobia receded slightly with this realization.

Calvin knelt and closed his dead friend's eyes, and carefully searched the tiny chamber in which David's body had been placed. The presence of the corpse did not seem to have any purpose other than heightening their fear.

"There's nothing in here that can help us," said Calvin as he stood up. "I pushed against every panel in there and none of them are hidden doors that we can open."

They kept the tiny door open regardless, as they began pushing upon every inch within the main room. They worked along opposite walls examining, until they were rejoined later at the center wall. Just like the two prior chambers, it also contained a rectangular panel. It opened, just like the others had, with a firm press upon its center.

"Another tunnel," said Collin with hopelessness. It was the first time that Calvin had seen his powerful friend despair.

Calvin stared at the wall, and the tunnel, and then back at the hidden space that held his dead friend. He then realized that there was hidden space between each of the rooms. This seemed certainly to be how the body had been placed ahead of them. "I want to try something," said Calvin with authority, and then shared his plan with his friend.

It was Calvin who went first into the new tunnel, but he had no intention of entering the fourth room. Instead he opened the far side panel when he had reached it, and peered inside.

"What do you see?" called Collin with a touch of hope in his voice.

"The room is smaller," he answered, "But otherwise it is the same - completely void of anything."

"Is there another panel in the far side wall?" asked Collin.

"Yes," said Calvin simply and then wriggled back into the third room as Collin pulled him out. They made certain to hold the nearest panel, although the one at the far side could snap closed at any time. It was a chance they had decided to take.

While still holding it safely open, Calvin turned around and slid back into the tunnel, this time upon his back. Collin again helped him along by pushing upon his feet. The far side panel did indeed remain open, but it was, for the moment of no importance. Calvin slid inward until his elbows were at the center. Once there he clenched his left hand and slammed his elbow forcefully against the side. He had mentally prepared to do so until his arm could take no more. Suddenly however the side wall opened, revealing a hidden passage.

"It opens!" Calvin shrieked as elation filled his body. "I see only darkness!"

"Get into it before it closes!" shouted Collin, as he forced his head and arms inward against Calvin's feet. He had no intention of getting left behind.

Calvin wriggled into the darkness of the new passage, first with his hand and then with his head. His weight pulled him downward into uncertainty, as he fell into the blackness below. When he hit, he looked above him, expecting to see Collin's face and light from above. Instead there was nothing and only silence, and the cloak of darkness that had swallowed him alive.

"Collin, come on through!" He called upward to the lighted outline of the closed passage through which he had fallen. Once upon his feet Calvin pressed upon it, but it was locked firmly in place. The silence told him the fate of his friend and he did not call out to him any further. Instead he felt along the narrow walls of the passage he was now within, and staggered along its side. It seemed to be a hallway, and he felt certain that he had been right. His hand found a doorknob which turned easily and he emerged into the freedom of daylight.

***

"You know the rest from the media, I'm sure," said Calvin.

"So you never saw the gray man again," stated the Doctor. "He may still have been inside of his labyrinth when you got out."

"I only looked around me for a few seconds, and then I ran into the woods. That probably sounds cowardly but I challenge anyone else to have done any differently," said Calvin. "After a few miles of running through the woods, I changed my direction to get back to the road."

"No, no, no, that isn't cowardice for certain," assured the doctor. "But where did they find Jake and Collin's bodies? I suppose Collin was in the third chamber where he had last been."

"His body was on the floor near the panel door. They said he must have inhaled poisonous gas and died instantly. Jake, likewise, was in the second chamber, and had died in a similar way. Only David had been moved for the purpose of inciting our fear. But I never did reenter the structure when we returned... The police knocked in the first door with a battering ram. For the rest of the chambers they simply cut through the side with one of those saws they use at auto wrecks."

"And if you'd have gone into that fourth chamber…" asked the doctor.

"Yes," said Calvin, "That is the great unknown. Because the panel on its far wall did not open, and there was nowhere further to go."

"Madness," said the Doctor, "And to think that the gray man had simply killed the owner and taken over his land. And all those other victims that had been buried in the ground nearby…pure insanity."

"Yes, insanity indeed," said Calvin. "And now I am left to wonder if he rewarded me with freedom, for solving his puzzle of fear…"

5. The Killer Unseen

Stan rolled white paint onto the warped wood of the old library, and then turned his head to watch the children as they played baseball in the park. He liked children, but also feared them due to a life of ridicule and relentless teasing which he had been forced to endure. And there had been also, from time to time the occasional angry parent who had chased him away from the playgrounds where he liked to sit and watch them play.

But Stan was more like a youth himself than an adult of age twenty-five, having been born with both mental retardation and a speech impediment which he had never fully outgrown.

But the old building would not paint itself, Stan knew, and so he returned to his work. He was a good and prideful laborer, and enjoyed most the days such as this one, when he was able to work peacefully alone. The presence of others only intimidated him, and he had often been manipulated or verbally accosted by the other men who worked sometimes at the job sites alongside him. Mr. Thomas, his friend and employer knew this, and therefore gave Stan all of the solitary jobs which were fit for a slower man. Mr. Thomas also praised his work frequently, which had enabled an unspoken trust to grow firmly between them.

This praise had become the primary source of Stan's self-worth, and it was the praise that inspired his diligent work throughout the day. And so, he continued rolling the white paint with precision, and only occasionally glanced to the children who played happily not far away.

He finished the wall within the hour, and then carried his ladder to the rear of the building where there should not have been prying eyes. But Stan noticed immediately that he wasn't alone, and began watching a man who seemed to behave oddly down by the river. There was a large drainage pipe which protruded from the bank of the hill, where it could drain unseen into the waterway below. The concrete pipe appeared to extend upward through the large hill where its gray mass emerged from the earth high above them, where the grounds of the park began. The man seemed to have come down this hill with his dog, where he peered curiously into the darkened hole.

It was the demeanor of the man which seemed to Stan as peculiar, as though the activity of his walk was now long forgotten, and something new had seized firmly upon his interest. The dog as well seemed engaged in the new task at hand, as it stood upon stiffened legs and with an arched backbone of pending aggression. As Stan watched, the man turned momentarily back toward the wooded shore line and plucked a stick from where it had lain. Then as though he were a curious child, this man began poking the stick timidly into the darkness of the hole.

Stan returned to his work somewhat hesitantly and spread the first patch of white paint onto the new wall. He would greatly have enjoyed watching the man further, and even with his handicap, he took pleasure in the usual things that ordinary people do. But once his back was turned, the man was soon forgotten, and Stan thought only of rolling the paint and getting the praise of Mr. Thomas. It was not long before the trance of work overtook him, for his attention span was short, and he did not hear the quick sharp cry that rang out through the air behind him.

Even when the dog barked moments later, Stan did not immediately recall the man. As he stood upon the ladder, the dog tore suddenly into a torrent of barks, so ferociously that he was at last made to turn around and look behind him. As he peered down to the river from atop the ladder, he could no longer see the man to be present. When the dog had not stopped its torrent a minute later, Stan relented and began to climb down.

He could no longer hear the sounds of the baseball game, and saw that dusk would soon begin to fall. He looked again for the man, but saw nothing except the black staring gaze of the pipe. Hesitantly he crept into the trees, cutting through them to the sounds of the agitated dog, and coming out upon the bank not far from the river. The dog turned its head and glanced toward him momentarily before turning back to the pipe and continuing its yelps of alarm.

Stan crept further onward, now between the large pipe and the dog, searching the blackness of the enormous pipe for any sign of the man. The bottom of the concrete reached his stomach as he stood before it at the bottom of the hill. Stan peered meekly into the darkness, planning to retreat quickly when he saw that the man was inside. But the man did not seem to be there.

Something then appeared momentarily within the shadows, becoming visible only for a second within the dim light. It was a shape of some kind, upon which the surface had briefly illuminated, when the angle had shifted and the edge had refracted against the mild illumination. He thought perhaps he saw also, a dark shape within the shadows.

Stan climbed onto the concrete and looked, trying intently to grasp with his eyes the strange shape which had so briefly appeared. Slowly as he strained and squinted, the outline took form once again. It looked to him like a softened crystal, whose clarity was so perfect that it nearly could not be seen. The size of the thing was not too great, and it seemed to Stan that he would be able to reach around its mass if he were inspired to try.

He then saw with certainty as his eyes adjusted, that it held at its center a darkness of solid matter.

Stan stepped closer and looked down through the shape, to investigate exactly what it contained. As he watched, a sudden flash of redness appeared, which then turned quickly to the darkness of black. Then this blackness began to lighten and recede until the encapsulated mass had turned a brilliant white. Stan could only watch in horror as the image of a human skull appeared before him, staring upward with the dead black holes of its eyes.

This image was more than he could bear, and so, a shriek of terror escaped him and he recoiled backward dropping to the ground, before running back into the trees. Once back to his ladder and tools, he kept running beyond them to the front of the building, where at last the terror that had filled his flesh began to unlock his simple mind.

In his impaired brain even he realized the truth, although each of his senses besides logic assured him that he must be confused. Stan knew that the life of the man had been taken, by the invisible thing which he could not see. The same creature that had dissolved the tissue of the man's flesh and now covered the hardness of his bones. His mind raced as he pondered a course of action, for he knew that no one would believe him, not even his dear friend Mr. Thomas.

When some semblance of calm had finally returned, he walked again to the rear of the old library where he peaked timidly down to the blackness of the pipe. The dog was no longer there, having fled finally away, knowing instinctively that its owner was gone. After another fifteen minutes Stan checked the time on his digital watch. Mr. Thomas would be there at any moment, and so with a flustered mind, he began to pack his things.

That evening he went early to bed, after television had failed to relieve his mind of the disturbing events of the day. He wondered within his simple intellect just what had happened within those few minutes after he had first spied the man.

During the ride home his face had shown the anguish, and Mr. Thomas had questioned him as to what was wrong. Stan had only shrugged and said nothing, for he was quite incapable of formulating an untruth. And since he had not told his one true friend, it was as much as certain that he probably would never speak of it henceforth until the end of his days.

And as the darkness of night overtook his bedroom, it was fear for himself upon which he began to fixate, because a return to that terrible place was assured. It was a certainty which would come early with the waking of morning. When sleep finally came upon him it was tainted with the darkest nightmares which his mind could conjure. He dreamed of the invisible mass smothering him and dissolving his flesh until only his bones remained. For much of the night he flailed at his bed sheets as he slept, the weight of which seemed to his subconscious, as though that terrible thing had found him.

But the routine of the morning allowed for a bit of a distraction, and he showered and ate toast with butter, just as he did on most of his mornings. He even played along with an act of good spirits when Mr. Thomas picked him up for his ride, during which they had spoken of simple and pleasant things. This mild chatter had actually begun to steal his thoughts from the unpleasantness, that is, until the truck stopped before the vacant library.

Once outside, Stan set his equipment in place and set to work without delay. He thought perhaps, that the trance of mindless work would fall upon him as the morning hours progressed. But the ever present curiosity of the darkened pipe bore at him, and his mind could not focus upon painting. After forty minutes of little progress he climbed down from the ladder with nervousness in his belly, and walked cautiously into the trees.

The darkness of the large pipe now appeared to him as overwhelmingly sinister. He stepped from the trees and peered cautiously into its blackness, waiting for some small ray of sunlight to reflect upon the invisible mass of the thing.

When it did not reappear Stanley thought perhaps, that it had crawled back into the recesses of the pipe. He felt a slight urge to take a stick and poke the darkness of the interior, just as the unfortunate man had done before him. This revelation made the skin of his neck crawl with creeping squeamishness, and he then felt a tremendous urge to flee quickly from the place.

But he had done his duty and investigated without success, and was then mentally able to begin his work for the day. He had nearly forgotten all of his fear by the afternoon when the exterior painting was nearly completed. The horror of the prior day even began to seem as though possibly, completely imagined.

This tranquility was soon shattered however, when his ears heard anew the familiar barking of the orphaned dog which had returned. It was an auditory stimulus that brought back all of the terror within an instant.

He looked toward the sound of the dog, and saw that a different man now stood upon the walkway within the park, high above the darkness of the ominous pipe. The form of this new man towered over the bank of the river, oblivious to the horror that resided in the darkness of the tunnel beneath his feet. The dog had returned to the base of the hill near the water, where it had cried out in alarm the day prior. It stood again in agitation, intermittently growling and barking.

This new man then spotted and looked intently upon Stan, who immediately reacted by averting his eyes. When he dared to look again, he saw that the man walked toward him, signaling with his hand in a friendly but determined manner.

"Pardon me," said the man with a forced smile, "I wonder if you worked here yesterday." The stranger appeared to be the age of thirty-five, and intimidated Stan with his confidence and handsome face.

"Y…Yes," said Stan warily with the stammer he had had for all of his life.

"You see, I'm looking for my brother," said the man, who studied Stan's appearance and silently passed a judgment. "I know that he left home yesterday to walk his dog somewhere in that park. The dog returned home without him sometime later… and acted very strangely." The man's brow furrowed a bit as he said this. "I thought that perhaps if I brought the dog back here…" The man's words trailed off and he looked briefly back to the park before looking inquisitively upon Stan again. "The dog may be signaling something at the river, I can't accurately say…"

"I...I... saw a man yesterday and that...dog," said Stan fearfully as his hands began to shake. "He looked into that p...p...pipe..." He pointed his hand to the ominous circular blackness encapsulated within the concrete.

"In that pipe?" said the man with some excitement, as he took a step back in the direction he had come. "Did you see anything else?" asked the stranger. "Was anyone else with him perhaps?"

Stan did not know how to answer this, and so stood silently looking at the ground. The handsome man had not waited however, but instead turned and walked quickly in a direct path to the river's edge. Stan followed the steps of the man like a child, through the trees at a distant pace and halting ten-feet from the lair of the thing. The handsome man looked into it briefly and then searched his eyes over the length of the water's edge. When he did not find what he looked for, he turned about, and again looked deeply into the blackness of the hole.

"He looked in here, you say?" said the man with great energy, both upon his face and in his words. He then stepped to the side of the giant pipe and climbed up to stand upon the concrete base.

"Yes," said Stan feebly. He was terribly uncomfortable, feeling guilt for not being more forthright, and equally concerned that he was somehow in the wrong. Frantically he searched his mind for a way to steer this man from the fate that had claimed his brother.

"Did he enter this tunnel?" inquired the man firmly, quite unaware of the creeping death which could be lying unseen at the tips of his feet.

"I think... yes..." said Stan. "Please...be careful."

The man did not question him further, but stepped within the concrete of the opening, and stared intently into the darkness. "Damn it, I need a light..." said the man, and then fumbled around in his pockets.

Stan stood upon the safety of the moist dirt, beneath the protection of the warm sun, where he did not think that thing could venture. The bottom of the pipe rose to his stomach, and he stood, with wide eyes and an open mouth, peering at the man above him.

"Ah yes!" the man yelled, somewhat to himself, as he drew a lighter from the pocket of his trousers. The scrape of the flint was heard as the trigger was rapidly depressed.

The man's endangerment now weighed mightily upon Stan's limited mind. He struggled for the right words as his stammer hindered his speech. "Watch out f... for the th…th…thing," was all that he could manage.

The man seemed unaware, and perhaps he did not truly listen due to the perception that he had of Stan. Instead he walked onward, slightly bent over, deeper and deeper into the intense blackness of the pipe.

"It m…m…melted him," said Stan timidly from his safety within the daylight. He watched as the man suddenly halted, and then moved the light of his fire from side to side, and then upward and down.

"There's *something*…," said the man aloud, apparently to Stan behind him. "Something transparent…," he said, with confusion in his voice. He then lowered himself and sat back upon one of his heels, as he studied the bizarre shape that had so briefly appeared before him.

"Don't touch…" said Stan, but he did not know if the man would listen.

"It's nearly imperceptible," he said, "And it does not lay flat upon the ground. It has… form…"

"It k…killed your b…b…brother," stammered Stan as beseechingly as his simple mind could manage.

"I see an object!" yelled the man, "It's my brother's watch, I think… I need a stick or something…" The man arose and retreated momentarily, the grabbed the same stick which his deceased brother also had foolishly wielded. He returned to the mass of the thing holding the stick within his hand. As he poked and jostled the invisible killer, Stan saw its form appear briefly to him within the light.

"Please," pleaded Stan with utter distress now filling his words. "Your brother d...did that …too."

"It won't come free," said the man. "Wait…here!" With this cry of premature victory the man thrust his hand into a clear breakage which had appeared in the peculiar mass. "I've got it!" he then called, but the clear tissue had already felt his flesh. The organic warmth had triggered its feeding desire, and the invisible cells crawled quickly up the flesh of his arm. "God, I think it's…!" cried out the man as he felt the invisible ooze move with quickened speed, under the shirt at his bicep, and then quickly over every orifice upon his face. All of his cries were then muffled greatly, as he thrust himself upward and back, smashing his head upon the concrete above, and realizing at last his folly. The pain of the impact he barely felt, for his flesh had begun to dissolve. The man fell to the ground fully engulfed, as his face turned a horrible red and his eyes stared terrifyingly through the invisible mass that was upon them.

Stan could only stare helplessly upon the pleading eyes as they quickly dissolved. And he did not attempt to grab the covered hand that the man thrust imploringly before him. For even Stan's slow mind could see that such an action would bring his own demise. Instead he could only step backward and watch the man slowly dissolve as his flesh was fully consumed. Eventually the remaining tissue of the man ceased its quivering, and the whiteness of the exposed bones were visible through the mass of the creature.

Stan scurried away when he saw the first hints of whiteness, and did not look back toward the pipe until he was safely at the old library. It was then that he remembered the dog, which had seemingly fled when the shouting began. It sensed now, Stan was certain, the sheer evil of the thing in the darkness.

That night again, Stan kept the events to himself, although his delicate nerves had degenerated into a terrible state. Mr. Thomas had simply assumed that some children had teased him badly, and offered generously to remain alongside him during most of the following day. To this arrangement Stan happily agreed, for on the morrow the job would be finished, and he would never again be forced to return to that place of terror. It would be only the morning hours, they agreed, in which Stan would be left alone.

The night brought an even greater ordeal, for the dreams could not be controlled, and as they unwound in their horrible fashion, they seemed to Stanley as entirely real. Each time he would awake, the sensation of relief would come overwhelmingly, at which point he thought of the few pleasant things in his life, before drifting back into restless slumber. But very soon the blanket of sleep would again steal away these pleasantries, and leave in their place the terrible visions of the killer unseen.

So it was from a second night of horrible sleep that Stan emerged from his simple home and climbed into the truck of his awaiting friend. He took a free coffee from Mr. Thomas gratefully, which the old man had already purchased in an attempt to cheer his pitiful friend.

"Finish up that upper tier," called Mr. Thomas after Stan, who had stepped from the truck without saying goodbye, "And I'll be back in three hours and we'll finish this ole' miss together."

Stan unloaded his gear from the back of the truck, and then waved a hand loosely before heading away. He set the ladder in its place from the day before where he had been too upset to finish the job. And when this was done he set promptly to work and did not allow himself even one look down toward the pipe. He was very close now to being done with it altogether, and fell instinctively into a state of denial.

By noon the exterior of the old building was nearly fully white, and only a few unpainted bits remained. The truck belonging to Mr. Thomas appeared soon thereafter and pulled to a rest at the end of the road.

"Well you're almost done now," said Mr. Thomas from the ground as Stan looked down to him from above. No sense in me setting up, when you'd have finished by then already." The old man lit a cigarette and ambled around the old building as Stan set back to his work at a greatly hurried pace. He had come through the ordeal of the previous two days, and very soon now they would load the truck and drive peacefully away forever. So joyous was this thought that Stan laughed out loud like a fool.

When the final surface of old wood had been painted, he looked down and prepared to make the descent. He did not see Mr. Thomas to the right where he had been, and so, turned to look down at his left. His old friend was not there either, and adrenaline shot suddenly through his veins. The paint tray fell upon the ground and splattered, as he scurried frantically down the rungs. Once on the ground he dropped the roller and hurried into the trees. At the other side he saw first the gaping mouth of the pipe, and then Mr. Thomas standing calmly at the edge of the water.

"What is it boy?" said the old man when he saw the look of fear upon Stan's face. Stanley stood sweating and stammering while no words could form in his mouth. "It's alright boy," said Mr. Thomas who had stepped over to his frightened friend. "Come on now, tell me what is the matter, and then we'll finish and have some lunch."

Stanley shook his head in refusal, but the old man simply would not let it go. The old man was intent now on solving whatever problem Stanley had imagined himself to have. So with apprehension, and possibly a desire for relief, Stan relented and told of all the horrid events from the prior two days. Tears were falling from his eyes as he finished, and he waited to see if the old man would laugh. He had been laughed at many times throughout his life, but never by this surrogate father.

"That's quite a tale," said the old man earnestly, and then clasped and shook the shoulder of his dear friend before him. "Well I suppose we ought to have a look then," said Mr. Thomas. "Carefully though lad, both of us, and we won't touch the thing or get near. I make you this solemn promise."

The old man turned to face the pipe which towered above him, and extended into it the flame of his lighter. "Do you see it boy?" he asked, to which Stan only shook his head. The spry old man then climbed the hill with Stan beside him, and stepped onto the concrete base. Again he struck a light and illuminated the area of pipe nearest to their feet. This process was repeated as they inched inward.

At nine feet into the darkness, the watch of the first victim could be seen lying overturned at the bottom of the pipe. Stan pointed and began his stammer, but the old man only quieted him and urged him along.

As they progressed further inward, the light of the flame at last came upon the invisible shape. Stan, who clasped tightly upon his friend, became rigid with fear throughout his limbs. "Th… There!" he cried, as he clutched the old man and kept him from stepping closer.

"I saw something…" said Mr. Thomas, who had until that instant of momentary sight, simply intended to quell the fears of his friend. "No, there is nothing there…" said the old man, as the outline of the shape then appeared once more. The creeping death was perhaps, pulling itself further into retreat.

"I see…something," stammered the old man, "Simply the reflection of oil and water from a puddle upon the ground... An optical illusion only…"

But the tone did not align with the words spoken, and Stan clasped more tightly upon his friend. The ominous shape then disappeared, returning several seconds later when the thing again moved and pulled itself further onward.

"Come away Stan," said the old man uneasily, as he began to turn his body but not his eyes. "It is only the light of my flame playing tricks on our eyes as we watch." The old man pushed Stan backward as they retreated, turning his head many times behind him and seeing only the darkness of the pipe. The flesh of the old man had begun to creep with revulsion, and the solace of daylight beckoned strongly.

"It…It was there…" stammered Stan, as he was hurriedly pulled out into the bright air.

"I saw nothing," said the old man adamantly, as he marched off in the direction of his truck. This strange reaction perplexed Stan's simple mind, but he did not pause to ponder. Instead, he simply followed in the steps of Mr. Thomas, leaving the thing forever in the pipe behind.

6. The Demon Seer

"It has been called a gift, but I disagree with this designation, for it has always caused me much more trouble than it has prevented. This was the case exactly when my wife and I first saw her nephew Edmund, as he was introduced to us as a baby. We had all been invited to my wife's parents' home, as was the rest of her family, for that very occasion."

"I had no premonition of bad things come, for you see, my ability does not work in that way. I had simply put on my best clothes as everyone else had, and driven quite pleasant mindedly over to the house with nothing more on my mind than the anticipation of a gin and tonic."

"That is not completely true, I suppose, because I did also look forward to seeing that beautiful old Victorian home. It had always filled me with a feeling of utter tranquility and a sense of prolonged happiness. Quite possibly because we may have been the ones to inherit it one day. So it was with a peaceful mind that we arrived and parked our car along the drive. I had helped, of course, my beautiful wife Nina from the vehicle and escorted her up the lavish steps to the door of the house in which she had lived for so many years."

"And when the door opened, still I felt no unease. Her brother Jack greeted us fondly with a smile, just as he always did. His wife Jessica even complimented us on how lovely of a couple we were together."

"And so I removed my jacket, and took Nina's coat, and prepared to hang them in the proper closet. For I knew very well by now where the guest coats were supposed to be hung. And as I passed the new parents seated upon the sofa, that is Randall and Nina's sister Justine, I believe that I smiled and wished them congratulations. But this is where a bit of the darkness began, for I did see a glimpse of the new baby."

"One thing that must be made clear, and I insist that you understand, is that there is no pleasure in my ability whatsoever. It is not a skill that one can take even a bit of pride in, for you certainly would never want anyone to learn of it and associate you with abnormality. And this is why I suppose, that I did immediately look away, as was my custom whenever I saw one of those things inhabiting the flesh of one's body."

"What's that you say? Oh no, it does not occur all that frequently. I shudder to think what life would be like if I saw them often at all. It would be like being in hell I suppose, looking everywhere and seeing a demon. It had been probably two months since I had last seen one, as I drove along to the office. It had been in a homeless man who stood at the entryway to an alley."

"Yes, it had seen me also. They always see me also, without exception. For you see, they sense my ability just as I can sense them. And the absolute worst part is that they are drawn to me, and do seek me out. Usually they would come knocking on my door or window in the middle of the night. A call to the police solves the matter, for the policeman think only that the person is a lunatic. I certainly cannot tell them that they are people possessed by demons, or it would be me that they took away, ha! Yes, but in all seriousness, it has been a tremendous wear upon my nerves. This is why I had to marry upward from my social status, so that I could afford a gated community. My dear wife Nina had always attributed my ever worsening insomnia and anxiety to the stress of work. Could you imagine what she would have thought if ever I had confessed the truth!"

"But I do digress from the main story, for I know very well that you wish to hear details of that terrible day. And so I did walk away and hang the coats in the proper closet, already feeling the anxiety for I knew what I had seen. All of the prior tranquility had begun to leave me by then, if it had not gone altogether. So when I did encounter my wife's father Richard as he emerged from the kitchen, I think he asked me if I felt alright. Nervousness has always shown on my face, you see, and I cannot hide it. I believe that I stammered some bit of partial truth, such as that I felt a bit under the weather. He was my employer after all and I did not want him to think I was mad."

"Yes, I did plan to look again at the baby, but from where I stood it was not quite visible to my eye. Everyone else, you see, was leaning over him and taking a look for themselves. When Richard handed me a gin and tonic I took it gladly, and was very pleased to find he had made it dry.”

“What’s that? No, no, alcohol has never had an effect on the ability one way or the other. Besides I only had that one drink and it takes more than that to change me greatly. But that is not to say that I do drink often, except before bed when I simply must sleep.”

“Anyhow I found myself alone again, standing there by the closet and still not realizing fully the implications that this new demon would present. It was at this moment that Nina called out to me in front of everyone, insisting that I come over immediately. So I clearly could not avoid it, not with everyone having heard her. And seeing their new baby, was after all, precisely why we had come.”

“So I drank deeply from my gin and tonic and surely pasted a phony smile across my face. For it was during moments of high anxiety such as this, that I felt most like the outsider, which was truthfully what I was. They were certainly, a rather well to do family and it had taken me a good deal of time to be accepted as one of their own.”

“Pardon? Oh no, I come from a much lesser to do family than the one that I married into. I met Nina at college, you see, before my nerves had given out so badly, and I had still possessed all of the confidence that I had once had. Suffice to say, that I had not so much as married into the family but was rather hired into the family business. Her father Richard was practically retired and Justine’s husband was indisposed with a career of his own. So I was the logical choice, so long as I proved to be of sound mind. Ah, but again, I am going off in a wrong direction…”

“So I did go over to the sofa, and I intended only to point my face at it, and not to focus my eyes at all. For you see that is the worst part of seeing the demon within the person, which is to say that the worst part is seeing their eyes. It’s a bit like a hallucination I suppose, although I certainly have never taken a hallucinogenic drug. So I did step up and take my turn viewing it, him I mean, and I saw his tiny baby’s face. I held that phony smile and said some nice thing I suppose, like, ‘isn’t he a darling baby’. But then its terrible voice began and I could not ignore it, although I certainly did try.”

"*You will burn in hell with us,* is what it said first, and God help me I looked it directly in the eyes. Within them I saw the wisdom of centuries inside that burning hateful stare. *There are more of us coming for you,* it said, but of course no one else could hear it. They simply kept chattering about and admiring what appeared to them as a beautiful boy. *Your wealth cannot protect you now, for I have infiltrated your family.*"

"Nina must have looked over at me, for I noticed that she stared at me with concern. She thought that the stress of the office was having at me, and asked me if I wanted to lie down and rest my eyes. I declined, for I did not want to raise any concerns. Richard was after all nearby and I did not want to appear as less than strong."

"*You'll be chewed upon for eternity,* it said next. *You will feel nothing but a dozen mouths burrowing into you and drinking your ever-flowing blood. But until you die we will continue coming for you, and the next one will be worse yet.*"

"I must confess that that last utterance from it frightened me worse than I had been frightened so far. For most things they say do come true in some manner, although I certainly don't believe that business about being devoured in Hell because I am an avid Christian with faith in God.

But most other threats that spew out of their foul mouths seem to hold a bit of truth.”

“*The next one will be your own flesh and blood,* it said next, *and you will never be able to escape it. Look at her belly even now, the demon is already there, intertwined with the growing flesh. It will be in your son, mark my words, and you will hear its taunting day in and day out.*”

“I peered at its awful little face and into the black eyes of the demon within. I felt also the sweat that had begun on my brow and I was certain my color had turned ashen. For this was the worst encounter yet in all of my life, and my mind raced for an excuse to get away. My heart was racing and I felt a strong faintness beginning to overtake my senses. All objects around me then began to blur, except those terrible eyes of the demon.”

“*No longer will you hide behind locked gates and night watchmen, we will be inside your very house! Nothing can now prevent it, for the child will go to term! It will be Hell on earth for you, until death delivers us your soul!*”

“Enough! I shouted at it at last, and the others recoiled in fear around me. Enough you devilish fiend, or I’ll strangle you here and now! I lunged at it with my hands outstretched forcing Randall, the father, to lunge upon me.”

“I may even have said some other terrible things, I can’t at this moment remember. The doctors at the asylum were called, and I was taken away to rest and for evaluation. Once behind their walls I made the terrible mistake of telling the doctors the truth of my lifelong suffering. Suffice to say that it had not gone over very well…”

“And the worst of it was poor Nina, for we had truly been very happy for awhile. But now she has served me papers and that portion of my life is permanently closed. She turned out not to be pregnant, at least that’s what she wrote me. I do suppose it is possible that she terminated it, due to the mental illness she perceived that I had.”

“No, I don’t mind these sessions, quite the contrary actually. They give me a bit of a rest from being among them. You see, an asylum is probably the one place I should have wanted to avoid if I had known. It is, after all, the place where most people carrying demons are taken in due time. A bit ironic, don't you agree!"

"There are dozens of them here, truthfully, and I could not sleep from their constant taunting. So to prevent my hysterics I was granted a private room. But the daylight hours with the others are now my torment, and I suppose they will be until the end of my days. I don't know why the good lord has given me this terrible gift as you call it, but I certainly will not question him for fear of an afterlife worse than here."

7. The Gatherer

The clock showed 10:15 a.m. and the television played the morning news on a tiny twelve inch screen. Ivan stood within his small kitchen preparing the morning tea. Occasionally he would shoot a glance toward the television set when a topic caught his ear. It was a ritual that he had become accustomed to during a sixteen month jail term not long ago, for the possession and distribution of illicit narcotics. The sentence had not seemed to him to be so terrible, except that one cannot make money while locked away.

He waited for the kettle to whistle, no longer watching the news but rather thinking of the judge's ugly face as it had looked during the reading of his conviction. "*Mister Stevenson*," the judge had said to him while peering down upon him like God, "*you will indeed realize that evil always finds its way back to evil men, and will seek its own revenge. You will be no exception to this rule*." Ivan had stood with a stone face before the judge that day, just as he did so now while awaiting his boiling water.

As the kettle began to whistle he heard the familiar and soothing voice of his favorite newswoman, and quickly forgot the face of the judge. "A third Westenberg child has gone missing in just two weeks," said the voice of the woman on the television. "Chelsea Palmer, age eight, was last seen outside of Chesterbrooke Dime Store on Ash Street and Mason, yesterday at ten in the morning. No trace of her or the other two missing children has yet been found. Anyone with any information should contact the Westenberg Police Department."

Ivan stared at the picture of the little girl on the tiny screen, and a most peculiar feeling settled into his belly. *"I saw her yesterday morning,"* he realized. *"Yes, it was her. I recognize the curly hair. And that yellow jacket, yes, it was that girl!"*

His kettle continued to whistle as the girl's picture cut away before him, to another newscaster dressed sharply and some business news which Ivan cared to hear nothing about. He poured his tea and walked to sit, now with the television off. *"That was her,"* he thought as he sipped from the delicate cup. *"She was a good four blocks from Ash and Mason, but that was her, I am certain."*

He went and stood at his third floor window, and peered downward to the street, just as he had when he had seen her on the morning of the prior day. *"Yes, she was standing there when I first looked down, right in front of the laundry mat."*

Ivan ran those few seconds from the prior day in his mind like a film, seeing her standing a bit oddly perhaps, although he did not think that he had noticed this before. *"Yes, she stood there staring down into the sewer drain,"* he realized as he sipped more of his tea. *"Perhaps she lost a toy."*

Ivan looked up to the clock and knew that he that must be off, lest he risk being late to meet a client. He set his teacup onto his second hand table and removed the hidden compartment which he had fastened within the drawer. He took out one of the bags of opium and then replaced the compartment as it had been.

As Ivan departed, two policemen corralled a homeless man into the back of their patrol car. Very few vagrants were left within the city, Ivan knew, due to a large shelter which had been constructed outside of town. Ivan found himself thinking about the girl as he stepped across the street. He walked over the gutter drain and looked into it while passing it from above. Inside he saw nothing but blackened water, drifting away into the darkness…

***

That night strange dreams came to him and Ivan was denied a peaceful sleep. He saw many things unfold before him, beginning with the cancer stricken face of his father as it had looked just before death had come. He saw his mother crying tears of sadness, and tears of self pity, for the even greater plight that now had been set upon her. But this vision did not last and a more peaceful setting overtook him. It was the view from his apartment window, and Ivan thought that he could, perhaps, even taste his morning tea within the dream.

He saw that little missing girl once again standing and looking into the gutter drain as though there were something down there to see. Behind her people would occasionally walk past, oblivious to the peculiar way that she stared into the darkness below. And then as though commanded she turned and walked suddenly away, her legs turning and marching along a path as straight as an arrow. She walked calmly although intently, past the end of the block and into the wild-grown field that led to the river. And then she was gone, having walked out of Ivan's field of vision, just as she had begun to descend the hill.

He awoke and looked at his clock, then rolled over for another sleep. *"She is down beneath the streets in the sewer system,"* he realized as he began to drift off again. *"She is either dead or lost down there, or perhaps just the victim of a head injury and now lies at the bottom of that hill."* It was not long before he was asleep again, for he did not feel any urgency regarding this new knowledge of the missing girl. And he would not call the police, not even anonymously, for he would not help the side of the law that that had locked him away, and probably would someday again.

In the morning he held the usual routine of sleeping late, followed with tea and watching the news. He would not admit it but he watched and listened with greater interest, waiting to see if he would be told the status of the missing children. As he sat upon his couch and sipped, the familiar pictures came upon the television screen. His favorite newswoman reported with indifference that none of them had yet been found.

Ivan didn't have any appointments with clients that day, nor had there been any word of the new shipment that he was awaiting. He arose suddenly from the couch and fetched his old rubber fishing waders from a corner in the closet. They made him think of his father and a few happy childhood hours of fishing eel. He put them on over his thermal underwear, and then an old jacket and gloves which did not need to be kept clean.

He opened the door to leave and then paused to think, before walking back to the kitchen drawer and removing his flashlight. From another drawer he removed a piece of chalk and then returned to the door. "I shan't need anything else, I don't think," And then added, "If I find her alive I'll take credit for saving her, and if she lies dead I'll say nothing at all." This all seemed entirely logical to Ivan, as he locked his door and departed.

Once he was at the bottom of the hill he felt relief that he could not be seen from any of the windows. He had always enjoyed greatly the sensation of being alone. The river was wide, and from the buildings upon the other side he knew that he would not be visible.

The drain entrance was a circle of steel within concrete, the diameter of which Ivan estimated to be six feet. A small trickle of water flowed out of it and dropped into the manmade stream which led to the river. It seemed that he would be able to walk the tunnel without much difficulty at all.

Ivan took a good look around the overgrown weeds before entering, just to ensure that the girl's body was not lying upon the ground. When he did not find her he clicked on the bulb of his torch and stepped into the darkness of the tunnel.

A slight crouch was all that was needed, for Ivan was not quite six feet himself. Behind him the daylight diminished with each step and he felt a chill in the air about him. At twenty feet inward the steel tube opened into a larger concrete channel which appeared to run the same direction as the street above. The length of this new tunnel seemed limitless, and Ivan remembered to take the chalk piece from his jacket pocket and draw an arrow upon the wall at his left, pointing onward in the direction he would travel.

He shown the light upon the ground in a back and forth motion, searching for that yellow jacket or any trace of the missing girl. The hairs upon his neck began to stand on end as he felt the adventure and the joy of something new. He was within an entirely new world; the underbelly labyrinth of the city above.

Every thirty feet or so he crossed an adjoining tunnel of smaller dimension, each of which seemed to be drainage tunnels coming from the streets above. He could see hints of sunlight shining distantly as he looked into them, but never did he venture inward to confirm if he were right. Instead he simply shone the light into each one and called out, pausing only a moment to hear returned silence before moving onward.

At every third tunnel he marked another shoulder height arrow, just for his piece of mind.

When he had marked his third arrow it occurred to him just what a bit of trouble he'd be in if his light should fail. This realization shot a bolt of adrenaline into his bloodstream and his neck hairs stood even further upon their ends. It was a risk that he decided to take, for he thought that he had memorized every turn which he had yet taken.

A mild sweetness in the air then became noticeable, like the distant bloom of a wildflower whose aroma could fill an entire room with its dominant scent. Ivan looked for the source of the odor as he shined his light but did not see anything new. Instead he began to follow the scent without realizing that he did so, and his steps beneath him became pleasant and light. The odor made him feel as though he were walking in a beautiful field beneath the bluest of summer skies. Perhaps to meet a girl with whom he was in love, and with a little imagination he could even see her beauty within his mind. She was a vision of absolute radiance, with flowing dark hair and pure skin as she stood ever before him, just beyond the reach of his grasp. She reached out to him as he strode forward, as the breeze blew across the field and the flowers, carrying the sweet fragrance all about him and he did not have a care in the world. It was the sensation of blissful eternity…

Without realizing, Ivan then stepped upon a raised brick and smashed his head upon the ceiling. Instinctively he placed his hand upon the wound and covered it to ease the pain. His eyes blinked several times and the dream world faded from his mind. He was again back within the sewer tunnel feeling great confusion as he stood holding his aching head.

He shone the light around him and realized that he was no longer within the same tunnel in which he had formerly been. The chalk piece had apparently fallen from his hand for it was no longer within the fingers that he pressed firmly against his head.

He was now in some type of chamber whose walls were lined with centuries' old red brick. It seemed to Ivan that he was no longer on the same level, but rather somewhere below where he had formerly been.

Great concern quickly replaced his confusion as he turned rapidly in a circular motion, shining every inch of the chamber around him.

He saw that one corner was engulfed with vegetation from which vines and tendrils ambled across the bricks of the room. Terror filled him as he viewed the adjacent corner and saw the long white hair of a man who sat against the wall. The man's eyes were open and staring, covered with the whiteness of cataracts or loss of pigment from a life of extended darkness. His white hair hung below his shoulders and the gaunt face projected filthy whiskers that dropped to his chest. Beside him the missing little girl sat in a similar pose, showing no emotion whatsoever.

Ivan's heart beat wildly beneath his ribcage as he stood there fighting the sensation of terror. He held his light out before him like a weapon and his muscles were taught and ready. He could not collect himself enough to utter any of the questions that flashed within his mind.

Then the gaunt old man's hands moved from his knees and slowly were placed upon the ground. Then the shoulders came forward as the horrible figure rose slowly to his feet. Within moments the old man was upright, his aged muscles showing like tough sinew between his torn rags of clothing. Ivan withdrew a step and prepared to fight, still trying to comprehend the image before him. The old man walked slowly forward and then stopped when reaching the center of the chamber. His terrible white eyes seemed to glow as Ivan's light shone into them. Then slowly the white eyes began to fill with a peacefulness that seemed to Ivan like glasses of pure white milk. Again the field and the girl appeared to him and he felt the terror fade and his heart rate slow. He did not want to fight any longer and forgot completely the source of displeasure which he had been consumed with mere seconds ago.

Just before the final image of reality was to fade away did Ivan remember the initial terror from the sight of the aged man. He fought within himself to feel the horror and not give in to the delight being forced upon his mind. Then the fantasy washed away completely and Ivan saw that the old man had approached further and now stood just before him. A rock was now clasped within the old man's hand, with which he intended certainly to smash Ivan's skull.

A new shot of adrenaline caused Ivan to throw his elbow at the old man, smashing into his temple, and sending the gaunt figure crashing to the ground. The rock dropped at Ivan's feet causing an echoing thump.

Blood spewed from the old man's head, running down his chin and dripping onto his chest. Ivan reached for the rock and raised it to finish the task at hand.

"J.. J.. Jonathon," said the old man with a stutter, "Jonathon…Prescott." Ivan knew not what this meant and did not care, raising the rock high and then bringing it down with a sickening thud. The old man crumpled to the ground as his blood spewed, and was dead before his body came to rest.

Ivan wasted no time and went to the girl, placing his hand across her cheek. "Are you alright?" he yelled to her, and then gave her a slap when she did not respond. The girl blinked to life and her face took on a look of great concern. "Who was that man," Ivan interrogated, "why are you hear?" The girl could not answer, and only looked around and appeared as though she would cry.

Behind Ivan the blood of the old man now flowed downhill toward the adjacent corner. Slowly at first, and then rapidly a sucking sound had begun. It sounded like a dozen cats lapping from bowls of milk. Ivan turned from the girl and shone his light, seeing the vegetation within the corner and dozens of its tendrils now upon the ground, writhing and sucking the blood from the puddle on the floor. The entire plant now seemed to breathe and pulse with life, as it fed itself from the fluid of the lifeless man.

Then once again the intoxicating fragrance was about him and Ivan began to succumb to the entrancing dream. He fought it with his entire being, but it was too powerful for a man of his limited conviction. Below the fragrance cloud the girl pulled upon Ivan's hand, but he was unable now to leave. She took the light from his grasp and ran out blindly, putting distance between herself and the lair of the monstrous plant.

This time Ivan was shown a new vision and he did not feel the peacefulness of the other. He saw the plant as it had seeded and grown to life many years ago. He watched as the old man had been lured down into the labyrinth while still a very young man. The scent had flittered out and seized him as he had hiked along the river, many years ago. Like a boy following the scent of apple pie to his mother's kitchen, he had entered the sewer in a trance.

Ivan saw also the hundreds of victims whom had been lured to the lair, by the lesser powers bestowed upon the old man. Ivan saw images of him standing in the tunnels beneath the gutter drains, staring upward with those white eyes to the chosen victims upon the street. They were then pulled telepathically to the sewer entrance where they were overpowered by the greater allure of the master plant. Most of the victims had been vagrants, but children had been taken as well. Especially now that the vagrants were in short supply, due to the new shelter outside of the city.

Ivan was now utterly powerless and only a hint of him mentally remained. The telepathic message from the terrible plant was clear to him, and Ivan knew his awful fate. He was to become the new gatherer of fresh blood for his new master, just as Jonathon Prescott had done for so long…

8. Doctor Kraus' Garden

"It is nice to have an exciting new neighbor," said Charlie's mother as she spoke into her telephone. "And I don't think we've ever had a professor move in before, which seems a bit odd too, now that I think of it, with the university right in town…" She sat at her kitchen table with the spiral telephone cord pulled tautly clear across the room. "Oh, no, no, I don't think so," said Charlie's mother, "But you know, he did tell Carol that he moved here for the climate. You see apparently his health problems require him to live in a climate as humid as ours. And you know he went right to work on that tall wooden fence in his backyard. Yes, it is obnoxiously tall I agree with you, but Doctor Kraus must be a private man…"

In the back yard young Charlie had a very serious task that demanded his attention. He had just come up from the basement and out through the cellar door, which opened directly into the backyard. He stopped a moment and listened, directly below the kitchen window to hear if his mother was still on the telephone. To young Charlie her yammering was a wonderful sound, for it was to him the sound of total freedom. And so long as he remained in the house or in the yard, he could do most anything that he pleased.

This did not of course, include the taking of rat poison from the basement, which certainly would not have been allowed. But this offense was easily justified, for it wasn't often that a young boy discovered that he was living next to a garden of giant flesh eating, murderous plants.

Charlie knew this because he had heard Maurice meet his end only three days prior. It had happened in the hidden place behind their yard, between the thick hedges that had come with the house, and the new fence of the doctor's yard. Maurice had been the friendly neighborhood stray, flawed only with an irresistible urge to trespass and feed from everyone's garbage. On that fateful day he had taken to digging a hole beneath the doctor's new wooden fence that towered high above the others. Charlie had come over when he first heard the growling, only to find the hind quarters of the dog shaking violently and sticking out from beneath the fence. Maurice had then made a terrible shriek before disappearing forcefully through the hole.

This remarkable incident was followed only by the noise of thrashing and the subsequent death yelps of the dog. Charlie had run away due to fear, and told his mother, who assured him that the frail doctor was a kindly man, certainly incapable of harming the animal. But no sign of Maurice had been observed since, and only Charlie knew where the dog had gone. The hole had mysteriously been filled by morning, with every inch packed tightly with soil so that Charlie could not peer through.

These strange occurrences were why, after the dog's death, the boy had taken his deceased father's antique hand drill from the cellar and set to drilling a hole in the doctor's new wooden monstrosity. A young boy's curiosity is strong, and Charlie reasoned that it was his duty to learn what had happened to the dog. He had found that the wood was thick but not hard, and the spiraled manual drill bit had cut quietly through with precision as he turned it.

The first spying glance had taken every bit of his courage, but Charlie was a courageous boy. When he first pressed his eye against the hole he saw only a blur of brilliant green. Then their terrible shapes had taken form, and he observed the bizarre green stalks swaying back and forth through the air. Their circumferences were as large as melons and their leathery stalks towered as high as a man. And this only measured the terrible green stalks, and not the thick tendrils that continued upward like the arms of an inverted squid. The mass of them swayed gently, and the tendrils pointed skyward made the garden appear as though it was seaweed beneath the water.

As Charlie peered through, a beautiful monarch butterfly appeared in the air and floated gently above the squirming mass of plants. It hovered gracefully a few moments and then descended, landing upon the side of a green stalk where the tendrils above were sprouted. As soon as the butterfly's wings ceased their motion, a tendril of the plant snapped quickly to life. With great dexterity the tendril latched upon the fragile insect and thrust it into a gaping hole that appeared suddenly upon the plant. It was a ghastly, gaping mouth at the top of the stalk, opening like the barbed mouth of a lamprey, preparing to consume a living meal.

The realization came quickly to young Charlie that he now lived next to a garden of carnivorous plants. For the world is to young boys still full of adventure, containing many monsters for heroes to slay. He imagined quite clearly how those sinister plants had awakened and consumed the poor dog Maurice. It was the only possible explanation and his youthful naiveté allowed him to accept this truth. It was not long after that Charlie had formed a plan to inject one of them with the pesticide that he had seen down in his cellar.

He had promptly taken the drill away and returned to the house, where he assembled the tools for the new task to be performed. The first of these was his mother's culinary syringe which she used to inject raw poultry with melted butter. He had crept into the kitchen and taken it from the drawer while his mother was in the other room. Down in the cellar, he submerged the needle point into the liquid pesticide, and filled it with as much of the chemical that it would hold.

He was back at the fence within half an hour, where he found that one of the giant plants was indeed close enough to the hole for the needle to reach when extended through. When he examined the thick leathery surface, he felt a chill come over his body. The skin of the stalks appeared to pulse with life, and it seemed that they would be perhaps, warm to the touch of his hand.

But he had no real desire to learn if this were true, and so, had slid the point of the needle quietly through the hole and drew an inward breath. When he felt the hardness of the stalk he thrust the needle forward, feeling it pierce the tough hide. He could not see because the hole contained the needle, but thought he felt the vibration of movement. He depressed the plunger hurriedly, driving every bit of the pesticide into the abhorrent mass.

When he withdrew the needle and looked again he saw the stalk writhing about like the severed tail of a lizard. Its four tendrils slashed through the air as they searched blindly for the source of their pain.

Charlie heard them smash against the fence and became fearful for his peering eye. He then pulled away and saw the tendrils clawing for him over the top of the giant fence. He could hear the hardness of the barbs upon the wood, scratching like an animal's claws. He cowered and waited as the horrible plant thrashed about, but alas, it soon regained its calmness and steadfastly refused to die. A creeping terror came over him as he realized that the plant had wanted to consume his flesh and physically ingest him. With this realization Charlie's courage became exhausted, and he dropped the needle unintentionally upon the ground and ran for the comfort of his yard.

But on this present day his courage had returned anew, and Charlie ran from his hiding place below the window. Once out of site and behind the hedges he quietly removed the box of rat poison from where he had hidden it beneath his shirt. He felt certain that the plants could not seize him so long as he stayed out of the doctor's yard.

He found the needle on the ground exactly as he had left it. He peered through the hole and confirmed that the devilish plant had indeed survived. Its leathery stalk again swayed to and fro, amidst the planted army of its brethren. It had tolerated enough pesticide to kill an entire lawn, and was somehow no worse for wear.

Charlie eyed the entire yard through the hole as best as he could to ensure that the doctor was not outside. Left he leaned, and then right, peering past the bloated stalks to the open yard beyond. Silently he looked, dreading the awakening of the abominable plants. He thought of their tendrils grasping for him through the air, and felt a shiver down his spine.

With uncanny calmness Charlie poured the poisonous powder into the syringe, and then topped it off with water from the hose. *"Anything that eats meat can be poisoned,"* Charlie reasoned as he thrust the point through the hole once again, and into the pulsing hide of the hideous plant.

Shivers of terror shot through him as its fat body shook immediately to life. The thrashing was more violent this time, as the barbed tendrils clawed at the fence top and tore pieces of wood from the planks. As much as the pesticide had hurt it, the rat poison seemed to hurt it more. A horrid shriek filled the air, followed by silence, as the tendril arms abruptly ceased their tearing of the top of the fence.

Charlie peered through once again and saw each of the tendril arms hanging loosely above the ground. The top of the plant gaped open and revealed a mouth that would not taste flesh again.

A new sound came into the air as the doctor's house door swung open forcefully. Charlie's body froze in its position with his face still against the fence. It was an equal mix of fear paralysis and curiosity that kept his eye to the hole. Then when the white hair of the doctor appeared, the curiosity dissipated and only the paralysis remained. He saw the aged bespectacled eyes burning in his direction, displaying great concern. Certainly the doctor had heard the death shriek and now saw it hanging limply among the others.

Doctor Kraus disappeared momentarily from view and then a new sound filled the air. It was the sound of mist being sprayed from a red device within his frail hands. Charlie watched as he sprayed the plants at the edge of his menacing garden, covering each with the mysterious mist as they reared up to latch upon him. After a moment their tendrils would fall limply, one after the other, and the doctor then stepped methodically between them.

The doctor lowered the red misting device and examined the plant that Charlie had killed. He felt over its withered green hide slowly with one of his bare hands. For several moments thereafter the old doctor stood silently as though mourning a euthanized pet.

Then as though within a nightmare, Charlie saw the doctor's gaze fall upon his peering eye. His face portrayed wrath more powerful than Charlie had ever seen. This induced mobility back into his limbs and he withdrew from the fence, turning and running through the hedges toward the safety of his house.

Charlie ran through his kitchen and beneath the spiral telephone cord that was still pulled tautly across the room. "Charlie it's lunch time,' she hollered at him, as he tore through the doorway to the hall. "Why yes," she said into the telephone, "He did have a wife when he first arrived. But apparently she didn't adjust well and had to move east to live with her sister. At least that's what Carol told me. After all those years, can you imagine, a marriage ending in divorce? Oh yes, I do remember that now that you mention it…"

Many things stirred about in Charlie's mind as he tried to calm his nerves. He pondered mostly upon the red device that had rendered each of the plants so harmless. Many courses of action worked through his young mind, none of them particularly pleasant. He wished then, as he did often, that his father were still alive.

A sound came from the doctor's yard and Charlie looked out through his window. He saw Doctor Kraus leaving in his car, disappearing as it pulled from the driveway. The sound came again as the unseen security gate closed behind the fence. He thought again about the red mist device and how quickly the doctor had retrieved it…Yes! It was clearly kept outside, Charlie was certain. He ran from his room quietly down to the cellar, and gathered what he needed.

The alley beside Doctor Kraus' yard would provide him shelter from the neighbor's eyes. He easily climbed the large oak tree and assessed the doctor's yard from the new angle. The sleeping plants were safely at a distance at the rear of the yard.

Charlie was careful not to jostle his backpack as he threw his leg over the fence. From there he shimmied quickly down and dropped to the driveway with a painful thud. It would be a difficult climb when leaving.

The plants turned in his direction upon hearing the sound of his landing. A moment later they seemed to forget, and drifted back to their swaying sleep. Charlie set immediately to work and looked over the doctor's tools near the garage. The red device was setting in plain view, and it seemed to Charlie a wonderful sight. He removed his pack from his shoulders and took the device in his shaking hands. He knew very well that the security gate could open without warning. There would be no safe place to hide.

As Charlie crept across the cement drive the plants turned to point their tendrils in his direction. They did not come fully alive but rather seemed to sense his presence as they slept. When he reached the tool rack he set his pack lightly upon the ground. Taking the mist device in both shaking hands he pumped the spray in the direction of the nearest plant. It reared up just as it felt the coolness, and then limply dropped its tendrils toward the ground. He exchanged the red device for the needle, which had been refilled with the poison. He would have to refill it many times from the box of poison within his pack and water from the outdoor faucet. Charlie stepped up to the drugged abomination before him and prepared to give it a lethal shot.

"They aren't monsters," came a grainy voice from behind. Charlie's heart shot into his throat as he turned and saw Doctor Kraus standing at the corner of his house. The doctor wore a gray suit which draped over his tiny frame. "You see, they are the result of many years of cross breeding all of the carnivorous plants from around the world. Each generation I have made stronger, and now I come to live in this part of the world where they will flourish in your moist climate. Already I've confirmed that the seeds thrive in this soil."

Charlie stood speechless with fear.

"I am just a man of science," said the doctor as he walked slowly, foot over foot to where Charlie stood. "You see, they are my life's work. So I have begun teaching again so that I might find the right young successor. It would not do for me to die and all of my work along with me."

Doctor Kraus crept up further and the space between them rapidly closed. Charlie looked over his shoulder at the plants, not knowing which of the fiends he feared more. Suddenly his young mind remembered that he held a concoction of deadly poison in his grasp.

"My wife also began to deviate from the vision," said the doctor in his eerily calm voice. "She became concerned when I began feeding them cats and dogs which I had acquired. But the silly woman failed to realize that I had the perfect method for her disposal. And now you, young lad, are causing me more trouble than you know. For a child that goes missing will surely bring an investigation from the police. So I will be forced to uproot my little children, and hide them down in my basement, beside their offspring beneath the lights."

The doctor outstretched a hand, the sight of which freed Charlie's limbs from their paralysis. He turned to the drugged plant behind him and drove his needle deep into its tissue. The plant seemed to feel the pain of the poison and awoke partially from its slumber. Languidly the tendrils slashed sloppily about at its sides.

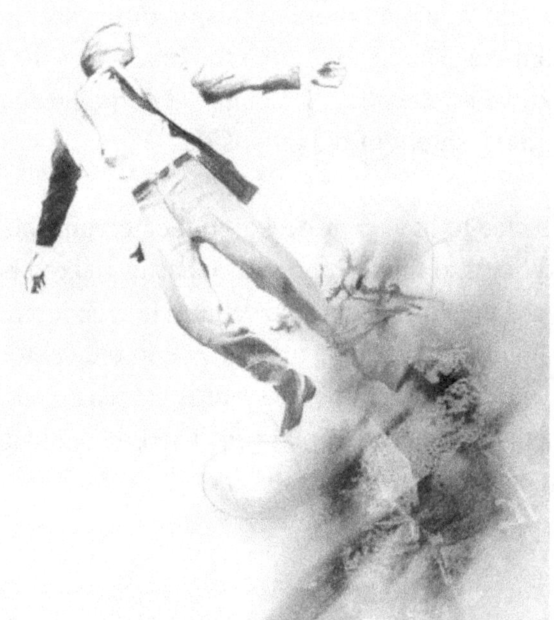

"No!" cried the feeble doctor, who rushed forward, pushing Charlie aside. The doctor collapsed onto the dying plant as it clasped him and held him tightly. Charlie scrambled safely away and watched as the doctor howled. "No, it is I!" he shrieked, "It is your beloved father!"

The entire crop of the foul plants came to life then, and thrashed about with tremendous hunger. Their tendrils filled the air wildly, and their mouths opened and closed repeatedly. Green fluid of salivation spilled out of them, and all of their white teeth were exposed for Charlie to see.

It was to the boy the worst vision he had ever beheld, as the barbed tendrils of several plants tore the doctor's clothes and flesh. Soon the old man was no longer upon the ground as his limbs were stretched and pulled upward. One of the hideous plant mouths seized his left hand, and another clamped his right. Each swallow drew his limbs deeper into their abominable masses.

When the mouths had engulfed him as deeply as they could, they clamped down and severed the arms. "No, it is I…" howled the doctor pitifully as his head was drawn to a waiting mouth which swallowed him to the base of his neck.

Charlie could watch no more of this revolting scene and seized his backpack from the ground. He ran to the fence near the oak tree and threw his things into the alley. He clutched at the fence and scrambled upon it, and to the safety of the other side.

***

"Yes it is nice to have a professor in the neighborhood," agreed Charlie's mother into the telephone as Charlie walked beneath the window toward the entrance of the cellar. He wondered how long it would take the plants to starve, and how soon the doctor would be missed. Perhaps it would be best to return, he reasoned, and simply drug and inject them as he had first planned. The boy decided that he'd have to sleep on it, as he opened the cellar door.

9. Farmhouse Terror

It seemed like a nightmare, and perhaps it had been only a terrible dream. You see, my girlfriend Mary and I were out on some country road, parked off the asphalt a bit, onto the shoulder. A stranger approached, and there was conversation between us, but what it involved we could never remember. Even now I have no knowledge of the verbal exchange that had occurred. But the stranger's demeanor seemed friendly and we did agree to go with him, back to his mother's house for reasons still unknown.

Upon arrival at his mother's farmhouse there was abundant activity right from the start. There was energy in the air, as though many people had been about, and had only departed very recently. And as I pondered this, the strange man's mother emerged and greeted us at the door. She waved us in, and we entered, just as one does things at random in a dream.

There was another man inside the doorway as we stepped inward; a large salesman in an ill-fitting suit. And although the old woman did receive us very cordially, her attention was quite divided. For she worked also to prevent the salesman from leaving, and I noticed the poor fellow to be in a pitiful, emotional state. He shuffled his hands in and out of pockets and appeared to be fighting a terror that showed plainly on his face.

And as I stood there observing this, a mighty sound came up through the floorboards and vibrated throughout my bones. The house shook with the force of it, but the old woman paid it no mind.

The salesman however twitched beneath his skin and he promptly fled past us and out through the doorway. As he shuffled past, his eyes met briefly with my own and I shan't forget what I saw there. There was a craziness in his eyes, and his foul salesman's breath ran up my nose. The utmost desperation filled his words as he said imploringly, "Get out of this house." And then hastily he ran down the tall steps, never once looking back upon us.

I looked to Mary but she saw none of these peculiar warnings, and it seemed that I was on my own. It was Mary's nature to be oblivious to such things, and presently I said not a word. Mary and the old woman simply chatted and exchanged pleasantries, the way that women do.

I looked around for the stranger who had brought us there, but he had long since departed. I suspected with quite a bit of certainty that he was headed back to the main road, searching for other travelers at that very moment, to be herded to the house just as we had been.

It began to seem that we were part of an elaborate charade, and that we were now dangerously submerged into the sinister plan. Even as I thought these words I looked up to see that Mary had already been led into another room.

Their conversation never halted, and their legs seemed to share a rhythm in which they were both entwined. The old woman would step backward slowly, her words pulling Mary along. It was as though an invisible rope was about my Mary's waist as she continued to be drawn onward. Just as Mary would finish speaking, the old woman would speak again, wrapping her words tightly around Mary's words so that I was never able to intervene.

Perspiration broke out on my neck as I waited for a break in the chatter. All I needed was a split second to interject that we must be off for the sake of time. But no break was forthcoming and my words were held mute in my throat.

The charade was very well rehearsed, perhaps running from dawn until dusk each and every day. And still we were drawn along with her, like lambs toward the slaughter.

My brain thought back to the salesman and pondered just how he had slipped away. He had had no girlfriend alongside him, and his tongue had not been bound. But he was now long gone, having escaped never to return.

Into another room they trod further, to a space void of furniture or discernable purpose. Only a large door on the farthest wall presented itself as a noticeable feature to behold. I remembered the house-shaking sound which we had heard moments earlier, and felt dread grow deep in my belly.

The old woman pulled still onward, and her feet inched closer to the door. Each step was well rehearsed, and I sensed the impending crescendo of what lie ahead. And still we moved onward...

A stammer from my lips would have sufficed perhaps, but there was simply was no room for it at all! I saw now a fact that I had missed earlier - that the old woman did not draw breath between her words! She was an inhuman ghoul and I knew this now to be true. It was clearly the secret to her ability to fill each bit of air with her words, wrapping them around the words of others. And I was forced to shuffle along foolishly and listen to their terrible sound.

I peered then to the crack beneath the far door and saw a hint of something there. It was a shifting of feet and a creak of boards, and I knew that our time ran short. My heart seized when the door flew open, but alas, I was not surprised! Another burly county born son had been hiding there lying in wait. His arms were massive and his face was covered by an appalling mask of black. The eyes peered out at us displaying malicious intent.

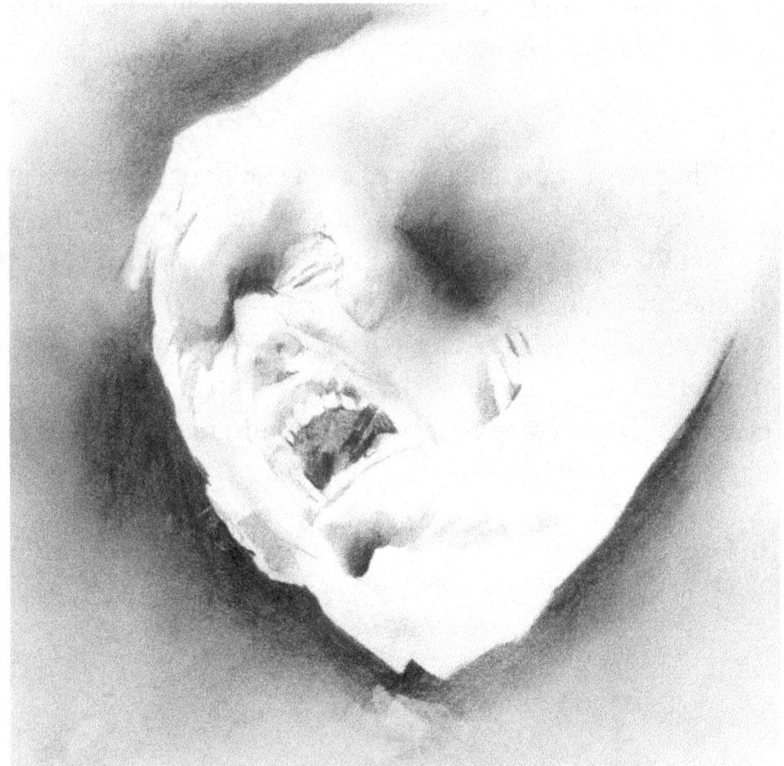

Mary shrieked and stood terrified, now for the very first time. The old woman stepped away to the corner and her false smile had disappeared. It was replaced by an evil smirk that showed her inhuman teeth. Her evil was now plainly presented to us, which my keen eye had already perceived.

In a flash the hand of the ghoulish son was upon Mary, and clasped her tiny wrist. He sought now to hurl her down into the darkness, to a certain impending doom.

I lunged and took his wrist into my hand, while forcing my other hand beneath his chin. Now at last all that had been hidden was upon us, and I was locked deeply in a battle of survival. With utmost strain I held him back, as his ghoulish head towered over my own. From the corner of my eye I spied the old woman as she wrung her hands, waiting eagerly with glee and delight.

The ghoulish son realized that he needed both hands to fight me, and released his grasp from upon my Mary's wrist. I stepped a leg between both of his, and pushed into him with all my might. The stairs seemed to be my only chance, but I knew that I risked greatly, tumbling down them as well. If I did so then whatever horror lurked there would certainly be my end.

I arched downward and pressed even harder until at last his arms did flail. I launched a blow with my hand now freed, and over the edge he began to fall. His ghoulish body tumbled hard onto the upper steps and he disappeared into darkness below.

The old hag shrieked an ungodly sound as we ran from that awful room. Retracing our steps, we rushed as though the Devil himself were at our heels. We tore out into the daylight toward our car, and drove off with the haste of terror.

Much later we decided that it was surely a shared hallucination, for such insane things simply do not occur…

10. Cavern of Death

There are limitless opportunities for adventure within the summer days of ten-year-old boys. The hard truths of the world have not yet pressed down upon them, and their imaginations have learned no boundaries. But there is also present the naïveté of youth, and danger is never far behind …

Young Paul was a bit timid when in the presence of others, but once out of view he felt as much at ease as the rest of the boys. Especially when he was out in the woods or down by the ocean, which was his destination this very morning. He picked up his trousers from the floor where he had dropped them on the prior evening, after an entire day of bliss and the bright blue sky. He took also a clean shirt from his dresser drawer, where his mother had placed them, neatly folded.

Paul scarcely saw her that morning as he simultaneously ran out and shouted goodbye, letting the screen door smack loudly behind him as the stretched spring pulled it closed.

His best friend Adam may not have awoken yet for the day, but this was a matter of no concern. Paul trudged languidly through his yard of brown field grass and toward the woods that bordered their land. It was a trek he had made thousands of times and could easily have done with his eyes closed.

Once he was inside the tree line, a dirt path became visible through the tall brown growth. Paul felt great pride as he stepped upon it and walked between the trees. He alone was the king of this domain, and he ruled the dirt beneath his feet. Young Paul knew the location of every stick and rock within that woods, and this provided him nothing short of the feeling of ownership.

His mind began to wander to the plans that he and his best friend Adam had made the night before. There was a small cave within the rocks of the bluff which they had never dared to explore. The boys knew very little about the mysterious rock hole, except that it filled with sea water each afternoon when the tide made the water roll high. Together they had climbed upon the rocks at its entrance their entire young lives, but never once had dared to venture into the cold darkness that lurked in its interior.

Caves such as this near the ocean shore were common, and both of the boys had heard stories of them throughout their lives. One tale in particular had haunted Paul relentlessly, when the darkness of night had filled his bedroom and he lay alone in his bed.

The tale told of a boy who had dared to explore one of these caves, and drowned deep inside when the tide had filled its depths. This schoolyard legend described how his body had never been found, having been pulled out to sea with the retreating water. It was further said that the dead boy walked from the sea each year at midnight on the eve that marked his death. The drowning and the subsequent rot was said to have damaged the boy's memory, and his corpse was unable to remember the way back to his home. And so, from dawn until dusk once each year, the rotting mass that remained of the boy was said to walk throughout the coastal town. He ventured to every house whose path he crossed, and his little rotten hand would knock gently upon the glass of each darkened window…

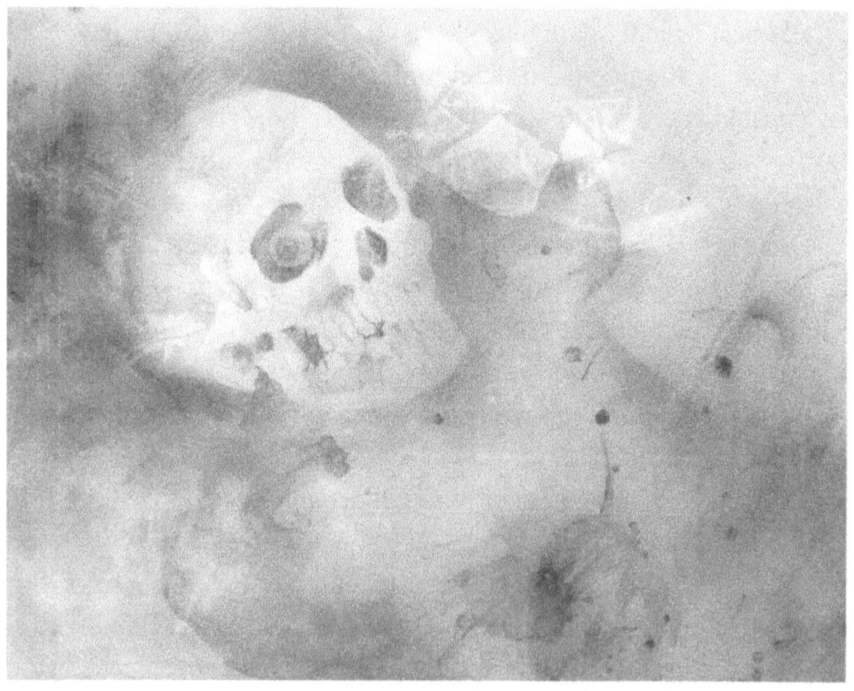

But he was not a small child any longer and Paul no longer believed these children's tales. He knew also the timing of the tide swells just as well as he knew the familiar trail beneath his feet. He could venture safely inside the cavern for a few minutes without really taking any risk at all.

Adam was already awake when Paul arrived, and was busied with a task inside his backyard shed. He was ten just as Adam was, but taller and more assertive. The door of the shed was propped open and Paul could see that Adam was searching upon an upper shelf while standing on the tips of his toes.

"Hey," said Paul as he walked up.

"Hi," said Adam as he took a flashlight from the shelf when he located it, and then started closing the shed door. Both of the boys had been excited about the plan, having lain in their beds imagining the great mysteries that they may find inside.

"It ought to be pretty clean in there, with the tide washing it out every day. Not like some bat cave in the mountains," said Paul. He had thought of various types of caves as he had lain in his bed trying to sleep. "Where's my light?" he asked when he saw only one in Adam's hand.

"This is all I can find," said his friend, as they turned and walked toward another trail that would take them down to the coastline. Above them the sun radiated summer heat amidst the perfection of a cloudless sky. Adam led the way down the bluff trail, as was their usual custom. Paul felt the tingle of great anticipation churning within his belly, and the raising of the hairs on his arms. This thrill of a pending adventure was the best sensation he had ever known.

They walked along the sandy trail and descended to the water, just as they had so often before. From their location, the mouth of the cavern lay only fifty yards northward along the ocean shore.

"The time is good now," said Adam when they had reached the hollowed rock of the bluff, with a tone like that of a lieutenant commanding a platoon. "The tide is at its lowest now."

Paul looked to the water's edge and said nothing, but he did not fully agree. He estimated that the tide had been lowest nearly forty minutes before they arrived. Both boys stood at the entryway of the water-carved rock that formed the mouth of the cavern. Many times before they had stood and looked inward, just as they did on this day.

Adam clicked on his light and shined it upon the interior walls.

"It's clean," said Adam.

"But how far back does it go?" said Paul. Adam did not reply, but rather stepped inward, leading as he always did.

The entrance was widest at the bottom and narrowed as it rose, but both boys could walk along without touching the stone. Paul reached out to it with his hand, noting how cold it was where the sun's rays did not penetrate.

Eight feet within the narrow stone corridor, the natural floor suddenly descended rapidly for a stretch of ten feet or longer. When the light was shone along the descent, they saw only a pool of standing water at the bottom. It seemed to Paul that the adventure had ended, before they had even gotten a good look inside.

"Well that's it then," said Paul as though he felt disappointment, but truthfully he felt relief.

"Come on," said Adam, as he began to descend the sloping rock, as though the thought of giving up already would not register in his brain. "Let's get a good look at that pool of water."

Paul followed his friend without question, as he had done so many times before. Adam's confidence seemed to him as contagious, and instantly the thoughts of turning back drifted out of his mind.

The cavern filled their nostrils with an unusual smell, one that neither boy had encountered before. It was partially the odor of seawater, but also the smell of rock and earth. It was neither unpleasant nor outright foul, but simply foreign. It seemed that they had truly entered into a new world.

The rock of the downward slope was slippery and walking became impossible. Both boys lowered themselves to a squat, and then slid down on the soles of their shoes while leaning back upon their hands. Paul looked into the approaching black water, and it looked to him like a pool of death. He imagined vividly how one could slip upon the rocks and fall unconsciously into that dark water, ensuring certain doom.

"Look, natural stairs," said Adam as he pointed over the pool and into the darkness. When the light was shown Paul took a better look at the distant new tunnel they had spied from above.

"Do you see it?" said Adam passionately, the thrill of the adventure churning now within his guts. "To the left there, it continues. There's plenty more to see!" Adam shone the light into the standing water and they could not see the bottom. "It must not be deep," he then said.

Paul wasn't so certain. He could think only of slithering and scurrying marine life that might inhabit the dark pool. Without a word more, Adam stepped a foot down into it and sank to his groin.

"Cold!" he shouted, and then trudged determinedly through the water. A few sloshing steps further, and he had reached the natural steps. "Come on now!" he called back, as he stood triumphantly on the far side.

Paul would follow, but first looked back and upward, to the light of the entryway from which they had come. The bright light and safety of the beach now looked to him, as though disturbingly far away. His shoe pushed into something soft as he stepped his right leg into the pool. His mind thought of the drowned boy and imagined the body decomposing beneath his feet. This horrible thought only helped to speed him along, and Paul was quickly across.

From the other side Paul looked across the watery divide, and it seemed to him as though something significant had been accomplished. It was the wonderful sensation of ownership again, for he and Adam had now claimed the cave as their own. It had become part of their kingdom, just like the beach and the woods and the trails.

The boys climbed the irregular steps and grabbed the porous rocks to guide their way. The corridor at the top was wider and they could move about with ease. They walked along it for ten feet or so, and then followed it around a curve. Ten feet further the overhead rock began to narrow, and they could not walk side by side. Soon thereafter the corridor closed completely, and came abruptly to an end.

"So this is the end of it," said Adam. "It goes farther than I thought!" Both boys took a better look around since there was no more ground to cover.

Paul found himself searching the corners for signs of anyone who had come before them. The single light forced them to remain together and the progress of examination was slow.

To his great delight Adam found something circular and metallic hidden amongst the stones. A closer look showed that it was a coin, corroded beyond readability. It was covered with a bluish coating, concealing the identity of the find.

"It's treasure," said Adam as he clasped it safely within his hand. "We'll get a good look at it back outside. Let's see if we can find anymore."

This made Paul think of the tide and he wondered how much time had passed. As he pondered it he felt emptiness in his stomach and realized that he was hungry.

"Lets head back," said Paul earnestly as he turned to look at his best friend. "We can come back in here if the water hasn't swelled too high."

"A while more," said Adam intently, as he continued shining the light about the ground. "There's something more in here, I can feel it!"

Paul pushed aside his fear and tried to match the courage of his friend. They found no other relics, and soon Paul's mind began to wander. Thoughts of the entry corridor would not leave him, and strangely haunted his mind. Then in a flash a realization came to him, and he felt terror fill his body. For the cavern had first dropped downward, and would surely fill with water from the tide. And then they had crossed that shallow pool and climbed higher than the sea level. It was all clear to him in an instant, that they would get trapped within the cave. And possible still was the chance that they had not climbed so high, and that the cave would be flooded completely.

"The tide!" yelled Paul. "It's going to trap us in!" Paul took the light from his friend's hand and ran back to the steps where the corridor narrowed. He both scooted and climbed downward as though there wasn't a moment to lose.

To his horror the fear was confirmed, and he saw that the tide had indeed already crept far inward. Already it had filled the narrow crossing corridor of the pool, with only a few inches of air remaining beneath the ceiling made of stone. "We've got to swim through it!" screamed Paul to Adam who was now behind. "We've got to or we'll drown!"

"The coin!" yelled Adam. "I dropped it up there when you screamed!" His friend snatched the light from Paul's hand and scurried back to the dead end cave. Paul was left standing in near darkness but could still see a hint of daylight through the water.

He did not wait, and submerged himself, feeling the coldness of the ocean water as his whole body dropped into the pool. With great terror he felt an incoming wave push against him, driving him back through the darkened water from which he may never escape. With all of his strength he fought and swam, keeping his flailing hands out before him so as not to smash his head against a rock. He followed that hint of daylight that called out to him, urging him to remain alive, and not die within that pool only to become one of the soft things at its bottom. He reached the slippery slope they had come down and popped his head out into the free air. The light was stronger now and he could see the water falling down the slope, as it tried to entomb them within the cavern.

Paul climbed fully out of the pool and then remembered that Adam was still behind. Frantically he breathed and waited, wanting only to see Adam's head and hands appear from the water filled channel. Second after second ticked away, and then minute followed by minute.

At last Paul knew he must do something and climbed back within the edge of the pool. He grasped the rock wall firmly and pushed his legs back through the water, hoping to feel Adam as he tried to swim his way through. Paul felt only water and rock with his feet but refused to flee without his friend. He continued this effort several more times, but was at last forced to save himself. He pulled his body again from the water and scurried up the watery slope.

Paul ran from the cave and into the daylight, and knew at last that he would survive. He could do nothing except call for help, and so, ran up the trail toward his home. Already the beach was mostly submerged and the mouth of the cavern would soon disappear. He thought of Adam perhaps within the safety of the upper corridor, breathing the trapped air where the water would not rise. Paul hoped dearly that the upper cave was above sea level, but he could not be certain.

It seemed an eternity before the police arrived, and Paul had lost hope. Their mothers gathered on the remaining sand as the police divers searched within the cave. They found Adam's body in the flooded chamber of the pool where he seemed to have fallen and downed while unconscious. Or perhaps he had smashed his head upon a rock as he tried to swim through the flooded corridor. It was impossible to determine with certainty if the head wound had occurred before or after he had died.

The coin however, had never been found, and it seemed an important detail only to Paul. It would now be lost for the remainder of its years until it corroded completely, within the chamber of the standing water.

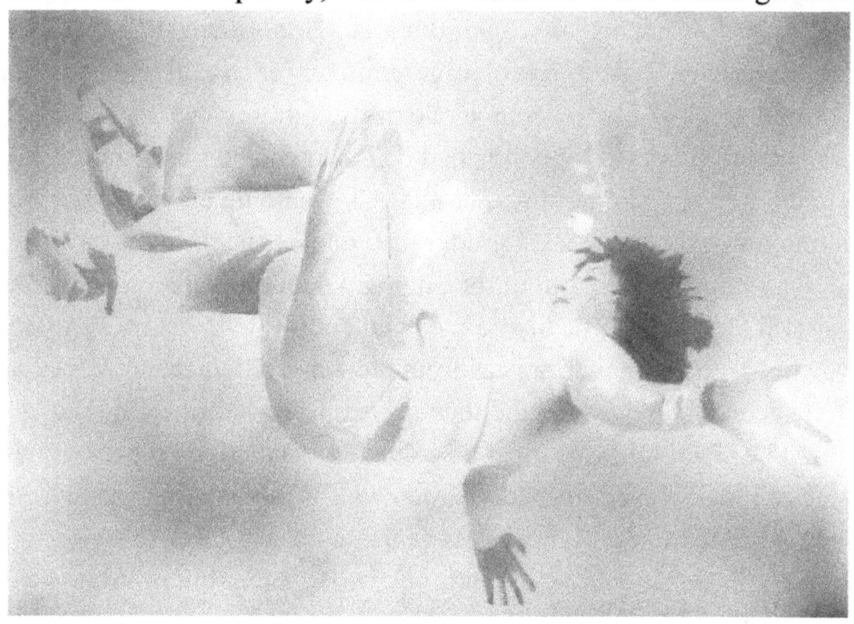

The nights were the hardest for Paul, because these were the hours when he thought most of his dead friend. Especially on the anniversary of the drowning, which was when Paul imagined Adam's corpse rising from its grave and walking throughout the town. For several years after he would be certain that he heard the rotting fingers upon his window. During the moments of this terrible sound Paul could only cover his ears. He vividly imagined that when dawn came, Adam's corpse would walk from the town, just as the schoolyard legend had foretold. Paul dreamed that his friend did not return to the cemetery, but rather to the cavern where he had died. There the corpse would leave the moonlight and disappear into the tomb of the standing water. There the dead flesh would lie and rot for another year, beneath the eternal blackness of that water.

11. Unearthed

The wind storm had formed quickly across the plains of the farmland, which was a sure sign that the hot weather of summer was soon to come. William looked out through the open door of his cottage and onto the vast field of his village's farmland.

"The wheat stalks all lay eastward," said William, to his wife Augustine who sat not far away, holding their newborn to her chest. "No funnel cloud must have formed, although I'd have thought from all that wind that one had." Augustine looked up to him momentarily as he spoke this, but did not look out through the door to the field. William was the authority on such matters, and she did not doubt his word.

"It did blow mightily, didn't it?" she said in agreement, as the babe cooed softly in her arms.

William ate the eggs which she had made for him and gazed upon the beauty of her face. Of the three other wives within the village, Augustine was certainly the most beautiful. It had been many months since they last engaged physically, and as he looked upon her, he anticipated greatly those times that would soon come.

A knock then came loudly upon his wooden doorframe, and William shifted his gaze to view which of the three village men had called upon him. Standing within the bright sunshine of the doorway, he saw the gleaming face of Edward, the village's youngest man.

"The lone oak was felled last night," said Edward as he both leaned upon and clasped the hinge side of the door, "The big one out there on the west side. It don't matter which way she felled, I reckon, cause either way its lays in the field."

William continued eating while Edward waited, and then finally stood and took his hat before walking wordlessly through the door. Edward waited for him to pass, and then trotted up to his side to walk along with him.

"It'll be a day's work just chopping through her," said the young man. "Then another one hauling the splints away. We ain't got no saw."

"We'll use the mule and what's left of the wagon cover, just like we dragged the rocks from the fields," said William. He stopped and took his ax from where it leaned against the side of the cabin. Edward saw this and realized that the labor was to begin, and so, ran to fetch his own tool. William continued walking to the remains of the tree, which he saw now distantly upon the ground, hearing soon thereafter the eager trot of Edward returned to his side.

Removal of the tree would indeed take the entire day, realized William when he had reached it, and stood studying the jagged base that remained. This was no great matter, for all the seeds had been sown already, and the man hours could be spared. He looked back toward the village and saw that the other men now approached distantly with their tools.

"I'd a liked to have seen it fall," said Edward as he walked along lightheartedly at the tip of the fallen oak. "I'll bet that it made a thundering crack followed by…" The voice of the young man cut off abruptly and a cry of fear escaped his throat. This noise was followed directly with the dominant sound of breaking rock.

William turned to look upon the young man just as the last of his head and shoulders passed through a hole upon the ground which had opened beneath his feet. It looked as though the earth had simply opened its mouth, and swallowed the young man in one gulp.

"Edward!" yelled William down into the darkness, when he had scrambled over the girth of the tree and stood peering down into the hole. Instinctively he kept his feet distanced apart, to spread his weight upon the ground. "Where are you boy?" He could see a thick layer of rock that lay beneath the sod, below which there was darkness and open air. Far below a portion of a rock cavern was visible, but he could not see the body of his friend.

"I am here," said Edward somewhat breathlessly, and then extended a hand out into the descending ray of sunlight that penetrated deep into the hollow space. "The earth just…fell inward," he said confusedly from twelve feet below the height where he had formerly been.

"Is it vast?" shouted William down to him. "If your skinny bones could break it, it's a wonder this tree still sits above ground."

"No, I cannot see much, but there is a wall of solid rock not far from where I am," said Edward. "I think I have fallen in at the edge of this thing, through ground weakened by the fall of that tree. I think my ankle is… yes… hurt."

"Hold on now and I'll call to Paul and David for rope and the lantern," said William, who then turned and yelled loudly into the wind that blew over the massive field.

Within a half hour a rope had been tied to the splintered stump of the tree, and then lowered gently through the hole in the earth with the lantern tied to its end. Edward had unfastened it and set it upon the smooth rock of the bottom before climbing to the daylight above as the others pulled.

"That cave's big I think," said Edward, as the men heaved the rope upward and he stepped upon the protruding rocks of the wall. "It is an easy climb, even with my ankle."

"Matches," said William simply to the other men.

"To think that we've been farming over this covered pit for two years now, and never known it was there," said Paul.

William did not have a reply for this, and so, clasped tightly the rope and disappeared into the darkness. Once his feet were upon the stone bottom he dared a look around. Except for the small circle of light in which he stood, nothing of interest could be seen. He stooped over the lantern and set it alight, with the flame of a match he had struck upon the ground.

"It is not so big," he called out as the light expanded and fell on the walls of the chamber. He saw immediately that the chamber had been constructed with symmetry, and was not a fluke of the natural land. In the corner nearest the tree, roots penetrated the rock walls and ambled throughout the room. The rock ceiling above puzzled him most, for it appeared to be made entirely of stone. The slabs seemed sculpted and arranged precariously as though their massive weight would topple at any moment. "They quarried the walls of the chamber and then covered it over with the largest stones," he said to himself as he held the lantern high and gazed into the light it cast.

"What's that Will?" called out David, as his voice betrayed overwhelming curiosity. "William, I'm coming down!"

William kept the lantern in this raised position and then turned a half step to his left. As the light crept over the wall an enormous figure was suddenly exposed, sending Williams' heart into a panic. Adrenaline filled his veins and a gasp escaped his lips as the image of a stone beast appeared before him. It held the figure of a man, although perhaps a third larger in size. The massive form was seated upon a throne carved into the stone of the ground. The great knuckles of the hands gripped the ends of the stone ledges upon which they lay. The tendons and muscles had been carved with the detail worthy of a great museum. The head of the carved beast displayed equal prestige, of which the scowling countenance was visible. The facial features held a look of strange hostility, although only the ears appeared inhuman. They were pointed at both the upper and lower portions, and shaped like no creature's ears which William had before seen.

"Great God!" exclaimed David when he had descended, announcing to William that he was there. "It's hideous!" David shrieked, and then stepped unknowingly somewhat behind the safety of William's form.

William stepped closer, perhaps now braver since he was not alone, and stood directly in front of the seated sculpture. With the light now fully upon it, he could see that the figure was unclothed, and each stone muscle was polished smoothly into lifelike perfection. And most disturbing of all its lifelike traits was the phallus of the beast, which extended in an upright stance. A shiver of strange fear ran down William's spine as he beheld this macabre detail.

"Look at that," said David as he saw the peculiar authenticity which had been given to the stone humanoid. "Why? It's ungodly!"

"We already knew that these lands had been farmed in the distant past," said William stoically. "It is clear those same pagan people worshipped this thing, whatever strange purpose it is supposed to serve."

"Perhaps it holds value," said David questioningly. "Or maybe something else was left here as well…" He began peering around the base of the carved throne, for any gold which may have been placed there. He crept up to the sculpture and placed his hand upon one of the stone hands, before pulling it back suddenly as though afraid. "Cold…" was all he said, and did not reach to touch it again. "There is nothing else here," he said when at last he had contented himself that no valuables had been left behind. "Perhaps the sculpture itself holds value," he then said with great hopefulness in his voice. "One of us could ride into Perryville and send word into the city."

"Perhaps," said William as he maintained his stare upon the sinister looking thing before him. "But first we examine this chamber thoroughly, and then we rest and meet as a group. All four of us will have to be in agreement on the matter."

"What have you found?" called the voice of Paul from above, down through the upper hole behind them.

"It is a stone sculpture," yelled William without turning except at his neck. "You can come down after we have climbed out. Now give us time to look about." William then broke the motionlessness of his stance, and both men searched the chamber from corner to corner. Neither man would stand with his back to the strange statue, and without the illumination of the lantern fully upon it, neither would venture even to that side of the room.

***

"It serves no purpose to us," said William across the table, to the three men who sat upon each of his table sides. "We are God fearing farmers, and that pagan symbol might be best sealed up as we found it." Augustine poured each of the men some tea, and then joined the other wives who sat silently nearby.

"It is a significant finding," said Paul as he leaned onto the table, showing great energy in his arms and his eyes. "Agreed it is the folly of the pagan savages, but it could be a thousand years old. We cannot simply pretend it has not been found."

"You men are in agreement?" asked William toward them as a whole.

"We should send for a scholar to determine if the pagan deity can fetch a profit if sold," said David.

"I agree with this also," said Edward, displaying the enthusiasm of his youth.

William looked over each of them in silence for a moment, while thinking of his next words. He felt perhaps a bit foolish for his caution, but he was certain also of the unease that rested in his belly. "Very well," he began at last, "We'll work in our normal pattern, and if any of you want to venture into the chamber, you will do it during your resting hours. Come Sunday David and Paul will set off for Perryville. Edward, you will rest your ankle and remain here with me. The two of you will send an inquiry to the university, and wait in Perrysville for a reply. If anyone will come, you will guide them, and we will see what value the sculpture can bring. Afterward we will seal the chamber, whether the sculpture be sold or not. These are the terms of my agreement."

"We agree," answered each of the men, but William's uneasiness would not withdraw.

That evening the wind had gone completely and all was silent when William fell at last into slumber. His mind was restless and full of questions, and the cold stone glare which had been in the statue's eyes was embedded within his cognition. His last conscious thought was that he would mark the outline of the hidden chamber, in the dirt of the field above. This would prevent any of the men from walking upon it, and eliminate any chance of additional collapse.

He heard then sometime within the night, the creak of his door as it was opened. Within the beam of the moonlight that was cast inward, he saw the figure of Augustine standing in the open doorway preparing to depart.

"Dear," he called out, "What are you doing there?" She would not turn to look at him, and did not answer his words. Instead she stood frozen in the doorway, seeming to ponder if she would take her leave.

"Augustine," he called somewhat louder, but trying not to wake the baby. When she continued her rigid stance, he swung his feet promptly onto the floor and arose to retrieve his wife.

When he reached her he put a hand upon the rear of her neck and gently led her backward. When she was free of the door, he closed it gently and fastened the bolt in place. She did not fight him, and went willingly back to bed, but never gave a word of reply.

In the morning she did not remembered even a moment of it, and William had not pressed the matter. He ate the breakfast she served to him, and watched her beautiful figure as she walked about the room.

"Can we be together soon?" he asked after some time, to which she turned to face him somewhat shyly.

"Yes, not long now," she answered, and then returned promptly to her chores.

A mighty knock then came upon the door, which had not been unlocked from the events of the night. The face of Edward appeared when it was opened, but the young man did not enter.

"The wheat!" was all he said, and then limped away from the door knowing that William would follow. William stood immediately and strode for the door, where he beheld an amazing scene. In each direction their fields flowed with towering wheat crop, where only sprouts had formerly been. They were robust and mature grains, ready to be harvested and sold. It was clearly miraculous, and his body filled with the appropriate joy that a proud young farmer should feel. It was then that he remembered the sinister gaze of the stone beast, and all joy was taken from him.

"It is a miracle!" said Edward, "We will be able to name our price at the market! And perhaps plant a smaller second crop, and sell again in late September."

"It is unnatural," said William stoically. "This is not meant to be. Have you forgotten that thing in ground? Do you fail to see the ungodly cause?"

"It is God's will!" replied Edward, whose arms were now outstretched.

"There must be a cost," said William solemnly. "I feel it in my gut that there is." But his warning fell onto deaf ears, even after Paul and David had been told.

But mature crop must be harvested, and even William set to this task at hand. The fallen tree was soon forgotten and left to lay unbothered near the hidden chamber of the stone beast. It could not be seen any longer anyhow, due to the wheat crop that reached mightily toward the sky.

That evening William was awoken again, this time from a terrible dream of pain and searing fire. He dreamt that the fields roared with flames as he stood outside the door of his cottage. The wheat burned ceaselessly and never relented, as though hell on earth had come to be. Then the eyes of the stone creature had appeared above the flames and walked steadily toward him, coming to seal his eternal doom.

It was not the creak of the door that awoke him from this nightmare, but rather the sound that came when the wind slammed the open door loudly against the wall. Beside him in the bed Augustine was gone, and he ran straightaway into the nighttime darkness. Near the edge of the field he saw her white sleeping gown, and ran to seize her arm. With his other hand he slapped her cheek, and then waited for her to speak.

"Will… what… where am I?" she asked fearfully and looked about her in a panic.

"Where were you going?" he asked, but in his mind he already knew the answer. She could not answer this verbally and only cried, and so, both returned to their dwelling.

William dressed hurriedly and told her to bolt the door, before running maniacally into the field with his hammer. He would destroy that thing while the others slept, and then seal the chamber in the light of morning. There was indeed a cost for the gifts it gave, and he would not partake of its evil.

Light emitted from the hole in the ground and the skin of William's arms began to crawl with fear. Then between howling gusts of wind his ears heard a woman, as she moaned loudly from pleasures of the flesh. It was unabashed and without regard for ears which might hear the sound.

William thrust the hammer into his belt and climbed down the rope with the speed of a man running into battle. There within the stone confines of the chamber, he saw all three of the wives of his village friends. The wife of David sat atop the stone creature with her legs drawn up to its sides. It was she who moaned with delight, and did not cease even when William called to her. The other women knelt near the throne, each placing a hand upon the forearms of the terrible stone figure. They would not look at him as he called out, but continued kneeling and earnestly awaiting their turn.

William drew up the hammer in his strong right hand and stepped toward the giant of stone. Perhaps it was a trick of the lighting, but the eyes of the beast seemed suddenly to dance with a flicker of life. The sinister gaze fell upon him and he saw images within his mind, all of power and great prosperity. He was shown items of luxury upon their once humble farm and each of the four women dressed in elegant clothing. Soon the dream had fully entranced him, and he blinked with open eyes many hours later, from within his bed to waking life.

He looked immediately to her side of the bed, and found his wife Augustine captured within a peaceful sleep. The events of the night remained clear to him, all except for his emergence from the chamber and the method of return to his home. He was more groggy than terrified now, and he sat for many minutes upon the edge of his bed.

It was an urge that he noticed then most sharply, and it came in the form of simply accepting peacefully the changes that had come to the farm. The urge to dress himself and sickle the towering wheat until darkness fell, tore upon him with tremendous pull. And after this pending day of great labor perhaps he knew that he would no longer awake in the night.

William stood and stepped into his clothes, and took his hat before exiting the cottage. There awaiting his emergence were David, Paul, and Edward, each holding their tools for the day.

"Good morning William," said David somewhat strangely, to which William did not reply.

"It is time to harvest the wheat," said Paul, with the same empty tone as his companion.

"Get out of my way," said William as he looked amongst his tools for the hammer.

"Your scythe awaits you," said Edward. His voice was as empty as the other's.

"I choose the hammer," said William with a voice of defiance. "What have you done with it?"

The three men did not answer him, and began to enclose him with their stance. Then with malice in there steps, they began to descend upon him. The wall of his cottage cornered him, and he turned to reenter the door. A small sound then came into the air, as the bolt was set into place from the interior of the dwelling.

"Augustine, it is me!" he called. "Augustine, open the door!" But his wife would not reply. He knew then that she had been entranced a second time that night prior, and had engaged physically with the beast of stone. He turned to face the villagers as they bore down upon him, each wielding their scythes in their hands.

12. Into the Hands of Evil

"Is this seat taken?" asked a young, well-dressed businessman as he pointed down to the brown leather seat of the train.

"No," was the reply, spoken by an old man who had been daydreaming out through the window of the train. His head was mostly bald, and the gray hair that remained was trimmed quite short. He politely moved his bag to the right side of his right leg, so as to lean it against the wall of the rail car.

"I would bet you are on holiday," said the businessman cheerily, "I take this route often and I don't believe I've seen you." The businessman feared that he spoke rudely and began again, "I mean you seem also to be enjoying the trip. I would be hard-pressed to say the same." Again he thought he had come off badly, but it was not intentional.

"It has been thirty-one years since I last rode these rails," said the balding man, with eyes that betrayed no emotion. "My last trip was… unsuccessful." His vision did not focus upon any one thing as he spoke these words.

"Not successful…?" said the businessman. "Do you mean a malfunction of the locomotive?"

The balding man turned to look at his young companion for the first time since they had spoken. "I don't know the cause of it, but it was mechanical in nature I do believe. And it wasn't the snow," he grumbled, "but there was one hell of a storm blowing about. But myself and my companion Carl, being only twenty-four at the time would sooner have feared a flock of pigeons, ha!"

The businessman relaxed a bit now, having decided his seatmate was not to be taken seriously, and seemed to be only an old fool. "Well we'll not have that problem tonight sir," he said and smiled largely to sooth the old man. "There'll be no harsh weather to fear." The businessman took out his newspaper and opened pages two and three widely in front of his chest.

"But the weather wasn't as harsh as the true evil we did encounter." The old man turned inward to his seatmate and stared at him now, and continued in a lower voice.

"You see we were not legal passengers all that time ago, but rather shipping car stowaways. When the malfunction came and the car rolled to a stop, we waited for several minutes until we felt it was safe to emerge. We listened until we had heard the workmen dismounting, and their voices trailed off down the tracks. Only then did we slip from our hiding place and follow their tracks in the snow back in the direction we had come. But those men had provisions and traveling gear, whereas we had nothing at all. Carl, my companion, was a bit of a headstrong fool. And my name, young sir, is Jack Rollin."

The businessman folded his paper upon his lap and waited intently for the old man to continue…

***

"This track runs east-west," said Carl as he pulled on his knit cap amidst the snow. "Thirty miles west of the station there's a small village called Hamburg. I say we had traveled near forty miles from the station before the train stopped, and I reckon we ought to veer northward."

Jack looked to his left at the north sky and saw only the whiteness of the storm. The men continued walking eastward through the snow as they debated. "I saw you nod off while in that car," said Jack gruffly. "You cannot know if we've traveled forty miles or seventy."

Carl, a larger man than Jack, set their pace with his long strides. "We can't cover forty miles of track back to the station before dusk. That leaves only the option of begging those men up yonder for a share of their fire and shelter when they stop for the night, *if* they stop for the night. You and I won't last a night out here walking in these clothes."

"I see nothing north of here but frigid fields," said Jack as he tucked his chin back down in the collar of his shirt.

"Hamburg is just north of us," assured Carl. "I bet my life on it. Even if I am wrong by five miles, we'll cross the farmer's roads and follow them on in. It shan't be more than a ten-mile trek at the most."

"Back in that rail car with the straw and a closed door would not be such a rough night," said Jack.

104

"We'll walk five miles north. If we encounter no road to Hamburg, we'll turn right around and sleep in the rail car. Give me ten miles, Jack, and I'll get you a warm bed and a hot meal."

Jack pulled his chin out and looked north again. "All right, five miles north," he said gruffly, and nothing thereafter.

The snow continued to fall, and this was not as much of a hindrance as the bite of the frigid wind. Neither man spoke as they trudged along, and they soon fell into the pattern of the smaller Jack following the lead of Carl. Jack's fear grew as the air before them grew darker, with nothing but endless fields of white freezing death inviting them to lie down and die. But he spoke not a word of this, feeling fearful of displaying this weakness to the man who led him along. Instead he bit down on his back teeth and breathed deeply from the freezing air.

In his mind he had already decided that he would walk one more mile before turning back around. He prepared the words within his mind, pondering the best way to speak them so as to not be an outright coward. It was at that moment that Carl halted and regained the posture of a confident man.

Aye, we've found it!" yelled Carl, with a shrill voice of excitement that betrayed his recently disposed of fear. "Do you see the wagon wheel ruts in the snow, surely not but two hours ago?"

"Aye, but which way did they travel?" said Jack. He scanned the eastward horizon and then the west. "The hoof prints are now all full."

Carl was silent having realized this also. His decision of direction could now determine their very existence, for with the snow still falling they would not again find the footprints that they had just made.

They trod eastward," said Carl, "I am near-certain this is true." He did not look into Jack's eyes as he said this, and instead, began walking with feigned confidence in the new direction. He did not turn to see if Jack followed, but felt relief at hearing the noise of his footfalls behind.

Jack looked around for an object to mark the intersection where they decided to make this directional turn. He saw nothing at all of distinction. He thought then of pissing a bright yellow marker, and then turned to see Carl rapidly disappearing into the whiteness ahead. He dismissed the notion and ran quickly forward, returning to the heels of his companion.

Two miles further onward, the sun was preparing to set and Jack felt certain that all hope was lost. He no longer cared about showing cowardice, and thought hard about declaring his intention to retreat. With every step the words grew nearer to flying out of him, when Carl cried out suddenly with joy.

"Ahead now! I see the dark outline of a dwelling!" Jack peered around his large companion and saw with his own eyes that it was true. They ran toward it until they were within thirty feet, and then walked with their dignity outward. Signs of life, however, were not forthcoming. Carl stepped upon the wooden porch, which gave a faint creek, and then knocked firmly but politely upon the door.

"If it's abandoned," spoke Jack, "then we'll be forced to break in for the night."

And then there was sound from within and the thick wooden door swung outward exposing the enormous face of a man. His forehead was broad and his eyes sunken and narrow. If the travelers had not been so chilled already, they would have felt this man's ugliness with a cold shiver down their spines.

"Yes," came the ugly man's voice, with a bit of surprising charm. He stood eye to eye with Carl, but it seemed to Jack that the man did slouch somewhat within his doorway.

"Excuse my sir," said Carl very lightly as he held his woolen hat up to his sternum. "Our train had a malfunction, and we are now on foot to Hamburg. Could you tell me please how near we are or if there is a boarding house nearby?"

The ugly man did not answer, and neither did his eyes seem to fully appear from the shadow of his brow. Instead the door opened wider and a woman came into view beneath the arm of the man. She was not so unpleasant to view as her apparent husband, but neither did she have any particular pleasantness about her. She seemed to Jack as possibly the plainest woman he had ever encountered.

"Hamburg is five miles east of here," she said with a voice that smelled of cigar tobacco. "You'll not be getting there before dark. But we have a room for you. Only one, you'll have to share. And it will be thirty cents apiece, thirty-five if you'd like dinner and tea."

"Agreed, ma'am," said Carl, still holding his cap so dearly and speaking with his charming voice. The ugly man stepped back into his dark house and the woman held the door widely.

Once inside she lit an oil lamp and halted them at the foot of an aged wooden staircase. She gave them the lamp and instructed them to their room, noting that they could pay at dinner. She then turned to her husband who stood lurking nearby, and said to him a touch sternly, "Yes, prepare a guest dinner." Neither man delayed their ascent, as Carl led the way and shined the light up the stairway.

"I'm not hungry," said Jack as Carl set the lamp upon the table within their room. "I'll be content to warm myself by that fireplace once I get it started. My stomach feels a bit ill."

"Not mine," said Carl. "Let's have your thirty cents, then. I'll pay it for you when I go down."

"Here," he answered, and then a silence came between them for a moment. "The town is only five miles, the woman said. That seems… comforting to me… somehow." He looked at his large friend and felt confusion at why he had felt compelled to speak those words.

"I'm starved," said Carl, and then, "We'll see what a five-cent dinner entails out here in the middle of nowhere." He was out the door without another word and Jack listened as his footsteps trod down the warping stairway.

A small fire was soon roaring and he lay there in his chair watching shadows dance upon the wall. He tried in vain to hear the sounds of the dinner below. As his blood warmed, a feeling brewed within him for which he could not readily find a source. It was the feeling of dread which sprang upon him suddenly, growing first in some dark region of his innards, and then creeping through every capillary and vein until it claimed the whole of his entire body.

The shadows came alive on the wall before him, and he saw the plainness of that woman's face. It was as plain as their simple wooden house, which sat in the middle of their plain white field. This shadow face soon molded into a new form, and within it appeared the brow and seemingly eyeless face of the enormous man. These shadows upon the walls consumed him, and surrounded him at every side. Their dance never rested as the flames of the hearth pranced about, constantly guided by a draft that flowed from a crack unseen. Jack hoped very strongly that Hamburg was truly only five miles to the east.

After the shadows had played their games with him, he rethought his decision about dinner and went quickly from his chair. He did not take the time to don his boots, and crept softly down the wooden steps. *I'll just excuse myself for having delayed*, he thought, and felt happy that he would again be at the side of his good friend. For it was just the cold that had brought on his hysterics, he reasoned, and thought that companionship would surely cure him.

Jack realized that he did not have his five cents extra; the money was in his workman's coat. He would simply apologize earnestly and pay promptly after the meal. And with this joy he rounded the corner of the ground floor and ambled toward the light that he saw ahead. Already he heard the sounds of conversation, and he was thoroughly glad that he had reconsidered.

He stepped into the room and saw Carl seated across from the plain woman, whose appearance was still off putting. Both sat at a large table, where his friend ate from a bowl as the plain woman's chatter filled the air. She seemed to be speaking of an event, perhaps their harvest from the year before.

A bed sheet had been hung strangely across the room, from which the woman sat directly across. Carl showed it only his back, as he devoured the hot food he had been given. Beside him Jack saw an empty chair where the woman had intended for him to sit.

Jack reasoned that the sheet was meant as a curtain, surely due to these poor farmers feeling shame for their pitiful house. And as peculiar as the sheet appeared, it seemed to him as logical, for the house had fallen badly into disrepair. He accepted this explanation and thought only of joining his companion and taking a portion of the remaining meal.

Carl and the plain woman both turned their heads to view him as he stepped from the darkness of the hall. Jack's hysteria had subsided fully until he looked to the face of the woman. Her plainness was now replaced by a peculiar expression of irrefutable alarm. The anxiety washed over Jack again in a torrent, and he was consumed with dread once again.

Before a word could be spoken a great shadow appeared suddenly on the opposing side of the sheet which divided the room. Through it Jack saw the large image of the man, who held something sizeable within his grasp.

Jack looked again to the plain woman and saw that the concern in her eyes had grown to outright panic. Her glare pierced him like needles, revealing some malevolence yet to be revealed. She turned from him suddenly and looked upon the curtain just as the great shadow drew up its arms. The hands of the figure now held the shape of a massive hammer, drawn back and ready to swing.

"Carl!" shouted Jack, as he threw out his hand, and the woman leapt from her chair. The thin curtain heaved forward and came to life, as a sickening thud filled the air. Jack could only watch as his companion's head fell forward onto the table. The body of his friend lay with lifeless certainty, never to partake of our world again. The hot blood spilled outward in a wave of death, spraying upward and landing visibly upon the white of the sheet.

"The other!" shrieked the plain woman as she pointed her knobby finger to Jack who stood now within the room. The curtain was torn from the ceiling with a downward slash of a giant hand. The terrible body of the murderous man appeared, with the sledgehammer still firmly within his grasp. The evil within his black sunken eyes made him appear like a creature escaped from hell.

Jack struggled to move his feet but found them frozen, as though trapped in a horrid dream. They would not heed his commands as the man stalked forward. From the hammer dripped a trickle of blood which fell upon the rotting boards of the floor.

The sight of the hammer freed his legs and like a shot he ran from the room. Jack ripped the thick wooden door open with the strength of twenty men, and fled out into the storm. He was without boots, nor hat, nor coat, but he did not feel the cold. Not as he ran into the darkness, instinctively to the east, toward the village of Hamburg, if it did in fact exist there. And all the while he was certain, that at any moment the great hammer would come crashing down upon him, opening his skull and dyeing the snow that same crimson color as his dear friend's had shown upon the white sheet…

Hamburg did indeed exist," said Jack Rollin, "And there were perhaps truly five miles in between, but I was in no mind to be able to confirm that with certainty."

Beside him the young businessman clutched tightly his newspaper, not realizing that he did so.

"Yes, I made it there and pounded on the first lighted house that I saw. But it was not until the first daylight of the next morning that the men folk would venture out to that terrible house. And although I felt great guilt for having failed to save my friend, I did not press the urgency for I knew that he was dead...

In the morning the town's men found the house to be quite empty except for my friend's remains… The man and woman had fled on horseback and the freshly fallen snow had covered their tracks. The story became national news briefly and was featured in every newspaper throughout the land. I can only assume that they had been after our money, but truthfully we were more destitute than they. And nothing more of the pair was ever learned, except for four shallow graves found out behind their barn, belonging to four other nameless victims…

13. His Majesty's Spectators

The prince had a complexion like no other; his color the white of utmost purity and no pores for the eye to see. He wore purple, as he always did for tennis, made of shiny silk that had come from distant Asia. His hair was dark and well-groomed, combed over straightly and held there with the weight of many lotions. He did not speak to anyone standing about the clay court; not to his opponent or the servant that lingered behind him, out of bounds.

"His majesty shall be victorious!" shouted one of the condemned souls, his head and hands locked into a restraining device and held tightly beneath the weight of sanded oak. There were three of them on this day, punished for unknown crimes of unknown severity, perhaps violence or burglary or standing awkwardly on the street. It did not matter presently for they were now all three together, the weight upon their necks very great as they strained their eyes upward to see. They could view the match although not comfortably, seeing every fate-deciding shot and preparing themselves for the impending horror.

Of everything these condemned souls saw, the servant was the worst, standing in his pink silk uniform and all of his muscles very much at ease. He served no purpose worth mentioning, at least none apparent to the eye, save only as a shiny-pink decoration near the portable mount that held the ax. It was a simple portable mount, of polished wood bleaching beneath the sun, built many years ago and just as smooth as the day it was planed. Upon it was the ax entirely of silver, bright and flawless in its design. It was of the purest metal, from handle to tip of blade, shining with gleaming perfection in the bright summer sun. A purer tool had never been forged, pristine in its design and weighting.

The prince did not perceive any of this, and did not look at the condemned men bound so securely. Rather he stretched and prepared for the match that no outside spectators were allowed to witness. Not even from a distance could citizens peer, through trees or the perimeter fence, for it was patrolled by burly men dressed fashionably in pink sequined gowns. Upon their feet were the finest of puffy pink slippers with silver blades protruding from pointed toes. They used them very often to ward off trespassers who came calling, kicking them swiftly in their arses as they ran, the toe blades piercing their flesh.

The opponent walked to the point of service, and held the ball highly upon his fingertips for the prince to easily see. The prince nodded his approval and prepared a dainty stance. The neck-bound men then cheered loudly as the ball was served. Their voices were frantic with fear and desperation but still sang the praise of his majesty. They yelled of his greatness with fine intent and prayed that it fell upon his ears soothingly, never stopping except to breathe, and then starting the praise anew.

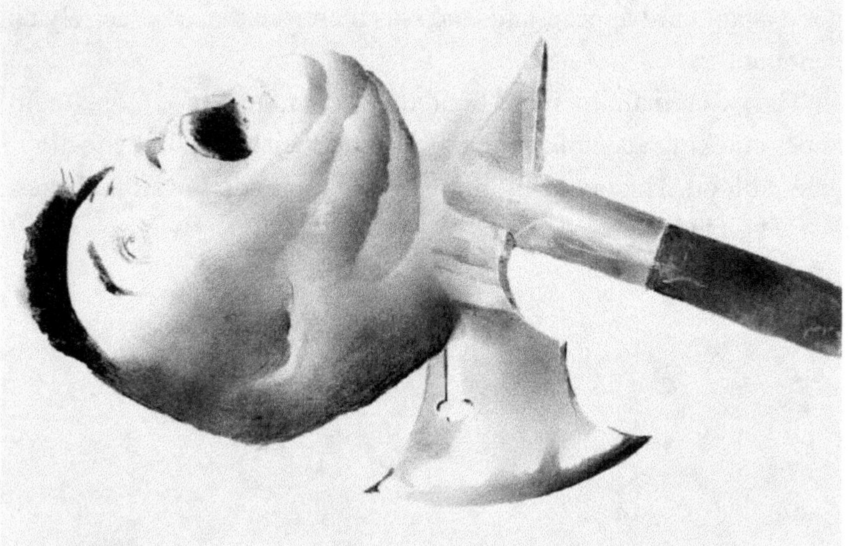

The prince returned the mighty serve, as the servant remained behind him with utter complacency, watching with great indifference as the match fell underway. The prince held his own for three returns, then floundered on the fourth, the racket nearly flying from his hand as he tripped upon his purple feet. And despite all of this he did strike the ball, with the utmost tip of the wood, sending it to the net where it hit softly and fell to the ground.

Still the neck-bound men clamored and screamed; the cords of their throat muscles stretching and tensed, and not an inch could they readily move. The servant stood as he had for several minutes now, arms behind his back and smiling upward to the sun. And by him the prince walked with tiny, angry strides to the mount where the ax majestically gleamed. He set the racket on the shelf above, just as he had many times before, and clasped the silver handle upon either of its ends. To the neck-bound men did he walk, raising the ax with an angry face and hoisting it upward with all of his might. He did not break stride or miss a moment as the blade came flying down, chopping through the neck of the first bound man with a gut twisting dismal crunch.

The prince then walked quickly back to the mount with the ax dangling within his dainty hand. It hung loosely over the ground as he walked, not far above the gravel and sand which could scrape and tarnish the perfection of the magnificent blade. But it would not draw blood again until appropriate, and was therefore placed precisely upon the mount as he had found it.

The two remaining men shouted and clamored once more, their voices cracking and spliced with fear, and their faces dashed with the other's blood. The opponent held the ball high into the air and again the prince nodded approval.

14. The Delivery

The request had seemed peculiar to Dmitri, but the income was direly needed, and he was truly pleased when the offer had come along. Three hundred dollars for a dozen rats was the proposition, to be plucked from the garbage dump and delivered to the old man's home, without much fuss at all. "And without a single cent of cost either," thought Dmitri, "At least not to me."

Although he despised his position at the county garbage dump, he was not above taking extra money for unpleasant or illegal tasks, to be performed on the side. But in truth Dmitri was fortunate to have obtained his day job, for he had little education, and his abilities with English were fair at best. It had been only the perfect timing of his application that had gained him the employment he currently held.

"Can you stick around for more than two weeks and not disappear like the last fellow I hired?" his new boss had said to Dmitri, on the morning he had come to apply. Dmitri had assured him that he was seeking permanent employment, and here he was now four months into the filthy career.

But the rats for this side job had been easy to procure, although he rarely saw them during daylight hours. After dark however, the heaps of garbage swirled and churned amidst a flea-ridden, rat covered frenzy.

Earlier that evening Dmitri had not gone home as he usually did. Instead he drove to a diner in his stinking work clothes and purchased a bowl of clam chowder and a turkey sandwich. When total darkness had fallen, he returned to the dump, knowing that no one would be around.

Reentry had not been a problem, due to the key he had been given for opening and closing the front gate as needed for his job. There was not anything of much value at a garbage dump, except possibly a few pieces of office equipment. But that was where the respectable employees worked, and Dmitri had not been given a key to that building.

The sounds of the dump had seemed different in the darkness when he returned, quite unlike the sounds of the daylight hours. Dmitri had heard the scurrying of the rats as soon as his engine was silent, and he knew that their feeding had begun beneath the cover of night. He felt a chill of uneasiness run down his spine as he listened, but convinced himself quickly that it was simply the coolness of the night air.

Dmitri donned his gloves, for he knew that the rats would defend themselves with the sharpness of their teeth. The gloves still bore the faded name Elijah, the man whose position Dmitri had filled.

The fittest of the vermin scattered quickly when the beam of light fell upon them. He held both the flashlight and the sack within his left hand, while grabbing the tails of those which were slow to run and hide. He dropped the vermin one after the other into the sack, feeling it grow heavier as each one fell. As the captured rats shrieked and struggled for freedom, a feeling of pleasure came upon him.

But alas, these events had all been half an hour ago and Dmitri presently drove to collect his money. He found that thoughts of the day were circling about his head, and always returned to the man who had hired him to procure the rats. He had been an elderly gentleman, chauffeured in a black sedan by an Asian driver at the wheel.

Dmitri had never seen the sedan before that afternoon, he was certain, for he would have remembered the symbol of wealth. The shiny black wraith had appeared suddenly, just as Dmitri prepared to lock up for the night. Its rear window had then rolled slowly downward, followed by the emergence of a decrepit hand. And as unusual as the luxurious black sedan had seemed, it was this decrepit hand that intrigued him most greatly. He remembered how slowly the fingers had extended, and how they had motioned him toward the car.

"My dear man," the elder had said, from a face as weathered as the frail limb, "I require the services of a young and able fellow such as yourself." The words had been spoken vibrantly, and identified the man as a South American. "Bring me ten to twelve rats," said the strong voice, "And three hundred dollars I will pay you. You see, I am from Brazil and I have brought illegally an anaconda from my homeland. You will be doing me a tremendous service."

Dmitri watched the eyes of the peculiar old man, whose white face and hair contrasted with the black interior of the beautiful car. His eyes danced with energy, which seemed to Dmitri as unusual for a man so close to the grave.

The peculiar old man did not wait for a reply and promptly spoke again. "Formerly it ate small mice, but these will no longer nourish her. I will require your services many more times if you agree, and find it worth your while. May I ask, are you married my good fellow?" The old man simply nodded his head when Dmitri had informed him that he was unmarried. "Ten p.m. tonight then. Please do not be late. Your payment will be waiting, and my address is upon this paper. But you must bring this paper with you I am afraid. For by returning my handwritten address to me I'll know that your word is good." The feeble hand had again been extended, and within it, a small card bearing an address was displayed.

Dmitri did not think further upon all of these strange facts, or rather, he attempted not to. The unpleasantness of the evening had already burrowed beneath his skin, and he wished now only to know the warmth of his bath. But Dmitri was no innocent lad, having performed after-dark feats many times before, when a profit had been attainable. Turning rats into money seemed to him, simply too good to be true.

He had never been so far north upon the road which he currently traveled. The homes here were very large and he became acutely reminded of the indigent that he was. He knew also that the police would surely stop his rusted car, if he happened to pass one along that empty road. But no such encounter did occur, and the desolation of the road continued.

There were no more houses for a stretch of several miles, and then the shape of an enormous dwelling appeared. His headlights shone upon a fence at the perimeter, which towered at twice the height of a man. Hidden within ivy upon a stone column, Dmitri found the address which had been typed upon the card.

The gate had been left open for him and Dmitri did not delay entering with his car. He drove upon the stone pathway in near darkness, parking against the curb within the circular drive before the entrance to the home. Once parked, he opened the trunk, and looked toward the house for any sign of greeting. Everywhere there was only darkness, and a sensation of foolishness came upon him, for he now felt certain that the old man was crazy with age.

Inside the trunk he found the rats running freely, having gnawed a hole just large enough so that their bodies could wriggle through. It was with a sensation of anger at this rebellion with which Dmitri again slipped the gloves upon his hands. Hastily he seized each rat, throwing them forcefully to the bottom of a second sack, which he had brought for just such a reason. He then encased the new sack with the old, a combination which he calculated would grant him an additional twenty minutes of time.

As Dmitri closed the trunk, a door opened suddenly from the house, and yellow light poured out vibrantly upon the driveway. He recognized the face of the silent driver. The man was, Dmitri realized now, extraordinarily large for an Asian.

The darkly dressed servant said nothing, and waited for Dmitri to approach the door. With neither greeting nor smile the servant simply motioned for him to enter.

Dmitri held the burlap sack outstretched before him, as far as his arm would comfortably allow. The large servant then closed and locked the door behind him, before leading him through the utility corridor, toward the central area of the home. This path of entry was preferred by Dmitri, for taking the front door while dressed in his shabby clothes would only have made him uneasy. The utility corridor ended at a second door, which the servant held open for him to enter.

This door took them into the living quarters, the kitchen being visible on the right. Directly ahead Dmitri heard the music of an organ, and saw soft light flowing from the hallway before him. He passed a look to the stoic servant, who only motioned him onward to the music with an upturned and extended palm.

Dmitri swallowed his pride and walked forward to the pleasant sounds, still carrying the sack before him that churned and writhed from the struggling rats. The room he encountered was nearly empty, and contained only the old man seated at his instrument, which he played as though in a trance. Dmitri surveyed the open room, which was highlighted with flowing white curtains and a brilliant red carpet upon the floor. It occurred to him that the peculiar room suited the strange man quite well.

After several moments of entranced playing, the old man removed his withered hands from the keys and turned slowly to face his guest with closed eyes. The lids then rolled slowly open, and the old man smiled to greet his guest.

"Good evening young man," smiled the Brazilian. "You are punctual, and I appreciate that greatly, for I must sleep soon after dark. As a younger man I was very fond of the nighttime hours, but those days, sadly, are past."

Dmitri relaxed his arm a bit, for the weight of the rats had begun to wear at the strength of his muscles. "Good evening sir," he said, "I think you'll be pleased with the rodents. Perhaps I could give them to your… butler." English being his second language, he had almost not known the proper word.

"Ah," said the old man as he arose from the black leather bench of the organ, "Vada detests rats. That will not do. You see, if it where that simple I could simply have paid my servant to procure the rats from you. But yes, you are right. And it does get late so quickly. And also there is the most important matter, which is that I am able to watch my beautiful pet eat."

The old man then stood upright spryly and began to cross the red carpet upon the floor. His legs remained hidden as he strode, beneath a silk robe that hung limply upon the floor. Dmitri's impatience began to fester as the old man crept slowly forward. He longed greatly for his three hundred dollars and a departure from this residence of oddity and age.

"Sir I apologize for the hurry," said Dmitri when he could stand no more, "But I must take my leave at once. I still have things to see to and the morning will come early."

The old man did not look at him, but rather placed his hand oddly around Dmitri's waist when he had reached him, and began to walk slowly at his side. "Indeed," said the peculiar old man, "Let's get to the feeding at hand. And your three hundred dollars, ah, now four hundred!" he declared this quite suddenly and with tremendous joy. "Vada, pay our nice deliveryman and let's be on with the evening's feeding!"

With this command spoken the servant walked coolly toward Dmitri and retrieved an envelope from his jacket pocket. The old man released Dmitri's waist and crept onward, and Dmitri then used his free hand to tuck the envelope safely away.

"And now you probably wish to be rid of those vile things," said the old man as he released his waist and stepped onward, before motioning for Dmitri to walk further along. "Even now, I can see them squirm through the sack you hold. But soon they will be so frightened that they dare not even breathe."

The old man laughed a bit at his exclamation as Dmitri stepped forward to rejoin his host. Their destination soon became clear, for a door at the far side of the room was the direction in which they ambled. Behind them Vada trudged along silently, perhaps waiting to catch his master if his frail form should stumble and fall.

The door's hinges groaned loudly as Vada pulled upon it, and a downward stairway was revealed. The air that escaped was damp and odorous, and it seemed even to Dmitri's nose, as unfit for any man to enter.

But Vada descended first when the lights had been illuminated, stepping downward and halting upon the third step below. There he waited until the old man reached out to the servant's shoulders, allowing himself to be lifted by the servant's arms and carried gently down. Dmitri did not wish to ponder just how peculiar a scene he had become a part of.

Gracefully the servant and master descended the stone staircase, as though they had performed this oddity many times in the past. Dmitri followed at a short distance, keeping them a bit apart from him, just like he did unconsciously with the bag of rats.

Where the stairway ended, a stone corridor began, and the old man was placed back upon his feet. "It is not usually this warm down here," said the old man, "but I warmed it throughout the day to energize my beautiful pet for her meal!"

Dmitri noticed the stillness of the sack and saw that the rats had stopped their squirming. He gave it a slight shake to jostle them, but they were intent upon remaining still.

Near the center of the great hallway, Vada stopped at a door which lay at the left of the hallway. When the old man was close enough the servant unbolted the latch and swung it widely open.

The claustrophobia of the stone corridor then began to wear upon Dmitri. He became aware that his brow now sweated, and he could feel the hairs of his neck standing upon end. *"I will not enter that room,"* he thought to himself, for it seemed to him like the cell of a dungeon. He knew that all had not been revealed to him, and he felt this truth resonating with certainty.

When the lamps of the room were alighted, Vada reached his large hand for the burlap sack. Dmitri saw that the servant now displayed for the vermin, none of his supposed fear.

"Look!" said the old man, "One of my little friends knows it is time to dine!"

Dmitri peered inside the wooden door and did indeed see a sleek, dark snake emerge from a shallow pool of blackened water. As he watched, a second snake emerged, and then a third came slithering forward. They were sleek in their movement, shining brilliantly beneath the electric lights as their hunger brought them forward.

All three of the snakes moved to dry ground, then halted and tensed as though trained. The servant Vada came then alive, taking the sack from the bottom and pouring the rats upon the stone floor. Dmitri stole a glance sideways toward the old man who grinned with tremendous delight.

"They are beautiful!" the old man shrieked as he held the side of the doorway for support while his frail frame remained in the hall. "They are the perfect killers! Watch and you shall see!"

Dmitri's heart was now racing, pounding up in his throat. He watched the first snake to have emerged from the pool, tense and then snap at the rat which had fallen nearby. The movement of the snake was much too fast for his eyes to follow. In the blink of an eye the serpent had seized it, and clenched the vermin with its body. In this manner the snake held the rat in a death grip, the mighty mouth still clasping upon the rodent's back as its life was squeezed away.

"It is born to kill this way!" shrieked the old man with pure delight in his voice.

Within moments the second and third snakes stuck also the first of their prey. The remaining rats fled frantically toward the open space of the door. With great strength Vada kicked at them, sending one flying with tremendous force into the pool of blackened water.

"Come now!" cried the old man, "We leave my beauties to their meal." Vada did not hesitate at this instruction, and stepped out to close the door. "Now you have seen how magnificently my beautiful pets can kill," said the old man, who looked fully upon the face of Dmitri.

Dmitri did not have much of a reply for this, and only stammered, "Yes sir, they are quite remarkable."

The old man smiled and rubbed tenderly upon Dmitri's muscular shoulder. "Then I will see you again when they are hungry next, but I shall only send Vada to call upon you. And now, my servant will show you out while I make my way back to the foot of the stairs. Good night."

Dmitri said nothing as the old man turned away, and followed the silent servant further along the corridor. The hallway ended thirty feet beyond the chamber of serpents, at a doorway bolted firmly closed. The servant opened it by pulling in inward, to the hallway in which they now stood.

Through it was great darkness and Dmitri would be very pleased to be outside in the cool night air. He stepped through, away from the silent servant, and the heavy door was swung promptly closed. Behind him, Dmitri could hear, the bolt being set in place.

The lights then flickered on, and Dmitri could see what was now upon him. He was enclosed within the walls of a larger cell, not unlike the room from which they had come. This chamber was larger but held the same damp stench, and a blackened pool of water which covered most of the floor. This sight filled him with terror and he threw his body forcefully at the fastened door. The heavy wood absorbed his weight and scarcely quivered despite all of Dmitri's force.

"Vada!" he screamed, "Open this door!" His accent was thick now as he screamed from his belly with horror. The servant, if he were still there, did not speak a single word.

A mighty black head appeared then at the middle of the pool, sending small ripples toward Dmitri's feet. Every instinct Dmitri had within him told him to freeze and cower, just as the rats had done. With macabre desperation he threw his weight again upon the solid door.

"You are one of many who have fed my darling," came the words of the old man, muffled from the other side of the thick door. "The last was a man you may know, a man by the name of *Elijah*."

In an instant Dmitri's brain understood, the pure terror of how he had come to such a terrible fate. Menacingly the giant head of the snake came closer, sliding into the shallow water.

"*So I truly am Elijah's replacement*," realized Dmitri, as he scurried along the side of the wall frantically, scurrying like a rat…

15. Purgatory

James finished reading the newspaper and then folded it carefully, before reassembling each section just as it had been when he had first purchased it from the vendor. He would not read it again, but thought perhaps that a subsequent passenger could find it upon the seat, and use it to pass their time. Instead James turned his attention upon the other passengers of the car, all of them now fully settled and unlikely to notice his gaze as he looked them over.

The lot of them traveled for business, he guessed, a fact which seemed to him as exceedingly dull. Except possibly the man across the isle from him, because his clothes were finely tailored and he wore an eloquent vest of silk. Soon James' vision focused solely on this interesting figure, and he attempted to fully assess the character of the man. He was certainly educated, for the shoes were made of expensive Italian leather, and he emanated the calmness that is so often coupled with wealth.

As James looked up again, he saw with great awkwardness that the man's gaze now aligned with his own. "Pardon me sir," said James immediately, as his mind grasped for some polite bit of small talk to fill the air, and relieve him of his discomfort. "Perhaps you'd like to read my paper?" He said this spontaneously as he grabbed his folded paper from upon the seat next to him.

"No thank you," said the man, it won't be long now, I don't think."

"Ah, you know the route," said James to prolong the conversation, because the awkwardness had net yet fully cleared the air. "You must be returning to Alberton."

"No, no, I live and work in Grandsville," said the man. "I don't often come into Alberton, but I do enjoy it when I do."

"I've lived there for nearly twenty years now," said James as he alternated between studying the man and looking about the cabin as he spoke. "My name is James Bishop. I'm a writer for the Alberton News, currently on my way back from covering a story down in Brady."

"Pleased to meet you," said the man. "My name is Dr. Edward Handley. I'm a psychiatrist at the Grandsville sanitarium. That's why I am traveling actually, that is to say, I am investigating a delusion which has become an obsession for one of my patients."

This statement seemed entirely interesting to James, and he suddenly forgot his prior boredom, and prepared himself to thoroughly enjoy the company of the doctor. "You must engage in a great many enthralling interviews," replied James.

"Oh, I think I've heard nearly all there is to hear," said Dr. Handley. "However every once in a while I am still told something that I consider shocking. That is certainly the case with this particular patient's fantasy."

"Perhaps you'd like an outside opinion," offered James, with a tone that made his interest clear. He did, after all, spend the majority of his days attending dull events, only to write about them later with false enthusiasm and an interest that was greatly exaggerated. He was quite beyond jaded, and this hint of a tantalizing story made the hairs of his arms tingle with excitement.

"Oh it is only the insane ramblings of a patient," said the doctor, "And a bit of an excuse for me to travel back into the city, and visit with some old colleagues, I suppose. If I thought that the tale could possibly be true, I certainly would not be going there."

"Well it looks like I've lost my chance anyhow," said James, when he saw that the train approached the station of arrival. Around him the sporadically seated passengers began to gather the bags at their feet.

"Ah, that was quick," proclaimed the Doctor. "My little adventure takes me to 5th Street and Wilson. If that is anywhere near your way of travel, you are certainly welcome to join me for a meal at the restaurant where my little adventure will lead me."

"I've a man to meet not too far from there actually," said James who looked upon his watch, wishing sincerely that his time was not burdened. "If it wasn't pressing I would certainly join you to hear the end of that tale. But I must warn you, that isn't a good part of town. You'd be best advised to stay out of alleys I'm afraid. I may know the place if you tell me the name."

"It is a local eatery," said Doctor Handley, "the name of which I don't know. The patient described to me a painted symbol that sits in the window, a sort of painting of a face within the flames of the sun. He said I would know the place only by the bright yellow color of the symbol."

"Your adventure grows more intriguing," said James with a smile as the train rolled to a stop. My appointment is with a man who directs plays, a pitiful assignment from my editor. I hope that you enjoy your stay."

"Thank you. Goodbye," said the Doctor simply, who then joined the others who stood waiting to exit the car. As James watched him he felt a sense of loss, as though a rare and memorable opportunity had passed him by. He finished gathering his things, and then stepped into the line of exiting travelers.

His appointment had only been a few blocks from the station, and he arrived nearly twenty five minutes early for the meeting. James took a seat within the upscale café and drank coffee while he waited. At ten minutes until the appointment, the waiter again returned, giving to James a handwritten note which had been taken from a call that had arrived.

"The nerve of that fool director," said James as he read the apologetic note of cancellation. But truthfully he was quite pleased, and motioned for the waiter that he wished to pay his bill. Within minutes he was within a taxi and on his way to Wilson and 5th. When the driver dropped him near the intersection, he was reminded exactly why he despised the south side of town. Everywhere about him was something of filth, even the smell in the air.

James scanned his eyes over the nearest windows, and then performed the same investigation across the road. He looked now for the yellow painting, or perhaps simply any diner near the intersection, if one should happen to be there. When he did not readily see one, he briskly crossed over 5th Street to the other side of the intersection. Hurriedly, local people brushed past his shoulders as he searched for the elusive yellow painting set within a window.

The color was noticed by his eye easily when his vision encountered it, for the bright yellow color stood out mightily against the other surroundings. James stepped toward and peered through the window that held the sign just before him, as the masses continued their hurried shuffle about him. The painting did indeed depict a face within the flames of the sun, engaging in an expression of great emotion, like the rage of battle or ultimate pain. As James stared upon it, it began to seem to him, not unlike the face of a man being burned alive.

The glass of the windows was otherwise obscured with a soft paper which had been upholstered from the ceiling down to floor. He pushed the entry door inward, which sounded a soft bell chime above, and then looked throughout the eatery for the psychiatrist from the train. The room was vacant of any diners, to which the doctor was not exempted.

Somewhat disappointedly James began to leave, when the proprietor emerged suddenly from the kitchen at the rear, still tying an apron about his waist that was stiff with the starch of laundry. "Good morning sir," said the man, whose ethnicity James could not readily identify. "Our best table for you here." The dark haired man motioned to a flawlessly prepared table as James studied the odd countenance of the man's face. "Are you from out of town sir?" asked the man, with a dialect that seemed to hold bits of Asian.

"No, I'm a local," answered James, "Tell me, has a very distinguished gentleman come by recently, wearing a silk vest beneath his jacket?"

"No sir," said the strange proprietor, "I see many here but not him." James looked about the room as he heard this, to the clean white room of empty chairs, and the window papers which blocked any view from the outside. It was clear to him now that the doctor had thought better of his initial purpose, and fled away to the north side of town. But James desired now to eat quickly, and possibly salvage some productivity from his day. He ordered breakfast without looking at the menu, and another coffee taken black.

No other diners entered the establishment as he ate, but he found the food to be quite good. James thought perhaps that he tasted a hint of sesame oil that had greased the pan beneath the eggs. The toast and sausage were superb as well, tasting of spices foreign to his tongue. He decided surprisingly that he might some day return, when his fieldwork brought him back to that degenerate area of the city.

As he paid his bill at the counter he studied the ethnically indistinct face of the proprietor once again. His hair was black and straight like an Asian's, but the skin color was pale, and the facial features held characteristics of amalgamation. No doubt, reasoned James, the result of a badly diluted bloodline.

Once back out on the pavement, the poorness of the streets was again imposed upon him. James, who stood at greater than six feet, towered over every man he passed. He studied now the ethnicity of this strange neighborhood intently, but they were all quite unlike any group of men he had ever seen. He decided finally as he walked along, that the ancestry was clearly from Asia, although he could not narrow this down even to one region of that vast land.

But this was no matter for prolonged pondering, and soon he was three blocks away and climbing into the taxi which would carry him from that peculiar place. The meal and the rest had invigorated him from his morning travel, and he was now intent on performing a bit of work.

Back at his office he set to writing the article for which he had traveled and researched that very morning. He found the topic suddenly quite interesting, and the writing flowed with ease. He was also filled with alertness, and could follow all of the conversations and traffic outside of his office door. Once, as he looked up without ceasing his typing, he thought that he saw momentarily, the face of Doctor Handley down the hall. He had caught only a glimpse of his face, which had appeared briefly when the traffic cleared, and then vanished again as a group of people obscured the path of his view. But James did not delay, and jumped from his seat to walk quickly into the long hallway. He peered to the far corner but saw no trace of the man from the train.

During the walk to his apartment that evening he saw the face of the doctor many more times. Each sighting was nearly identical, in which the distinguished man appeared in the direction he looked, always nearly thirty feet further onward. James had waved to him the first time, but no motion of greeting was returned. When he had approached, a crowd blocked momentarily the view, only to clear a moment later by which time the doctor had vanished.

On the second block the image appeared anew, within a view that was perfectly clear. James did not wave, or even blink for that matter, but the elusive figure still had not remained. At ten feet of distance the doctor had begun to fade, vanishing altogether like the mask of a fog when one steps near.

By the time James had reached the block of his apartment, he had grown weary of this frightening charade. He stepped into Underhill Pub when he had reached it, just as he did every day when his work was finished. He was quite unable to enjoy the merriment, but smiled cordially to his mates seated at the bar. His sharp mind pondered his sanity, as he gulped stout and looked out the window and across the road, where the gaunt form of the doctor stood and stared.

The next morning James stumbled to the bathroom where he took four aspirins before opening both of his eyes. He then lowered his mouth to the faucet and drank the cold water until he was full. The blinds of his windows had all been closed, for he felt no desire to look down to the street. The apparition would not appear in the apartment, he felt quite certain, and so he was at least offered a reprieve.

Within the hour he was shuffling down the street with the other working masses, and looking only at the concrete beneath his feet. When he felt foolish for doing so, he would glance upward, only to find that the apparition of the doctor was there. It always faced him with its distinguished gaunt face, never looking elsewhere, attempting perhaps to convey some message of which James was unaware.

He drew the blinds of his office window before sitting down, so that the view of the hallway could not be seen. James procrastinated all of his field research and spent the morning hours attempting to type and edit all of the unfinished articles that remained. Two hours later he took a look down the hallway, and then vowed never to look again, until the specter or figment of this temporary insanity left his presence for good.

At lunch he went to the corner pub and had a gin and tonic to calm his nerves. All the while he was watched by the doctor from the opposite corner of the adjacent street. It stood motionless and unblinking, the face a pasty white color. It was under this unceasing stare that James realized what he would do, and that was to take an early evening train ride west to the city of Grandsville.

Doctor Handley would not be there, he felt reasonably certain, and knew that it was the man's ghost which chaperoned him now. But perhaps, he thought pleadingly, the doctor's intriguing patient could be found and convinced to tell all that he knew. It would be a start, perhaps, to appeasing the doctor's spirit which seemed trapped in a state of unrest.

He paid his tab and felt the heightened confidence of alcohol within his blood. And so, with respect and good intentions, did he nod his head to the ghost of the man. It only stared back at him unchangingly, with an appearance of complete despair.

He did not see it from the train car, as he looked out through the windows, to the fields of the passing land. Perhaps he had already appeased it when he had boarded the train, he reasoned, but later saw that it awaited him, in the lot of the Grandsville station. He did not acknowledge it this time, but simply hailed the first taxi from the street. "Grandsville sanitarium," were the only words which he spoke to the awaiting driver.

The asylum was enormous, and although James had never seen photos of it, the institution seemed worthy of its prestigious reputation. The construction of the building was not dissimilar to the old stone mansions which filled the northeastern region of Alberton. The lobby was equally large, although plain, and James did not delay approaching the receptionist and asked to be seen by Doctor Handley. She did not question him or act in any peculiar fashion, but instead picked up the phone and spoke plainly to someone else unknown within that massive structure.

"Someone will be right down," she said pleasantly, and recommended that James take a seat on a bench nearby.

From where he sat the entire courtyard was visible, but the spirit of the Doctor Handley chose not to make its presence known. He had not seen it, as a matter of fact, since it had appeared to him in the lot of the local station.

Within minutes a man appeared from a pair of heavy doors which led into the secure portion of the asylum. His appearance and clothing affirmed to James that he held the rank of psychiatrist, even before a word had been spoken.

"Good evening sir," said the man, "I am Doctor Richards. I'm afraid that Doctor Handley is unavailable. Did you have an appointment with him?"

The man seemed to eye him inquisitively, but in his nervous condition, James could not determine if this suspicion was true. "No, not officially," said James. "I met him yesterday on the train into Alberton, and we had a rather interesting conversation. I'm a reporter for the Alberton News. My name is James Bishop." James then offered his hand, which the doctor shook cordially.

"Doctor Handley spoke a bit about the intricacies of some patient's delusions," said James, "And I sensed possibly that it would make a worthy story. No names would be used of course, and all patients' rights would be protected. He invited me to call upon him to discuss it further, and so, here I am."

The doctor before him and peered into his eyes and surely performed some type of analysis upon him. James stood his ground despite his weariness and nerves, and rose to the occasion, just as he always seemed to do. These few seconds seemed greatly extended until at last the doctor spoke again.

"Well, Doctor Handley was delayed in the city," spoke the doctor. "He was supposed to be in today, but did not arrive. But I think we can sign you in as a visitor and have a chat, so long as you have some identification."

James removed his wallet from his pocket, and proved that he was exactly who he claimed to be. The doctor studied it intently, surely due to the unusual coincidence of his visitation coinciding with the doctor's disappearance. It was then returned it James' awaiting hand.

There is one patient in particular whose delusions seem fascinating," said James, once they had passed through the heavy doors and entered the walls of the asylum. I do not know his name, but Doctor Handley described a vivid fantasy of a diner with a demonic painted yellow moniker. I would like greatly appreciative to speak with this man."

"You are referring to Douglas Chadwick," said the doctor as they walked. He came here only six months ago as a very disturbed young man. I think that you could interview him, if he's willing, so long as I remain present. How much of his story do you know?"

"Very little," said James, who now felt the joy of knowing that his ruse had worked.

"You see," said the doctor, "Douglas believes that he unknowingly consumed a human heart at the diner with the yellow moniker. Further, he believes that it was this consumption of the organ, and its ingestion, that triggered the onset of his madness."

"Quite macabre," said James with a shiver of repulsion, as he inwardly recalled the spiced sausage which he had devoured with such enthusiasm.

"Indeed, but it is not just the cannibalization, the patient believes that he is now haunted by an apparition, in the form of the man whose organ he believes he consumed. He is not my patient, so I do not know the further intricacies of the case."

James was shown into a simple room which held only a table and matching chairs. The doctor excused himself, and returned shortly, with both a nurse and a disheveled man who seemed not to have slept in weeks.

"Douglas," spoke the doctor, in a voice somewhat more noble, and with a resonating tone. "I would like you to meet Mr. Bishop. Please excuse me for just a few moments, there is a matter which I must attend to. This nurse will be in the hallway if there is anything that you should need." Doctor Richard then stepped from the room, much to James' elation and surprise.

The patient was visibly manic, giving the appearance of one who would not survive long in his condition. "There isn't much time," said James to the disheveled man, as he hunched over the table between them and looked into his crazy eyes. "I've come to tell you what I know, and to seek your guidance if I may. I know of the diner with the yellow painting. I know of the strange owner, and the sausage that they serve.

I've eaten there, and I have one now who follows me. Please tell me what can be done."

The disheveled man stared across to him unblinkingly, and took his time forming a reply. "Nothing can be done," said the wild-eyed man with a sadistic grin. "You have bitten off more than you can chew, perhaps, yes I think so!" In reaction to this feeble wit, the man carried on with chuckles of delight before he would speak again. "Do you see only one?" he asked at last.

"Yes, only one," James answered confusedly.

"I've two," said the man. "You see, I've eaten the heart of a man who has also eaten a heart. Now I've inherited both souls, and will carry both until I die…"

"How do you mean, I…" began James, but the man interrupted and continued his manic fervor.

"Where is the diner man from, do you think? Of what race does he herald? The answer is *several* now, I tell you, because he has taken on bodily features of the men whose hearts he has devoured. I assure you, I've had many hours of waking night to ponder these things, and I am now certain that he eats only a portion of each heart that he takes. It is in this way that he can maintain his youth in small portions, while causing another to carry the burden of the displaced and murdered soul. You have been his pawn, Mr. Bishop, just as was I. You consumed the meal, whereas he took only a bite! Ha, ha!"

With this exclamation the disheveled man slammed his fist onto the table, and began the hysterics of a madman. Doctor Richard appeared in the window glass soon thereafter, and burst in to attempt to calm the antics of the madman.

"He will walk in purgatory until your death, until at last his soul will be freed!" howled the man, as James retreated from the room amidst the madness and the commotion. A nurse freed him from the heavy locked doors of the front, when he showed his badge of visitation. The receptionist then phoned him a taxi, which he awaited with his back to the window.

James arose the next morning feeling somewhat better, and then peered through the window to the street below. The specter of Doctor

Handley was indeed there upon the sidewalk showing a face of utmost misery. "Perhaps he wishes that I take my life," thought James, "But what then would happen to my soul?" He released his blinds and walked away to the kitchen, to heat his morning tea.

The proper actions became clear to him as the weariness of waking passed, and the warmth of the tea began to fill him. He would simply report the suspected murder of Doctor Handley to the police, citing his encounter with the doctor coupled with the claims of the madman with whom he had visited. He was certainly free to exclude all aspects of the supernatural. Yes, the course of action shone with clarity within his mind and he began to feel quite a bit better. Perhaps that would appease the soul of Doctor Handley, he thought hopefully, but knew deep within him that it would not be so.

But he found that he desired one last look at the devilish building of the eatery, and somewhat spontaneously took a taxi to the south side of town. Once there he was not content to peer from the confines of the automobile, and so, paid the driver and excited to the street.

The papered windows of the eatery appeared completely innocuous as he looked upon it from across the road. So fascinating was the morbid place that he did not notice the strange looking locals who now peered at him from every angle about. They looked upon him from alleys and windows and doorsteps, as he stared at the yellow face which seemed to be alight with the fires of hell. Slowly they began to engulf him, closing in from either side of the concrete walk, until at last he realized their presence. As he turned, his fair-hair towered above them, amidst a dark sea of swarming malice, and ethnically indistinct faces that showed true evil. Then, a blow came upon his head, and the blackness of oblivion overtook him.

James felt the incision below his ribcage, the pain of which tugged at his swollen brain and attempted to rouse him to a state of alert wakefulness. But his eyes did not open, even when the greater pain of the thrusting hand drove beneath his ribs and clutched his still beating heart. Then there was only numbness and he saw once again the form of Doctor Handley at his side. It remained close to him and did not dissipate, and still held the hopelessness within its eyes.

"You fool," said the image of the doctor. "Your soul has now been claimed, while still intertwined with my own. And soon they will become entangled once again, with the unfortunate soul who consumes the next meal. We can hope only that the cycle is broken many years from now, when the next pawn succumbs to a natural death. Until then we are lost souls, incapable of joy or a will of our own."

16. The Myth and the Snow

The snow had begun to fall soon after daylight had come. Samuel stood at the lone window of outpost no. 8 and felt the presence of great uneasiness within his mind. He watched the new flakes settle onto the ground and attempted to push this uneasiness back into the dark regions of his mind where it could be ignored.

Loneliness and anticipation are what he felt most strongly. These sensations had grown with each new day during the isolation, and he was now just as aware of them as he was the cold draft that seeped constantly beneath the door. However this was not the end of his displeasure, for there was a new fear which had begun building within his belly three days prior, when surveyor James Brasson of outpost no. 9 had failed to report before the ninth day of November. It was not like a surveyor of the North country to miss the deadline marking the season's end and the beginning of the journey home.

"It is time for a difficult decision Tobias," said Samuel to his lounging dog without turning away from the window. The wind just beyond the thick glass of the pane howled as he sipped coffee from a tin mug clasped in his hands. "Perhaps he miscounted his days," spoke Samuel, "but even so, he is now two days past the planned date of arrival." His eyes searched automatically the whiteness of the exterior plains, seeking the dark shape of his distant colleague, although Samuel knew that he would not be there. For the distance between the outpost cabins was a full day's walk, and arrival at this early hour would have meant that his colleague had walked throughout the night. Attempted travel through the early winter darkness would certainly bring a sentence of death.

Tobias the dog moved only his eyes and continued lying upon the elk hide, on the cabin floor by the dwindling fire. He looked upon his master's back within the center of the incoming sunlight and sensed the man's unrest. The dog felt this truth within the very innards of its belly. There is no emotion that man can hide fully from a beast whose senses are keen.

"Brasson has not come, and now shall not," said Samuel to his dog and the loneliness of the still cabin, as he continued his stare through the thick glass of the small cabin window. "He is dead or injured, I am certain, and at a distance of sixteen miles to the north, quite a bit further than we are presently, from the beckoning of the village of Champlain."

Samuel had not spoken aloud often during these past months. The sound of his words shocked him with their vibrancy and made him long even more so for the civilized sounds of village Champlain. And it was at this moment that his decision became soundly forged, and the guilt as such began to wash over him. He would not deviate from the surveyor's policy and search for his companion, and now James Brasson would not survive the harsh cold of arctic winter. If he still lived at all…

"Perhaps the Nukpana Istas got him," said Samuel with a joking intention, but he regretted the words as soon as they were uttered. "Evil from the snow," he voiced dryly, and then turned away from the falling snow outside of his tiny cabin.

Now that the fire of departure had been lit within him, there seemed no reason for further delay. The temperature would begin falling more rapidly and descend further with each day's setting sun. And the light of morning would be warmed to a lesser degree with each successive sun that would rise.

Samuel, having been packed for departure already, had little remaining preparation to do. He bundled the remaining food provisions which had been left out, and took the matches from the crudely planed mantle above the hearth.

"I have given him two whole days already," snapped Samuel into the still air of the cabin. "It would be one day's walk in either direction, and then another for search lest he lies conveniently dead in his bed."

He looked then upon Tobias and the beasts eyes were wide and still. "Even if his leg is only broken and I gave him my rations, he could not fetch his own wood!" The eyes of the master bore into those of the dog, forcing the beast to look away.

Samuel could hear the reply of his conscience speaking, *"Unless you winter with him and care for the injured man. There would be food enough, if you supplemented hunted meat with your shotgun.*" But Samuel would not acknowledge this inner voice.

Within minutes his gear was prepared for the day's walk southward to outpost no. 7, to which he was not officially due until the sun went down the following day. He left the dying fire to fade into the oblivion of a half a year of lifeless cold.

"Dog!" he called from where he stood in the opened doorway, now with snow shoes fastened beneath his fur lined leather boots. Tobias arose apprehensively and without enthusiasm and then trotted out into the brightness of the snow. The force of a new wind howled across the plain and onto Samuel's back as he slammed and bolted the cabin's door.

The air warmed throughout the hour as the sun began the daily ascent overhead, and this combined with the warmth of energy expenditure, began to fill their bodies with fleeting warmth. Samuel's legs were strong, for he had spent the spring and summer walking great distances surveying the lands to the east and west. He longed greatly for the healing warmth of a bath and a woman, both of which he would purchase at the village of Champlain before venturing further South to the city of Saulk.

Saulk, it seemed to Samuel, was a town properly suited for passing a winter. He had a brother there, and an uncle, and friendships with many of the whores with whom he could ease the passage of the coldest season. There he could live cheaply for several months on the pay that awaited him within Champlain. That life of inner city squalor and sin seemed to him now like heaven as he walked through the snow.

Ahead of him Tobias suddenly froze mid stride and peered sharply to his left. Samuel then did the same, seeing only the white hills and sporadic trees. Wolves were the only predators this far north, and he knew that the natives would not depart from the shoreline now that the season had grown so cold. But still, the shotgun sticking from his pack provided him comfort, and he kicked Tobias upon his rump and the two of them walked southward again.

At six paces further the dog again turned its head but this time did not cease its motion. The skin of Samuel's arms then tingled with an energy he could not explain, and he was forced once again to look in that direction. There was only the same silent whiteness of hills, and the gentle powdering of fresh snow which fell softly from the sky.

"Onward!" he yelled to the dog, and then listened to his voice as it echoed throughout the vastness.

He estimated that three hours of daylight remained when he first saw the smoke escaping the chimney of outpost no. 7. Samuel did not wish to admit so, but within him he felt a great relief. His compass had steered him southward, but he had begun to fear that he had deviated to the east or west and passed the cabin altogether. It would not have taken more than an hour more to reduce him into panic, with the terrible decision he would then have had to make. It would have been the decision of whether to avert his direction to the east or west, or to trust the compass and continue further to the south. And this panic would have brought with it as well the horrible urge to turn back and retrace his steps to outpost no. 8, in a hurried attempt to reach it before the cold would extinguish his life.

But these fears fell quickly away and were replaced by the joy of knowing that he would soon converse with another human being, as lonely as he was himself. Samuel walked to the thick wooden door and pounded with the underside of his fist. The door of outpost no. 7 opened nearly immediately, displaying the heavily bearded face of Jerrold Brier. The smiling man looked first at Samuel and his dog and then past him, beyond into the snow.

"Where is Brasson?" spoke Jerrold as his bright smile was replaced with a shadow of darkness. Samuel did not immediately answer this, and instead pushed past Jerrold with Tobias at his heels, into the warmth of the cabin.

"I gave him two days beyond the deadline," said Samuel a few moments after he had reached the fire, keeping his back toward his colleague, as he stood before it rubbing his hands. "Just as our operating procedure dictates…"

Jerrold closed the outer door of outpost no. 7, and much of the light within the cabin was diminished. This barricade between the men and the muffled noise of the exterior wind brought a sense of morbid stillness into the room. It was this uncomfortable shadow which fell between them, which prompted Samuel to speak out once again.

"If the temperature had not already begun to fall, I would have taken the day's walk north…" His statement was left to trail off, and he resisted the urge to speak again.

"Here, have a whiskey," said Jerrold, and stepped toward the table to seize the bottle. "This is dangerous work that we do," the bearded man then said as he poured out one tall drink apiece. "Take the other chair and sit by the fire." He kicked softly at the butt of his own dog, shoeing it from where it had lain.

The light from the lone window faded as the sun began to set for the day. The small fireplace was soon filled with new wood, and Jerrold dropped the excess logs upon the floor against the wall. As he retook his seat, the forms of both men blocked most of the fire's light, leaving the remainder of the room more darkened than it had been prior. They sat mostly in silence and sipped upon their whiskey, one of the few pleasures each had known during the long months which had passed.

"Have you seen the footprints?" said Jerrold dryly after some time, as he stared with a tightened face that appeared like stone, into the crackling fire.

"I have seen wolf prints and I have seen wolves, and I have seen elk prints and I have seen elk," answered Samuel a bit sleepily.

Jerrold sat silently and did not move for several seconds. "That is all you've seen?" he then questioned.

"I don't know what answer you seek, my friend," said Samuel who followed this with a yawn. The fire crackled and blazed, and the new logs which had been added were now consumed by the flickering flames.

"I have seen the foot prints of the Nukpana Istas," said Jerrold plainly, and took immediately a sip from his cup. The bearded man then returned the cup to the top of his leg, and paused a moment or two before scratching at an inch upon his other leg. The motions of his limbs were stiff and awkward. "You have seen them also," said Jerrold amidst this peculiar fidget, and then returned the gaze of his eyes into the fire. "They are like none I have ever seen, and show the elongated thumb of each foot just as the native people document in their legends. And I have seen them far to the north of my cabin as well, which places them within your zone."

"I have seen the peculiar foot prints of a mutant wolf," replied Samuel, "and you have seen only the same. Or perhaps it is the ploy of an unusually cunning native boy who ventured far from the shore as he hunted at the side of his father."

"I've seen no human tracks of hunting natives," snapped Jerrold with the tone of irritation filling his voice. "And now you arrive at my door with our friend Brasson strangely absent." The now sleepy eyed Jerrold began to rub at his hair and eyes with the palm of his hand. "No," he then snapped more authoritatively, "It has returned to guard the land, just as the native's legends have warned that it shall. It has returned to guard its land from the tainting of the white man, and it has begun with dear Brasson."

"I followed operating procedure," spoke Samuel, "We all take risks with this work…"

Jerrold drank from the cup and maintained his unwavering glare into the red coals of the fire. "They say it will not venture into the forest of the low lands, but rather keeps to the high ground and the frozen plains."

"The fools say lots of things," said Samuel who arose from the crudely planed chair and lifted his tin cup before him. "To Brasson," he called aloud, "A good fellow whatever his fate." As he pressed the cup to his lips and drained it, Jerrold said nothing but spat a mouthful of the whiskey into the flames, causing an uproarious blaze that thundered wickedly. He then sat mutely and watched the coals until long after his intruding colleague had begun to sleep.

But despite all of this strangeness both men did indeed sleep more soundly than they had in months, each snoring loudly into the ears of the other and neither of them hearing a sound. Each of their subconscious minds sensed the presence of the other and interpreted this companionship as safety, allowing their bodies to fully relax and descend into the blackness of a peaceful slumber.

Samuel dreamt of the Nukpana Istas and its terrible form in pursuit always just behind him, looking just as it had in his nightmares when he had first dreamt of it as a small child. All was silent as he ran, except for the pulsing of his heart within his chest and the pressure of hot blood pounding in the veins of his temples. It seemed always at his heals, a beast of savage origin, stalking him as he ran noiselessly over the countryside and straining futilely to escape.

All was white about him as he ran blindly into this vast brightness, appearing like a cloak which sought to entangle him and strangled him from every side. Out of this cloud glimpses of the terrible beast could be seen, the whitened fur hanging from elongated limbs, showing fur which had weathered the cold of centuries long past, before the feet of man had walked the earth.

The menacing form emerged from the great whiteness behind him, prodding him into a quickened run which could not be long maintained. The white eyes of the beast were immense as its head poked through the thickness of the snowy haze and appeared lifeless like the eyes of a demented old man, and fairer than sun-bleached bone. Closer and closer it drew toward him, the hot breath of it falling upon his neck with an overpowering and rancid stink, which his lungs struggled to seize as his stamina began to fail him. Then just as it seemed ready to pounce upon him, he convulsed mightily and awoke, back safely again upon the floor of Jerrold's cabin, and nearly crying out like a frightened girl.

It was not long after that Jerrold arose from his own bed and tossed new logs onto the remnants of the smoldering coals within the hearth. Samuel spied upon him as he did so in the near-darkness, through eyelids barely parted. Jerrold then climbed back beneath the blankets and furs atop his bed, while both men waited for the fire to arise and create and a room temperature that was habitable.

At breakfast they ate fried cornmeal with syrup and coffee stronger than Samuel would have tasted. But he did not complain and neither did Jerrold speak a word about Samuel's outcry within the night.

Jerrold, as Samuel had been the day prior, was already fully prepared for departure. Neither man spoke a word this day of their fallen colleague.

"Malloy!" called out Jerrold to his dog as the men opened the door and initiated the act of leaving. Tobias arose with the other beast before the hearth and both trotted out into the whiteness.

"It looks to snow today," said Jerrold once the door had been secured. "I'll not like the look of it." Both men peered to the north horizon where the dark clouds of impending snow dominated the sky.

"It is bright to the south," said Samuel, who stepped away and left his companion hesitating at his doorway.

The first two miles passed well, and the snow upon the ground was a problem neither for their snowshoes nor the dogs. Malloy walked at the front of his master, followed by Tobias and Samuel at the rear. Samuel watched the posture of his colleague relax a bit as the miles began to pass, as though there were some weight that the man left behind. Occasionally did Jerrold turn and look behind them to the dark clouds, through the narrow slits of his eye gear that prevented the glare from blinding his eyes. Samuel felt relief that he was not forced to see the man's eyes and began to anticipate greatly their parting upon arrival at the village.

At approximately four miles Jerrold took a slender cigar from his pocket which he immediately lighted. It was perhaps, a celebration, for a quarter of their return was now completed. At twenty paces further Samuel watched him halt and stiffen, as did Malloy keenly at the front. Jerrold fixated his gaze downward at the snow.

"Here!" he then called out, to which Samuel approached without delay. Both of them peered downward at a track of prints that could not be denied. They showed the mark of the protruding appendage that could not be mistaken. "They'll not believe us in Champlain," spoke Jerrold coldly as dread reentered his entire being.

"Move on," ordered Samuel as boldly as his voice would allow, but the hairs upon his neck beneath the layers of wool and fur stood on end.

The snow from the north began to descend on them which Jerrold spied and then turned to Samuel, and the look of the man's slitted eye gear seemed to extrude agitation and growing fear. Samuel watched as the man's head turned this way and that and even to the rear occasionally, perhaps to see if Samuel himself were still were there.

At six miles the snow came down in giant flakes, stacking upon the heads and shoulders of the men and upon the backs of the dogs. But the chilling wind had not rolled in with it, and for this fact Samuel felt gratitude. Their vision was now being overtaken by the snow, and it seemed that a whiteout was upon them. The form of Tobias was still clear to Samuel, but the shape of Jerrold had begun to fade. Each of the party began to feel waves of isolation as they would momentarily fall a step behind and lose the form of their precursor. Jerrold would run a step or two toward Malloy who drove them onward, followed by Tobias and Samuel at the end.

Samuel now walked with his compass within his left hand and checked their direction of progress at successively rapid frequency. It was during a gaze down at this tool that he momentarily lost the group and looked up to see only the whiteness of the haze. Panic filled him and he ran onward for several paces, nearly upon Tobias who stood finally at Jerrold's heels.

"Malloy is gone!" screamed Jerrold as their three forms huddled together. "Malloy!"

"His tracks?..." yelled Samuel, who then stepped to the front to find the beast. There was nothing discernable within the snow, except possibly a trail of churned powder. Both men peered at this rapidly disappearing anomaly which intersected their line of direction but neither uttered a word.

"I'll lead," said Samuel simply and checked his compass. "We cannot stop," he spoke simply, and stepped onward again.

At ten miles the wind began to tear at their backs, through all of their layers of clothing, sending spikes of pain throughout their extremities. The airborne snow now whipped violently past them and a complete whiteout was at hand.

"It comes with the snow!" yelled Jerrod maniacally from the rear, to which Samuel turned but would not acknowledge. "It comes with the snow!..."

The wind howled madly now over his shoulders, filling his covered ears with its moan and drowning out the muttering cries of his colleague. When Samuel turned about further on, the form of Jerrold was not there.

"Tobias!" he called sharply to the dog who had taken the lead, which halted the dog immediately. Neither man nor beast wished now to be alone in these terrible conditions. Samuel stared over his fur clad shoulder but Jerrold's form never did emerge from the whiteness. He did not call out to the man but rather ran pushed onward hastily with his dog.

"It is not far now," his mind told him, *"You can make it...the warmth of outpost no. 6 awaits…"* But his conscious mind was not fooled. The sun was now upon its descent and there was no more room for error.

At this moment the snow eased its descent as if to answer Samuel's calls of desperation. The wind cleared somewhat and in the air before him he saw the brilliant green of the evergreen tree-line which grew thick and lush a mere hundred feet away.

"The outpost is just beyond, and they say it will not depart the flatlands of the snow!" his mind told him, as his heart pumped and his breath struggled as he ran as fast as his snowshoes would allow. *"Almost! Almost!..."*

Tobias halted suddenly just before the first evergreen as he heard the mighty shriek escape his master's throat and howl across the frozen land. The muscular back of the dog was arched with preparedness and terror as its yellow eyes saw some form of violent motion from within the screen of falling snow. It thought perhaps that it saw something of tremendous height and pure whiteness brilliant enough to match the purity of all that snow upon that endless land. And perhaps the dog saw the redness of its master's blood erupting and filling the air before splattering upon the powder.

The new flakes fell quickly upon the newly crimson ground, burying it until the thaw of spring that would come several months in the future. The dog turned southward toward the vast forest and ran into the safety of the evergreen trees. Tobias smelled the scent of an alighted fire within the hearth of outpost no. 7.

17. Ancillary Parts

Trapped room syndrome – that is what Edward Oswald was experiencing. A great panic sensation and the bodily freeze that accompanies it, his eyes locked forward and acutely aware of everyone and everything around him. And as aware as he was of all of these things, Edward was even more aware of his own body and his own mind, a sensation quite to the opposite side of the spectrum where content and bliss reside.

But he was no stranger to this, and at thirty-five years of age this particular panic attack was certainly not his first rodeo, as they say.

"The barbs are out," he thought, referring to the brain waves he was projecting out to the other passengers, which their brains in turn were registering and beginning to feel the psychological discomfort without directly knowing that Edward was the source. But of course they would know nothing of the barbs and the extra-sensory manipulation of their minds. They would only determine that *the tense man on the right side of the train car was making them nervous*. But such was Edward's lifelong burden.

He reached into his jacket pocket and removed a piece of delicately folded white paper, undoing one fold and then another. From inside two orange pills slid down into his hand and he promptly swallowed them. For the first ten years they worked wonderfully, but now the effects were unpredictable they and were only partially beneficial. But there really was no other choice…

Within ten minutes the barbs were withdrawn, pulled back into his brain and tucked away for the time being. But he was now mentally dulled. Edward tested his cognitive ability with mathematical exercise. The dulling side effect of the pills was of great concern. They were destroying his brain and he knew this with certainty.

But such thoughts were counterproductive to his purpose on the train. It was to be a holiday away from stress, and so he had purchased the train ticket at the station in Shelby, Kentucky for a peaceful ride through the south-central portion of the Appalachian Mountains. He would arrive at Dante, Virginia in just a couple of hours where we would be free to take a walking exploration of the old town and seek out a spontaneous dinner and night's board. In the morning he would decide whether or not he wanted to continue on down the line to Kingsport, Tennessee, or wait until later in the day for the return route back home.

By the time he filed out of the car at the Dante station he felt reasonably well and not as hazy as the medication sometimes left him. He had only one traveling bag, the beautiful black leather carrying case which had been gifted to him so many years ago. He had always liked the way the stained wooden handle felt in his hand, and he enjoyed this sensation as he walked down the steps with the others who excited, following their path out beside the station and onto the street beyond.

He was not yet hungry and walked several streets past the station in very little time. Everything here was a new experience. There were no pre-existing memories of the discomfort of awkwardness, for he had never before walked the streets or been among these people. And it was with this rare sensation of natural tranquility that he looked up and saw the sign for the clock smith's shop which read plainly "Stroeger Watch & Clock Sales/ Repair". Edward peered through the window and saw all of the displayed time pieces clicking away in regimented unison, and a peculiar spine tingling sense of quality came over him. *So few people paid attention to the fine details nowadays*, thought Edward as he entered the shop. The aged man he assumed to be Stroeger smiled up at him from his large circular-lensed face.

"I happen to have a broken watch with me," said Edward to the man. "It was a gift from my mother many years ago," he further explained as Stroeger acknowledged this with a pleasant sound and extended his hand to take the timepiece. The aged man then wound the device and held it to his ear.

"I believe this repair will not be too difficult," said Stroeger after a few moments. "If it is what I think it is, I can have it done for you within two hours at a fee of $30, and perhaps even in less time."

"That sounds very reasonable," replied Edward. "Do you think it's just a matter of swapping out some of the mechanics?" Edward knew nothing of which he spoke.

"I believe that you have only one piece of hardware which has slipped. It is a common repair on these models. Here, I have one here…" said the old man as he waved Edward down to the end of the counter. Awaiting them was an exposed watch whose exterior had been pried in half to expose the mechanical innards. "This is a similar repair, although not identical," stated the Stroeger. "You see when this delicate little shaft here begins to stick for whatever reason, the entire working of the watch in terminated." He pointed to a tiny portion of hardware with a miniscule probe within his hand.

"It's so tiny," said Edward, "It hardly seems as though it could literally stop time."

"Ah, indeed it can, small or not," said Stroeger. "And as detrimental as it can be to the function of the timepiece, watch as it is removed…" Stroeger then grabbed a miniscule tool resembling tweezers with needle-like ends and proceeded to masterfully pluck the tiny shaft out of the workings of the device. Edward watched as the watch pieces instantly came to life with movement. "So you see," said Stroeger, "we have removed the bind. Now gently pick it up and flip it over."

Edward did so and peered at the face of the watch. All hands of the device were alive and ticking with motion: the hour, minute, and the second hand. "They move again," said Edward to the aged man and attempted to hand the timepiece to him.

Stroeger did not immediately take it, but looked at the customer before him. "Do you not see?" he asked. "We have removed a piece of the device and yet all hands function." The old man's tone hinted annoyance.

"Ah, yes," said Edward, cursing himself silently and the dulling aspect of the pills. He was once a smart man and felt ashamed of the medication and their failure to allow him to fully observe and comprehend. "I should have noticed, forgive me. So what does that piece do then when it is in place?"

"One could argue nothing," said Stroeger, "but technically it ensures that all hands remain synchronized in full. But a quality watch should not require this unnecessary regulation – it is redundant.

"Ah, I see," said Edward with a bit of a chuckle. The old man did not join him.

"Do you?" he rather yelled to Edward, and finally took the timepiece back from him. "I think perhaps you should view another piece." Edward accepted, feeling the awkwardness which was now certainly present, but respectfully followed the old man into the back room. He saw a work bench and stool and an old looking wooden door at the far side. "Are you traveling on?" asked Stroeger, to which Edward explained his uncertain and solitary travel plans. "So you did not come to Dante to seek out my shop and have your watch repaired, you have only happened by?"

"Indeed that is how I arrived here," agreed Edward, to which Stroeger lifted a rubber mallet from his work bench smashed it down upon Edward's skull above the temple.

Edward heard a muffled moan and realized that it came from his own throat. He found that he could not sit up and became aware of being tied upon some sort of bench with his arms immobile above his head. His legs were equally transfixed, and a taut cloth had been tied tightly around his head between his open teeth. He was in some new room, unfinished and ugly, bearing the appearance of a cellar. He guessed that he had been brought down a stairway that was beyond the old door of the workroom. A clock hanging upon the dirty wall told him that it was 11:25 a.m. and not much time had elapsed.

His head ached mightily and the stretched corners of his parted mouth burned. Strangely he did not panic as was generally his nature. Edward tried to free his hands but was unable. It was then that he heard the door above and the sound of descending footsteps.

Stroeger entered the room somewhere behind Edward's head but he was unable to turn his head far enough to see the old man. After a few seconds the man stepped into view with an appearance of great indifference. Stroeger lifted some type of glass from a shelf and then turned to face him.

"I believe I have categorically placed you my friend, into the grouping which you truly reside," said Stroeger. "You are quite like that tiny shaft of hardware which I removed from that watch. You exist, and breath through your days just as any man does, hopping onto trains and shuffling along amongst the other masses. But there is nothing noteworthy about your existence. Here you are on a Wednesday afternoon, a man in his thirties no less, without a wedding ring upon his finger, apparently shuffling along as though you have no value to add, anywhere, to anyone. Yes, you are quite like that extra shaft which was engineered into the design of the watch which we viewed. You are an appendix, a limb that was born lame. You are yourself sir, an ancillary part. This world has no use for you." Stroeger reached into a drawer and withdrew a cloth which had been folded neatly. "I do not hold any dislike for you personally but I have always disliked the unnecessary extras. You inherently bear an insult to those of us who have found success through our toil."

Edward began to voice a retort through the gag, stretching his mouth to speak and shambling through several mumbled words without any notion of how his sentence would end. "Silence!" yelled Stroeger, and then rapidly calmed himself. He stepped alongside Edward with both a bottle and a now crumpled cloth. "My father was a surgeon and I would often watch him work on entire masses of wounded men, one after the other, during the first Great War. You would be amazed at how well the human body can function without so many of its unnecessary parts."

Edward attempted to shout through the gag, but the old man paid him no mind. Instead he tipped the bottle downward into the cloth while stating simply the word, "Ether," and then lifted the doused cloth over Edward's mouth and nose.

Consciousness slowly entered Edward's brain. Edward did not remember waking but rather slowly became aware that his heavy lids were blinking open and closed. He saw the repugnantly indifferent face of Stroeger sitting at his side upon a stool. "Tick tock, tick tock," said Stroeger, "like a clock regaining functionality, the mind awakes." Stroeger then lifted a mirror from his lap and held it for Edward's gaze. Both of his ears had been removed. Edward screamed as though he were being burned alive. "Tick tock, tick tock…" said Stroeger as he set down the mirror and lifted the cloth damp with ether over Edward's face once again, smothering his protests.

Again consciousness slowly returned. The blinking of the narrowly opening eyes again told Edward the horror of his situation. It was as though no time had passed but the clock on the wall told him that it was now 12:20 p.m. He could not form words, but rather screamed uncontrollably through his gag.

"Your hand," said Stroeger with just a hint of joy as he sat upon his stool at Edward's side. Edward, still screaming, lifted his now free left hand from his chest to see that all four of the fingers, and the bones below them within the hand, had all been surgically removed. Only the thumb remained and the wound had been stitched closed precisely. As Edward stared upon the macabre remainder of the thumb a flood of tears began to stream from his eyes. "It will soon be dinner time," said Stroeger as he arose and grabbed the cloth, "Tick tock, tick tock…"

1:12 read the clock as Edward blinked to consciousness, feeling again as though not a moment had passed since he was last awake. The speed at which he was diminishing seemed to him as horrible as the acts themselves. Like an organic mass dissolving quickly within a jar of acid…

"Toes," said Stroeger as he motioned nonchalantly to both feet which had had all digits removed. The limbs had been untied so that Stroeger could lift his feet up into Edward's view. "At this rate you'll be just a torso of essential organs by nightfall. Tick tock, tick tock…"

The old man then braced himself to stand, still holding the scalpel in his grasp. Edward's scrambling brain saw then an opportunity, with the crumpled ether cloth that lay upon his groin. As Stroeger stood and stepped forward Edward threw his legs upward and seized the old man about the neck and shoulders with their length. Instinctively he locked the foot of one behind the knee of the other, both squeezing Stroeger and pulling him forward toward himself. Edward lifted the damp cloth of ether will the remaining macabre thumb and pressed it into Stroeger's face while maintaining the lock of his legs. The old man shouted and struggled, but was soon no match for the strength of the potent liquid. The ether quickly rendered the old man limp, and the scalpel grasping hand fell limply upon Edward's chest.

The blade would have made a perfect weapon if Edward's free hand could have grasped it. He attempted as such but the lone thumb was useless in this regard. But he was now only bound to the table by his right hand, and was after hurling the limp body of Stroeger to the ground, able to gain his freedom.

Stroeger was just beginning to blink to consciousness as Edward clasped the scalpel in his untouched right hand and sliced the throat of the old man. He felt strangely content as the blood of the aged fiend gushed out upon the floor and seeped all around his bared and toeless feet. Edward found that retaining his balance was challenging without the aid of toes, but then again, challenges were nothing new to him.

18. Gone Skiving, Back in an Hour

Business wasn't slow, just intermittent. Henry Kessler sat on the stool behind the counter at his hunting and fishing store, and began to feel a familiar yearning. Well *began* is a bit of a lie, for he had awoken with it, and like a newly opened gash it had festered throughout the morning. He now felt it in his legs and backside, the sedentary weight of atrophy combined with the psychological hunger for the thrill of something more.

It was not a bad life, which he certainly knew, and it was in fact the very best his father could have provided for him. Purchasing the shop for him to engage in retailing his passion, the freedom to come and go as he pleased, and every miscellaneous purchase which he should happen to desire along the way. But the ache of atrophy and desire still clutched at him and no amount of fidgeting upon the stool would do away with it. He thought that perhaps he would truly be happier not being the privileged son of such a successful entrepreneur who employed the majority of the county and quite a ways beyond. People certainly knew where their next meal was coming from, and from whom, and this did have its advantages. It was in this state of self -pity and contempt that young Adam found his friend and employer.

"Good morning," called Adam to his privileged friend as he entered the store and prepared to assist working the shop.

"Hmmm," grunted Henry. This seemed generously polite to ignoring him completely. They had after all, been friends since the age of eight.

Adam looked at him and stopped a second, then looked away and adorned his merchandising apron. "Got an itch I see," he said to his friend. Henry looked upon him now somewhat kindly. Adam was, he realized, the only person in this world with whom he could communicate fully, and receive in return a compassion which was void of judgment.

"I believe I woke up with it," said Henry.

"It's probably not early enough for trout," said Adam, "but it is a cool morning. I'd be willing to head up river and have a go at it."

"Skiving," said Henry as plainly as he could, but his yearning still revealed itself. Skiving was a game they had made up when they were boys.

"We're getting too old, this county has gotten too modern," replied Adam. "We've been lucky in years past, and I've moved on from that thrill."

"Well I have not," said Henry. "I am Henry Kessler and my father employs nearly every yokel in this town, and every town nearby, and every town nearest to those." He owns the people like he owns the land, and therefore I own them as well!"

To this Adam chose not to argue. He knew his thick-headed friend all too well.

"Do you think those retards still swim on Tuesdays during the summer?" asked Henry. He did not often ask questions so earnestly.

"I couldn't say," said Adam, "but perhaps it would be good of you to call and ask. I've given it some thought over the years and I think we'd have been good to have called ahead before. That Matheson woman for example, we could've avoided that whole ordeal. Who'd have ever thought she'd have missed a damn retard so much? Anyhow, if you call the institution beforehand, it'll give them time to phone out warnings. By the time we get there, all of the loved ones would have been plucked out for the day."

"They've all been plucked out permanently already," said Henry. "We have to pay the institution for the revenue they've lost. They are down to half enrollment."

"Only half?" thought Adam vocally and a bit sadly. "It seems as though it should really be greater. I honestly don't know what I would do. Like I said Henry, we have gotten so much older. "

"All right, call them," ordered Henry. "Tell them we will be there in an hour."

Adam did not argue. There was a limit as to how far you could push the sociopathic son of the wealthiest man in the state. "All right," he simply replied, and walked to the back room to place the morbid call with a bit more privacy.

It would be an awkward call certainly, but he was surprised that it was only general uneasiness that he felt. Perhaps he had not grown at all these past years as he had thought. And this fact became painfully clear to him, for it was the gleam of the circular saw blades that he saw in his memories' eye, shining brilliantly beneath the summer sun as he and his dearest friend stood on the rock peninsula extending into the great lake behind the asylum grounds. The look upon the faces of all of those silly retards and their malformed heads popping out of the blue water filled him with both repulsion and the great anticipation of that familiar killing thrill. Then like skipping stones across the surface they would politely take turns hurling the silver razor-discs at the extended heads of the men, women, and boys and girls who had the bad luck to be born without capacity of lone survival.

It was during the moments just after the saw blade left the hand that the true thrill was felt, for it was within these moments that the fire of anticipation resided. Most throws would not meet with a target despite the years of practice which both men had engaged in. It was during these misguided throws that the blades would slow a bit with each landing that they made upon the smooth water, until all momentum was lost and the great blades sank gently toward the bottom.

But there were the great throws also, in which the blades did connect with one of those oblivious faces. The round blades held a surprising weight and would embed themselves deeply into the skulls of the mentally challenged. They stuck usually with a tremendous thud, followed by the frantic motions of a distraught and quickly-dying victim.

But this was not always the way. Sometimes death came immediately and the bodies would sink quietly into the water, dropping gracefully like a beautiful silver blade during a miss-throw, and disappearing with little more than a ripple.

Henry smiled as he lifted the phone. While he dialed it occurred to him that it would be necessary to place a sign upon the front door of the store. He imagined a sign that read: "Gone skiving, back in an hour," and the numbness of years past again filled his veins…

19. Hotel de la Mort

"Carlton Hotel 5 miles" read the little wooden signed painted white with black lettering, and so I pulled off the county highway and followed this new road. Wife said nothing but I could feel the ice from that side of the car; cold silence mixed with *I told you so*, mixed with the chilled breeze of the air-conditioning blowing at maximum force.

It was indeed precisely 5 miles, and as I drove up, I was immediately a bit put off by the apparent age of the hotel as it came into view. *Run-down* wouldn't quite describe it, because it was just a massive stone building which doesn't run-down per se, but all the same my stomach signaled an immediate sense of displeasure. But we parked and unloaded child one and child two from the back, wife carrying one and me the other. The summer heat was beyond oppressive, passing well into the domain of certain death if one were left stranded for any length of time without water and shelter.

The inside of the lobby seemed like a bit of a madhouse with the luggage carts strewn about at odd angles and some visibly peculiar folks, busy doing exactly what, I still am quite uncertain. So I turned a blind eye to it just as one does when it is easier to do so than to acknowledge or deeply comprehend, and so, I stepped onward toward the front counter.

It was quite void of attendance save for a young black man in the usual bellhop uniform, and he wasted no time in telling me that the desk clerk would not be around.

"Just take a key off the rack back there and write it on the log, and it'll all get squared up later," he assured me.

The man seemed like a pleasant enough fellow, and displayed that he certainly belonged there from his attire. So I promptly did as he instructed and chose room 212 at random, which I recorded on the oddly-stained paper of the desktop log.

I then walked my family past the elevator, not quite trusting it for some reason unknown, and headed instead for the stairs. Wife followed silently but appeared agitated; her brain unable to piece together all of the various peculiarities as I had done, into a single indisputable signal that something here was amiss.

The stairs were uneventful but the second floor was immediately disturbing, with characters of all sorts seeming to be milling and scampering about. I saw Asian men with long hair and great face-spreading smiles, more black folks of both genders, and all of them somehow revealing clearly that they had jumped mentally off of any sort of rational agenda.

To my bad luck I saw that the stairway opened quite far from room 212, and so we began to shuffle as best as we could through all of this filth and chaos. Wife seemed to cuddle up a bit closer to me as we entered it but remained silent, showing quite certainly the opportunistic bitch that I knew her to be. I caught a glimpse of child number two in her arms, head snuggled down and eyes shielded, and that seemed just fine to me since I was doing the same with child number one.

Near room 234 and 235 a revelation occurred to me, and it was that the madness, or poor breeding, or whatever infected these people, seemed to be universal. The look of their eyes did not differ from one person to the next. Upon their faces I saw the same watery eyed, elated gaze adorning each stranger that we passed.

But it was then that we passed some sort of lounge area, and all pretentions of normality crumbled away. For sitting quite normally upon one of the padded chairs was the decapitated head of one of the Asian men. I assume wife saw it also but she said nothing, creeping then even closer to my back so that I was practically carrying her then too. Other strangers both sat and stood around the lounge area, neither taking an interest in either my family or the head of the deceased long-haired man. Instead they simply continued their business of continuing, whatever existence within which they endeavored.

The head of the dead man was very near to us as we passed it, a situational fact which could not be avoided. And so I pulled child number one even tighter to my chest. I myself studied the macabre thing intently and felt a very strange mix of thoughts and emotions as my eyes met the dead man's gaze. Why was the face of this poor dead man smiling like all of the others, showing a sort of loving embrace for the premature death that had been pressed upon him? And why the long hair so neatly combed, certainly post mortem? The internal inquiries went on and on.

But we were then at our room 212 which we mysteriously entered, instead of going onward to the stairwell and running hastily out of the lower door. It is an action which to this day I truly fail to comprehend. Wife even changed the diaper of child number two while I myself sat upon the bed and went about relaxing and unwinding from the drive we had just made. One positive fact I can attest to is that the air-conditioner blew mightily, quite contrary to what I would expect from such a hotel as I have just described.

Even the television worked, and I truly did begin to feel all those uncomfortably-driven miles beginning to unwind from within me. The great wind of the air-conditioner blew directly upon my face as I lay there, inhaling it right up my nose, and I do at this very moment remember having to suppress a tremendous urge to giggle aloud.

It is at this point in the bizarre tale that I am unable to recall the details quite as clearly as I would like. And now the policeman only frown their faces down upon me and do not appear to believe my tale of insanity one iota.

Only one final detail can I explicitly relate to them, and that is the horrible aching of my face from the permanent smile that had adorned it, at the moment when they say that I arose from my position of relaxation within that hotel room, and began to do all of those horrible things…

20. Indeed

Duncan did not know how long he had been blinking his eyes. It seemed now that he had awakened some time ago and had been sitting unaware, if such a thing is possible. But regardless, there he now sat, blinking in the lighted chamber and slowly gathering his bearings.

He did not feel rested as one does when wakening from a nap. This was his second realization. But from there it did not take him long to realize that other things were amiss.

Next to him sat a simple wooden table on a dirt floor. Upon it was a small electrical lamp which was turned on, and plugged into a cheap looking extension cord that ran along the dark soil. He did not at first look fully around the room, but did realize that there were some additional objects nearby.

When he stood at last, he felt a great haze impeding his mental ability, but he was able to stand and did so without any real difficulty. As he turned about he saw that he had been sitting upon a metallic folding chair which had been declined backward a bit. It seemed that this was how he had not fallen down while sleeping.

He turned further and gazed about, the sound of his shoes grinding upon the dirt of the floor. This did not seem at first peculiar, but merely baffling as Duncan felt quite certain that no one he knew had a basement with unfinished ground. But this pondering regarding the dirt floor did get a line of thinking started, and as he blinked more fully into a conscious state, the first hints of alarm picked lightly at the base of his brain.

He looked around the odd little room and saw that although mostly vacant it did contain some items of apparent storage. And at least one section of the porous white wall was discolored with a dark, scarlet sludge for which he did not see a source. But continue looking at the various items he did, walking from one to the next and so on. There was a rusted bicycle frame, God knows how old, leaning against the wall next to some gardening shears. There was also a wood-chipper, apparently quite new, with the cord unplugged but strewn messily upon the dirt of the floor. And lastly a very old and very used tennis racket, discarded into one of the corners. Excluding only a single wooden door which was closed, this was the entire inventory.

"Shambles indeed," muttered Duncan as he took a step toward the wooden door. As he strode he attempted to retrace his memory of how he had arrived at such a place. Too much drink seemed most likely, combined presumably with some comedic antics by his friends. But he was unable to recall a social event which had preceded his odd awakening.

Once at the door he was struck by the extreme age of its appearance. The portal had a small metallic knob and was constructed with many vertically running narrow boards, attached by two horizontal wooden pieces of much greater width. Duncan had not seen a door like this since he was a boy playing in his Grandfather's cellar.

But he did not stop to ponder this and simply reached to turn the knob. It opened, and within his hazy mind he tried to determine whether or not this fact surprised him. He was still uncertain when he stepped through to the other side.

Another chamber. However this one was narrow and shabby, as though constructed by a child. At the far end ten feet away was a second door.

"Madness indeed" whispered Duncan and shook his hazy head. And with this action came a memory from earlier that(?) morning. It was of breakfast and two soft boiled eggs he had eaten. *Absolutely nothing extraordinary about that.*

And then more came back to him. Images of his wife and son, and with them just as always, came the undercurrent of burden. But this did not help him now within the dirty chamber-hallway, and so he pushed further onward both to the second door and through the quagmire of his mind.

His wife had wanted to go shopping he recalled, and so the child would be his responsibility for a few hours. But it was Saturday and the sun had been shining, and so he had taken the young one and the pre-packed bag of baby supplies provided by his wife, and ventured outside.

Locked. The old knob would not turn. This door seemed somewhat more durable than the first, but Duncan was no small man. He felt quite certain that he would get through it quickly one way or another. In his current mood he would feel neither ill-advised nor guilty for smashing his way through.

There was a man who had approached him in the park. Yes indeed, it was coming back a bit now. Older, with graying hair, but burly beneath an excessive amount of clothing. There was something that had prompted the stranger to approach and speak to him, but the precise memory would not immediately come.

Duncan thrust his shoulder into the wood of the door and the old metal of the lock gave easily away. He then pushed through and stumbled heavily, onto a wooden staircase ascending to an exterior cellar door. The light of day came streaming down upon him through cracks and holes of the decaying wood. Duncan hastily scrambled upward and burst through them, into the sunlight and out of the hazy torment of the dark.

About him was nothing spectacular. Only the shell of an abandoned farmhouse, having been clearly vacant for many years. The surrounding fields were abundant with wilderness and the growth of neglect. Duncan saw then an envelope pinned between two large rocks, and so stepped forward to grasp and tear it open. The typed note read:

"Some folks don't appreciate what they've been given. I too, did not during the time in which I had it. And so your cursing of the burdens of parenting which I overheard urged me drug you with a sodium pentothal inhalant and bring you and your offspring to this place. I did nothing which would render me any bit guilty except ask you if you would like to be free of your burden. That I suppose and also the act of plugging in and engaging the motor of the wood chipper which you stood before while holding your son..."

21. Post Mortem Comm.

"Then you pull it out of the broiler and let it *rest* for five minutes," said Specialist Royal, "this is very important." A plasma blast came then over to their left side and both Specialist Royal and Private First Class Reater hunkered down against the hard ground. "Your turn," said Royal.

"Yep," said Reater who then popped his head up over the metallic barrel that they were hiding behind and took a look at the enemy's distant position. He then turned his head to look behind them, where Private Nolan was positioned. "Ok, five minutes, then what?" asked Reater as he flopped back down into the slight hole beneath the barrel. The enemy had not advanced.

"Well that'll finish the cooking. It keeps cooking *internally* after you remove it from the heat," said Royal. He had a way of emphasizing certain words. "So don't overcook it. Ya gotta pull it off a bit early and let it finish itself – this is very important. The juices will redistribute as it sets."

Another laser plasma blast came and half the barrel was molecularly gone in an instant.

"Christ!" yelled Reater and both men rolled and then ran to the small rock pile off to their left. As he ran behind Royal, Private First Class Reater used his free hand to feel that none of his right arm had been molecularly pulverized. It felt whole, but he knew that this was not necessarily proof. The plasma beams never caused instantaneous pain.

Both men flopped down behind the low-lying rock pile and pressed their faces to the ground. They could not look to see if Private Nolan was alright.

"So then the steak is done?" asked Reater as he clutched his plasma rifle, outstretched before his head.

"No there's one final step – very important," said Royal. "Listen!" I hear their turbines firing! Check their advance!"

"Not my turn!" snapped back Reater, to which Specialist Royal could not retort. And so Specialist Royal peered his head around the chunk of granite before him, saw briefly the nuclear-turbine powered tanks of the enemy advancing dangerously close, and then promptly had half his head, rifle, and left hand converted into free floating molecules.

"Fuck!" cursed Reater who rolled farther to the opposite side, upon his back to get lower, while clutching his firearm to his chest. The blue of the sky showed brightly above him, and then it was filled with the near-silent God-blessed form of his side's airstrike machines. Reater saw the plasma wave emit from the underside and then closed his eyes from the tremendous flash of illumination. Silence followed.

"Got lucky!" yelled Nolan as he ran up and then knelt upon the ground.

"He didn't" said Reater coldly, surveying the remains. He saw then that half of Royal's brain remained untouched, including the brain stem and a portion of an upper lobe. "*Musta been hit by only the edge of the blast*," thought Reater, "*Bad Goddamn luck*." He looked in silence a moment more, and then had a sudden idea. He ordered, "Get the post mortem comm."

Nolan looked to Royal's exposed brain and then to Reater. "What in hell for?"

"The final step," said Reater. "I had that rib-eye on special order for three months and Royal was a head chef back home. I'll be Goddamned if I'm gonna guess on it."

Private Nolan trotted back the fifty yards to the gear and returned with the gadget. Reater took it and pulled the mouth of it open, and slid it down over the exposed brain remnants. It closed upon the partial-head when he released it, and then whirled to life when the power was switched on. Both soldiers watched as the transparent cavity of the dead man's cranium was filled with the fluid, pressure driven to replicate the pumping of the heart so as to force oxygen into the remaining brain matter. The device was originally designed to allow battle-wounded soldiers to arrive safely to the medics, after suffering more mild wounds to the head. However it had been discovered that the device allowed the bodies of the severely brain injured to live on indefinitely, so long as enough of the brain stem remained. The geniuses of the world had then seen fit to add a communication device which would allow in some cases for post mortem communication with the fragments of remaining brain.

"You determine if communication can be established," barked Reater, who was now senior officer of the division. Nolan pushed at more buttons and then spoke into a telecom like appendage.

"James Royal, can you hear me?" spoke Private Nolan into the device. "James do you hear my voice?"

A silent moment passed and then a monotonous voice croaked quietly from the tiny speaker.

"Louder!" commanded Reater, a command to which Private Nolan promptly turned a dial. "Ask it what the final step is, for cooking the perfect steak!" The young Private did so, ensuring that he used the dead man's name, in an attempt to counter his commander's dastardly reference to the deceased as "it".

The men waited eagerly, both staring at the plastic slits of the tiny speaker. "Fuck, we've lost it…" Reater's bark began, but was then cut short by the monotone croaking of the death voice.

"Brush with *balsamic* vinegar, and top with sautéed mushrooms…" The monotone voice from the device seemed to display a hint of pleasure when relating the wisdom from a livelihood which he had once enjoyed.

"Balsamic vinegar," repeated Private Reaters, "I never would've guessed that."

22. Tomb of Souls

The air was surprisingly moist in the tiny village near the edge of the Atacama Desert. The local Chileans outside seemed to be involved in some unseen task. Whether walking or simply standing, their faces gave me the impression that they toiled for some greater, unknown cause. They did not ever seem to lift their eyes to my own.

"What else Señor?" asked the shopkeeper. I looked down at the counter and saw that the cigarettes and dried food supplies had been placed there. "Canteens?" said the middle aged man a moment after I did not answer.

"Ah, yes…" I replied, "Two. And I'll need a guide. Any one of the willing men should be fine."

"Where do you go Señor?" asked the shopkeeper.

"It is some sort of burial ground," I answered, "They say it has no name. I was told any man in your fine village would know the location."

The shopkeeper looked at me with a gaze that I couldn't quite judge. "It has a name Señor," the man said at last, "but we do not speak of it. There is quite a difference." I looked back at the man and searched within myself for the words best to speak next.

"I work for a very wise man at a university," I told him. "He is the father of the woman I aspire to marry. He has sent me here to observe and document the ancient burial ground located outside of this village." The shopkeeper's eyes did not shift even after the words had gone and silence hung in the air. "I was given a map," I said when I could stand no more of the dead air, and then reached inside of my canvas vest. A yellowed paper was produced, which I unfolded and placed on a vacant portion of the counter. "I was told quite explicitly that it is due precisely forty miles northeast of your village, here into the first plain of the Atacama Desert…" I bent and pointed my finger along the hand drawn map.

The shopkeeper then turned and walked from the room, returning soon after with two large canteens, each of which hung by a separate strap. "Two cantinas Señor," said the stoic man, who then placed them lightly upon the other supplies before looking upon my face again. "You can fill them from the hand well out back. But no man of this village will guide you. It is now a forbidden place. But your map is fair."

The shopkeeper took a pencil from the register and drew a small "x" southwest of the indicated destination. "This is a wall of rising rock; the first you will see on the horizon. Here are many old trees," he spoke as he drew a circle. "The first you will see after many miles of the dry earth. Between these two horizons is what you seek."

Outside, my Jeep now sat alone as I busied myself placing the full canteens and supplies in the back. The road was now absent of all of the locals who had been milling about.

As I departed I saw endless brown earth and rocks, except for the brilliant blue of the sky. The dirt street turned into only a hint of a road, with two aged tire tracks that grew less distinct with every mile that passed. Soon I was driving out into the nothingness, keeping one eye on the dash compass while trying to memorize the ridges of rock that decorated the distant horizon.

And then the thoughts came, and I saw my fiancé, a beautiful virginal brunette from old money. Then this vision transformed into her father; a museum owner or curator or some combination of both. I think of the conversation between myself and this aging man, in which he implied that I could marry his daughter if I were to partake in, and successfully complete, a dangerous archeological expedition. And then this man whom I distrusted, and hold an even greater dislike for, opened an old book and showed me a drawing of a dagger which I was to obtain. When we shook on it I saw his lizard smile and balding head, and thought only of his beautiful daughter.

The mountainous rocks of the horizon were no longer so far away, and I found that my Jeep seemed as though guided, like a herd of cattle through a final corral. Soon the great rocks of the east and west nearly pinch the sides of my vehicle as it crept over the rock and sand. Claustrophobia came then, lightly at first and then in great waves that fluttered about in my stomach and filled every nerve. But this sensation came quickly to a peak and then faded, as the front of my Jeep climbed the final hill and then fell down the decline of the other side, revealing the site for which I strove.

It was a flatland of only fine sand upon which stone buildings had been constructed. They appeared to be complex structures made from unpolished stone; crude rocks stacked upon more of the same, with archways of ancient engineering precision. Upon these archways the rocks of the ceilings were set, standing securely for only God knew how many years.

As I stepped out of my vehicle it was the stillness that struck me most poignantly, as though the wind were not permitted to blow. And with this stillness came a great silence that was only broken by a great shot of steam from within the engine of my vehicle as an essential gasket failed. I turned and watched the billowing steam as it rose and then quickly disappeared.

"One day," is what I thought to myself, because it was this amount of time that it would take me to walk back to the small village. And because there was ample water in my canteens I gave it no more immediate thought, and instead approached the rock structure to tend to the task at hand. Once inside the arched doorway I felt immediately the cooler temperature upon my skin.

Everywhere about the strange crypt was something interesting to behold. I saw weapons, art pieces, and perhaps books, all covered with thick dust of the desert. I brushed the sediment from the first artifact I saw, a beautiful bronzed armlet that sparkled from the light of the open doorway. And as I saw this I looked back to the great arched stone entry hall, and felt quite perplexed as to why everything remained so undisturbed. There was no security whatsoever, I remember it seeming at the time.

The true purpose did not readily present itself as I walked about the treasures. The hair of my arms stood markedly on end and I felt the wonderful sensation of complete titillation. But still I did not see the dagger as I walked slowly about the room.

Then I found myself before a great slab of polished stone, upon which rested the aged corpse of a large man. The age of the human remains appeared abundant but somehow the bones still bore remains of the flesh. Perhaps it was a result of the never ending dryness of the desert air.

And then in a flash I saw that which I sought, in the form of a knife's handle protruding from the sternum of the dead man. As I reached for it I saw the lizard-smile and bald head of my vile father-in-law to be, and it was with this unpleasant vision in my head that I pulled easily the knife from the dried bones and flesh. The pile of withered tissue scarcely vibrated as the tip of the old blade was pulled into the light.

It was a simple type of weapon, although beautiful, with a simplicity that suggested utility rather than adornment. The handle was thick so that my entire grasp could hardly encompass the girth.

The jaw tissue of the corpse seemed then to crackle as the old lips parted ever so slightly. I thought I heard a bit of wind blow then discretely as I stood eyeing the dead thing. Then what occurred was simply so remarkable that I knew not exactly what transpired. The wind noise came again and I realized that the dead thing attempted to draw in a breath. A putrid liquid began then to seep from the old chest wound and the entire corpse began to pulse and twitch with life.

If I had been a wiser man I suppose I should have thrust the dagger back from whence it came. But instead I allowed the burden of the mission to oppress me and I ran from the structure with haste. The engine of the jeep did turnover with ignition, but I knew the damaged vehicle would not take me far before failing for good. With the dagger in the seat beside me I put the vehicle in gear and saw just a hint of the dead thing appearing upright in the darkness as it stalked after me through the archway of the door. I gave a look into the rear view mirror as I climbed the hill of escape, but saw nothing of the dead thing. Soon the grays and browns of the mountainous rocks were about me as I hastily began a retreat.

It was perhaps three hundred yards before the Jeep overheated completely and rolled to a permanent stop. But I did not sit idle, and instead seized the dagger and forced it into my leather backpack, and fled with these possessions only, and the addition of the two full canteens. When the vehicle was ten feet behind me I allowed myself the privilege of one quick look back to the ridge, but saw nothing come over it except the image of the vast blue sky.

Losing the trail was impossible due to the tire marks, and after five-hundred yards or more the adrenaline began to fade. My pace dropped into a brisk walk as I retraced my way through the jagged maze of upright rock, and drifted onward somewhat passively. It was due to these frequent rock appendages that I could see neither far ahead nor much behind. And so I kept at my pace steadily, all the while with the vision of that thing standing upright and mobile, striding out into the first light of the arched door.

I estimated perhaps one hour of daylight remained, at which point the channel of rocks at my sides withdrew so as to widen the path, and my urge to rest could no longer be ignored. I sat upon a single large boulder and drank a full thirty seconds from the first canteen. When the lid was re-screwed I set it with the other upon the ground and then removed my newly obtained dagger from the sack. Its weight was immense and the craftsmanship impeccable. It was like no weapon I had beheld before, with ornate grooves carved into the gold of the handle so that it fit remarkably well within my hand. There was a single ring of thick gold that protruded from the hilt, so as to protect the index finger of the bearer. The blade itself was thin but sturdy, and felt impressively sharp upon the caressing the digits of my other hand.

It was then after this extremely brief bit of rest that a subtle audible noise came into the air, like a nearly indistinguishable creaking that the ear could scarcely discern. There was perhaps also a clicking noise of such subtlety that I could scarcely say for certain if I truly heard it.

And then a bit of motion caught my eye as the arm of the thing came first into view from behind a rock, followed by the entire corpse as its mass rounded the corner. How it physically was able to move I cannot hazard a guess, but it seemed now somehow less withered than before. It bore at me with increased haste as its dead eyes saw me, and I tore at my possessions and ran immediately. It was this very haste that rendered me unable to grasp both straps of both canteens, and the full one was left regretfully behind. I could not help but turn and peer at the thing that certainly wished me dead, and desired its precious knife returned. I saw it pause as it reached the canteen, then clasped it and tore the cap and nozzle away rather than unscrew it as a man would have done. I both ran and watched as it forced its jaws apart and poured the contents into the gaping and repugnant orifice of its mouth. Some of the water ran down the chest of the thing, but perhaps half did enter the gullet, some of which then spewed from the holes of the neck flesh. But surely some reached the decayed belly of the terrible beast. This image both sickened and terrified me, and I did not look back again until I was certain that I had run far enough to ensure its removal from my line of sight.

But how had it caught me so quickly, I wondered, for I had both run and walked briskly for several hours, with mine legs of living flesh compared to the rotten limbs of that thing. It was certainly this question that haunted me then most, coupled with its ingestion of much of my water and the probable strength that it would now gain.

I did not resist the urge to drink my single remaining canteen, and soon it went from half full to a quarter, and then to only a remaining bit that sloshed at the bottom. The sun was now nearly gone and it was with great relief that I saw in the last remnants of dusk-light that I had emerged from the rock enclosures and the open desert was before me.

The tire tracks I had made were soon lost to me, as I must have walked off along some hard-packed soil that my feet could not discern for road. But the general direction of return I knew, or at least I believed that I did, and I kept onward without delay. When my feet stepped into sand I simply stepped to the left or right, repeating the process until I felt firm soil that minimized my toil in the dark. Never did I hear any more of that dreadful clicking from behind…

By dawn the last of the water was gone, and I must admit that it was with a feeling of some relief that I dropped the empty cask to the ground. It seemed at the time to be liberating; one less thing to worry about, and my mind was then free to simply walk and out pace that *thing*…

But there was also dismay, for the old road and the tire tracks I had made the day prior were now nowhere to be seen. I had veered either to the right or to the left of them, and I was now possibly quite lost. And with the hills and the sand… my legs began to tire. Up one dune and down again, only to have another to climb. After twenty or so I simply could go no further, and deemed a rest to be both deserved and necessary. I chose to sit, perhaps foolishly, at the lowest point of one dune's descent, right where another incline began. Just a few minutes, I reasoned, and then I would climb again to the top where perhaps the vantage would be greater and I could see either my destination or gather my bearings.

As I sat in the softness of the sand gasping, one minute ran out into several, until even my mind began to stray. I looked up at the top of the dune I had just come down and meditated upon this horizon, until suddenly the head of that *thing* came into view. I believe that I even saw it spy me, and God help me, the eyes seemed to roll and focus upon my form. And then just as before the pace of the thing grew swifter and I was up and running like a shot. The familiar clicking came then softly upon the breeze, as the withered joints ambled toward me. The adrenaline it gave me would not last, I knew, but it did get me up and over that first dune and I did not have the courage to look back again.

"Perhaps I shall give it the knife," my mind reasoned, but the thought of my fiancé would not yet allow an act of probable defeat, and so I kept at my frantic pace. The higher vantage point had yielded nothing of advantage except to show that the ground began to flatten and grow firm, which psychologically gave me an advantage. I tore onward away from the clicking and did not waste the energy it would take to gaze back until the ground was solid as rock beneath my feet and as flat as a billiard table. I did then turn and see the blackness of that rotting thing far behind me at the horizon, never ceasing, never even for a single second, and it was this realization that filled me anew with a deeper dread than before.

Somehow I had passed the day and found myself covered with the darkness of the second night. My strength would not keep up I knew, and so I stopped abruptly once every remaining bit of daylight had gone. Then within this cloak of invisibility I retrieved the ornate knife from my pack and drove the tip of it into the firm ground. I then took my pack to a rock not thirty feet away and cowered down against it, where I

removed the kerosene lantern and matches, and began a wait of
unknown length.

I believe that I actually nodded off and slept a bit as I waited. And
improbable as this sounds, I assure you that it is true. I dreamt of that
ear-writhing clicking of the dead thing's joints, hearing the phantom
sound in my brain and then returning to waking life.

The sliver of moonlight shone down upon the hilt of that beautiful
knife, and twinkled softy up at me in the darkness. And then the sound
came in reality, across the silence of the desert hills, and a shiver ran up
my spine. It was a sound that my ears would carry with them to my own
grave.

Closer it drew, ever closer, but I could not see anything of the horrid
thing, although my eyes did strain in that darkness. "Click, click,"
sounded out, closer and closer, as fingers clenched a solitary match,
ready to strike when my terrified mind gave the order. I must guess
right, but nothing could I see!

Then it came, a hint of blacked shadow, like darkness of night
creeping slowly forward! "Click, click." Closer and closer to that subtle
gleam from the knife went the sound, and I then struck my match. How
deafening the noise from the combusting sulfur seemed! Quickly I
touched it to the waiting wick of my lantern and felt pure joy when the
torchlight beamed. I lowered the glass like a man possessed and erupted
from my skyward place of hiding. Down, down I ran in three swift
gallops just as the long dead thing had reached its beloved blade. I swear
it let out a hiss of wrath at the sight of me, but in one great circular loop
I swung the alighted lantern over my head and down upon the exposed
skull of the rotting terror. It broke and erupted with a brilliant light and
gave a cracking like kindling wood which had just caught flame.

I'd have not thought that it would have stayed upright for as long as
it did, but the Godless thing actually tried to continue its vengeful
pursuit of me once I had reached down and seized the knife from the
earth where it had been stuck. It was not nearly so frightening now that
it had become a great beacon in the night from which I withdrew hastily.
The last I saw of it, I believe it had finally stopped its forward
progression, for the flame appeared then to be a fading, stagnant pile

upon the ground in the distance. I gave one last glimpse at it as I rounded the top of a great hill, back toward the tiny village and the stoic shopkeeper who had tried so subtly to warn me.

23. Objective: Malice

"Wind chill. What a perfect and accurate description," thought Henry. He no longer cringed when it blew but it wasn't because the urge to do so had receded.

"What a cold December," he reasoned as he looked out over the mostly treeless field and meditated. Truthfully the wind only stung his face. All else was kept relatively warm from the layered clothing and Carhardtt bibs and coat. His head was kept warm by a muskrat fur-lined hat with earflaps. If the wind would only cease to gust periodically, it seemed to Henry that he would have been quite content. Except of course for the lack of deer…

Movement. Something large alternated between fully obscured and nearly-fully obscured 80 degrees off to his left. He could see bits of it most clearly near the top of the shrub line. It didn't seem to make enough noise for how large it must have been. He stiffened to rise, gripping tightly the rifle in his thickly gloved right hand, and then relaxed and decided to stay put.

"It comes to me," he realized, and then only slipped off both gloves and waited. Henry listened intently for twig pops from heavy strides which didn't ever come.

Then it revealed itself, stepping rather intentionally into the open, facing Henry fully with its eyes already focused upon him. His first reaction was joy that he had not fired a shot blindly, for it was a man that his eyes reasoned they must be seeing. But within a few moments this assessment faded and Henry could only stare in bewilderment. There was no fear within him until it moved again, stepping one stride closer to where he stood.

The blackness of it struck him most significantly, and the full and muscular humanoid form which moved with ease and grace. And then he realized that the masses behind it were wings that simply hung in a relaxed posture.

The eyes of the thing were lifeless like a shark, although perhaps not so entirely black. They seemed to smolder with a bit of un-illuminated redness that had faded to a morose burgundy. They looked to Henry as though that they awaited some trigger that would cause them to alight.

When it took another step Henry could take no more of this peculiar humanoid, and so then, raised his rifle and called for it to halt. His mind until that point had been holding onto the now impossible notion that the thing was somehow truly human, somehow a man engulfed in a horrendous guise.

It was then that the right hand of the silent black specter was raised, and as it pressed forward toward Henry he felt the barrel of his rifle grow heavy before pushing strongly toward the ground. The darkened eyes of the thing did then alight, becoming a burning red that glowed through Henry's own eyes, through them and back into his own confused brain. Their radiance filled his mind and a message was silently passed.

The silent black creature lowered its right hand but Henry's rifle barrel remained pointed limply to the ground. His eyes did not follow it as the wings snapped to their full span and the creature flew off into the cold wind of December.

The next blast of cold wind did rouse him however and he then blinked back to a wakeful state. Henry stepped leisurely away from the large oak tree which he had nestled up to, leaving all of his belongings except for the cartridges in his pockets and the rifle within his hands.

Due west he walked calmly, toward the distant sound of the freeway and the early holiday traffic which had begun to burden the road. He was neither warm nor cold when he reached the edge of the tree line that yielded to the asphalt channel. He simply walked in the same leisurely manner to the shoulder of the great road and turned to face the nearest cars, which sailed past him from the south.

Henry raised his rifle and took aim with a very calm and naked hand, upon the driver of a blue Toyota. The driver leered at him with confusion but not fear, with a look that seemed to shout *"take that aim off of me you damn fool!"* but not *"Christ I'm about to be shot!"*

But without any further time for the driver to ponder it, Henry squeezed the trigger and a shot rang out, cracking and clouding the windshield as the bullet passed through and caused the driver's head to promptly explode. His Toyota continued along upon the asphalt for about one hundred yards before veering into the grass of the median. From there the extended damage came quickly as the vehicle spun out and crossed violently into the oncoming path of a Dodge carrying a family of six. The loud sounds of devastation filled the air but Henry did not turn to view it. Instead he took aim upon one of the next cars coming at him and gently squeezed the trigger again.

His pockets were still full of additional cartridges although he never had the opportunity to reload his weapon. A rather astute and quick thinking college boy recognized what Henry had in store for him, and so, jerked his steering wheel to swerve his car violently to the right and run poor and kind Henry down as he attempted to fire again. His legs were severed at the knees where the boy's vehicle impacted him and his body (along with the rifle) came through the windshield and filled the vacant passenger seat with their bloody mass. He lay for a few brief moments before his body's life force expired completely.

And so it was that no one ever learned of the silent black thing that had stepped from the bushes and simply gestured and gazed upon poor old Henry, implanting some horrible message of malice into his normally kind and merry brain.

24. The Offering

"Justin's has been taken," said Paul with melancholy.

Behind him Ryan peered over his friend's shoulder to be certain. He too saw that all had been removed.

"We knew that it would be," said Ryan, who then patted his friend's shoulder reassuringly.

Together they walked to the bottom of the descending rocks, and then stopped to sit on the flat area above the lowest point which housed the entrance to the lair. Ryan, who carried the medical kit, lowered himself to sit as well. It would be the epitome of bad form to attempt to rush his friend on this day.

"These dreary clouds certainly fit the occurrence," said Paul once Ryan had settled beside him. The metal box of the medical kit made a clanking sound as he placed it against the rock.

"There is no appropriate weather for today," said Ryan. "The wedding is what you should be thinking about."

"Easy for you to say. You've still got two years until your marriage...."

"That's not the way, friend," said Ryan. "Mandy is very much in love with you. She'll still love you after you've done your duty."

"Yes I know," said Paul. "But things won't be exactly the same." He looked down at the gigantic forged blade upon the rock floor below them. It was, in a way, a work of perfection, having been hand crafted by the blacksmiths of the village. The rectangular base of the silver sculpture rose upward from the rocky earth, narrowing as it ascended, before curving slightly away from the entryway of the lair. The metallic form continued to arc and narrow, until it could narrow no more, forming a flawless razor's edge.

"Mandy had feelings for Dickenson," said Paul. "She might have them again. He has yet another year."

"No, not a chance," answered Ryan. "You know it's forbidden."

"I'm not saying that she'll go to him," said Paul now with anger, "Only that she may *yearn* to do so. To be properly held, by a real man..."

Beside him Ryan said nothing. He had been coached and prepared as Paul's guide to let him expel frustration if need be. They had said that it would be healthy for him to do so.

It had had to be Paul that guided him after all, since Paul's older brother Alexander had already performed his duty for the village, and so could not now. But it was Alexander who was Paul's best friend, and Ryan had assumed the responsibility accordingly.

"You know Ryan, you might think me a coward, but I've very nearly fled the village and left Mandy and Ma-ma and Pop behind. The unending acridity of the wastelands and probable starving don't scare me nearly as much as the ritual of the offering."

"I don't think you're a coward," comforted Ryan to his brother's friend. "And there's nothing probable about starving in the wastelands. It would be a certainty, and you'd be dead within a month." He then added, "All of you."

To this statement Paul did not reply. Instead he sat mostly silently, as tears of self-pity rolled from his face. Ryan neither touched nor looked upon his brother's friend. He himself did not feel the urge to cry, but a tremendous knot had filled his guts and now turned into a strong urge to wretch or vomit. Paul busied himself fighting the horrible sensation, while his older friend cried beside him.

"Why?!" screamed Paul suddenly. "Why must that *thing* be there?"

"It has always been," said Ryan quietly. "Since our people awoke from the vehicle which transported the embryos of our ancestors through space, away from their dying planet. It was then, the only way for the continuation of our people's bloodline, and the survival of our race. And you know that our offerings are now the only means to appease the creatures that were here long before us. If we had anywhere else to go - anywhere..." and Ryan's voice trailed off and did not state that which they already knew.

Before another word was spoken, Paul jumped suddenly from the ledge and down into the rock laden pit. "Get that kit ready!" he then screamed, as he stared fixedly upon the forged blade. Above him Ryan clutched at and fumbled with the box, rushing to prepare the tourniquet.

Paul then tore off his shirt and began breathing in great, audible gasps, with which he shouted amidst the breaths. Then with a great scream and a lunge forward he cocked his left arm back and threw it forward as though he were throwing a stone a vast distance ahead of him. The young and muscled arm flew up and around to the front of his body and then crashed down upon the shining blade, landing forcefully upon the razor's edge just above the elbow. The severed limb fell over it, to the other side of the great monolith, where it lay motionless upon the ground. Further beyond from the blackness of the creature's lair the darkness seemed to peer out at the horror which had just transpired.

"I am here!" yelled Ryan who reached Paul as he knelt on the ground, squeezing his right hand around the bleeding stump of his left arm. "I am here!" he yelled again and snapped into action fastening the tourniquet, just as his training had taught him.

In mere seconds he had the limb squeezed with the strap and the bleeding was stopped like a tightened faucet. He thought then of the creature down in the darkness and lifted his older friend by grasping beneath his armpits, wasting no time in helping him ascend the hill of rock.

"If only, if only..." murmured Paul, whose face was ashen with shock and loss of blood. Behind them they did not see the terrible creature crawl from its resting place and take the generous offering which they had left behind.

25. Twice As Good

The wind let loose with a new gust, throwing farmer Floyd's church necktie up over his shoulder, and setting his senses all askew. He took a moment and smoothed his hair, pulled the tie back down, and then kept walking out through the corn field. The storm had been a real torrent but the crop looked mostly alright.

"Corn roots hold like darned oak trees," thought Floyd, and felt thankful that they did. His wife Betty had verbally worried most of the night into his ear about the corn, as if there were something he could do; as if he were some kind of fool if he didn't. And here it was the next day looking just about as fine as a field of corn could.

Truthfully Floyd had worried plenty too, but he just didn't see the point of giving in to the fear and making it an entity unto itself. *"Give your fears to the Lord, and things will always work out fine,"* he thought.

Church was still forty minutes away, so Floyd kept on walking through the corn rows, maybe enjoying the fresh morning air or possibly just enjoying Betty being far behind him at the house. *"Man, that woman can worry…"* thought Floyd, as he rounded and exited the first sectional of his irregular lot and started walking into the back field where the trees obscured the view from the house. It seemed at first to be more of the same; strong and massive corn roots rising from the earth and clutching it tightly, with roots like the gnarled hands of an arthritic widow.

And then as Floyd walked by and peered into a corn row he saw what appeared at first to be a section of damaged crop. "Well, I guess she was partially right," Floyd acquiesced begrudgingly, as he turned abruptly and entered a row that would lead to the damaged corn.

Upon entering the area of distressed field Floyd saw to his disbelief, a creature the likes of which he'd never before seen. It looked to him like a bloated lizard with gray skin and blue eyes, sitting nonchalantly with it legs crossed, upon the edge of some type of small craft. Floyd had frozen mid stride and peered at the thing as you'd expect a simple farmer might do.

"AhFlingeGlaFlang," said the thing as calmly as you please, directly followed with, "That means good morning."

Floyd might have mumbled a sound in his throat, and then nervously smoothed his hair and straightened his tie.

"I'm to find an earth human and give to them this RahgKanMayLem," said the gray creature who then motioned to a device sitting upon the ground which Floyd had not as yet noticed. "I suppose you'll do."

The lizard-creature remained seated upon the edge of its craft with crossed legs and seemed to be waiting on how Floyd would react. When Floyd simply stood and peered at him, the gray creature decided upon a change in the line of conversation.

"My name is PhlauGunn," said the creature, "and this RahgKanMayLem is a gift, should you choose to accept it. You see it makes copies." PhlauGunn uncrossed his legs, and further waited for Floyd's reaction, or possibly, any sign of comprehension.

"What are you…?" asked Floyd as his mind raced and tied itself into a knot of tussles. "What's a raw-can-may-lem? What do you want with me? Where in Hell are you from fella…?"

"It makes copies," said PhlauGunn again, with what looked to Floyd like a hint of annoyance or impatience. "You see this planet has been chosen for a….. trial run…. a bit of an experiment I guess you'd say. But if you'd rather pass," said PhlauGunn, "I'll just save us both the trouble, wipe your memory clean, and move on to another specimen."

Well what do I need copies for?" asked Floyd. "Copies of what? Besides me and Betty got church in near half-an-hour..."

"Here," said PhlauGunn, now standing and stepping toward the device. "I'll show you once and then you'll decide." With a small flash and a puff of displaced air, Floyd's Sunday-best necktie disappeared from around his neck and appeared lying gently across the outstretched hand of the bloated gray lizard.

"Wait, how'd you…?" stammered Floyd as he looked at the creature's hand and then down to his belly and then back again.

"Behold," said PhlauGunn ignoring him, and set the garment upon the outstretched arm of the small tripod-like device upon the ground. In an instant a small flash of light came, and a second tie appeared in an instant, hanging in an identical position over a second symmetrical arm of the device.

"And so it is," said PhlauGunn, "A second one of these things where formerly you had only one. A copy as I had said."

"How in the Hell…?"

"It inverts the KalThuKayVem energy around each particle….." the visitor began to explain, then stopped immediately upon seeing the utter confusion upon Floyd's face. "It creates a molecularly-apparent replica by inverting energy which can only once be inverted. That is to say," clarified PhlauGunn, "that each piece of matter can be copied only a single time."

Floyd, despite his whirlwind of confusion, instinctively knew that this was the extent of the pitch, and the strange visitor would now either make his gift or depart as he had stated.

"Well, what's it cost then?" said Floyd in his bartering tone as his hand came up and clasped upon his chin. "I've only got a little in my wallet, plus I s'pose our tithe offering, if you need *that*…"

"No, no, it's at no expense," said PhlauGunn. "Your assistance will…aid us. But be aware that each replication will etiolate in time."

"Well what are we arguing about then?" asked Floyd, ignoring the last part of the statement as he wondered why such a thing would be free.

"Good day then," wished PhlauGunn abruptly, as his lizard-like countenance displayed something like the appearance of a smile. And then just as quickly the bloated lizard disappeared with a flash of light, and his craft then did the same. Amidst the field stood a mostly-perplexed Floyd, alone again plus two Sunday-best neckties and a new raw-can-may-lem(?) device. This was really all quite a good deal more than he had anticipated for a Sunday morning.

Back in front of the house Betty busied herself picking up some towels that had blown from the cloths line. "Well there ya' are," she said when she saw her husband approaching. "I thought maybe you'd forgotten about service." Floyd had the RahgKanMayLem in front of him, resting against his gut as he walked. "What in the world did you buy now?" asked Betty as she straightened up clutching a towel. "And how's the field?"

Floyd kept on walking to the porch and set the RahgKanMayLem upon it above the top step. The thing was remarkably light. He looked at the dual arms of the thing where both ties had been. There seemed to be a sort of a sensor at the tip of each. *That must be the part that has to make contact,"* he surmised.

"Good Lord Floyd, are you going to keep me in suspense?" said Betty who now walked up behind him.

"It's all right dear," he said at last. "I met this… feller in the field." Betty looked upon his face and saw an uncertainty the likes of which she hadn't seen on her husband's face since their wedding night. "It was this feller you see, and he gave me this…. thing."

"All right, well, what's it good for then?" she asked.

"It's said to make copies," and he then held out the ties for the woman to see for herself.

At just that moment ten year old Abel came out of the house wearing his only set of church clothes with his only-blue tie, and let the screen door slam behind him. "Wow, what did we buy Dad?" asked the boy with enthusiasm. His cow-lick ridden hair had been wetted and plaster-combed across his head.

"Well, you see…" began Floyd, "But it was all just a bit too much to experience once, let alone replay it again verbally right after the fact. "It makes copies," he said again. "I guess the thing to do is go down to the bank and withdraw our full savings account in cash money. But he said we could only copy anything once. I don't know if you can copy a copy."

And as he pondered this the boy reached down suddenly and touched one of the sensor-arms of the device. There came then the same small flash of light as before, and then suddenly upon the first step stood a second Abel, with plaster-combed wetted hair and a Sunday best only-blue tie.

"Good Lord!" shrieked Betty. Beside her Floyd was incredulous and his mouth hung open. Both of the boys looked at one another in seeming bewilderment.

"I didn't want this," said Floyd. "No sir, this is not what I signed on for!"

Both boys then stepped down off of the porch and took a few steps while still cautiously eyeing one another. "Can you talk?" asked the first Abel.

"Yes of course," said the copy. "Let's go play at the tree fort," the copy then suggested, apparently sharing full knowledge of the original.

"Good lord!" said Betty, "It knows what our boy knows!"

"Well… it is a copy…" replied Floyd. "The brain molecules and all I s'pose."

"Alright," said the first Abel, and then walked hesitantly across the yard to the nearest tree, with the copy beside him.

"My boy!" cried Betty, as she watched her more accepting son hoist up his new twin. "He's my boy!" She was quite inconsolable.

"But he's fine!" countered Floyd. "He isn't any less…. we just got… two now." Up in the tree house both boys appeared to be forgetting the awkwardness and simply played.

"But, but…!" stammered Betty, "It's not… the same now… somehow…."

"Well, he's still our boy. He's still going to grow up and marry, and the like…" reasoned Floyd. But Betty could only hold her hand to her brow and collapse into a sitting position upon the steps.

"How are we going to explain this to the community?" pondered the poor woman. "Who was this man that gave you this thing?"

"Well he uh, well he… he weren't from here Betty!"

Up in the tree the boys were sitting side by side and engaging in a conversation which the parents could not quite hear. Betty watched as they sat side by side, identically. It was at this moment that she realized with horror that she had taken her eyes off of the boys and they were now effectively, indistinguishable.

"Abel, get down here now!" she shrieked. Both boys snapped to attention and then began to descend. "No! Stop!" she yelled. "Only

Abel!" But again, both boys began to climb. When they got to the porch she demanded to know which of them was her true son.

"I am mother," said both boys in near unison, and then looked at one another.

"Stop it, she means me!" yelled the boy on the left.

"She's my mother!" yelled the other.

"Oh good Lord Floyd, don't you see!" yelled the terrified woman. "We've lost all certainty!" Floyd could only blink his eyes and shuffle his feet around nervously. This was quite the puzzle indeed.

"The scar!" he said after a moment. "The burn on his arm. Roll up your sleeves, both of you." To this command both boys immediately complied, rolling up their right sleeves. The forearms of both displayed identical scars.

"Oh heavens!" cried Betty. "We'll never get it straight! You've brought this evil into our house! You… you abominable man!"

Floyd's feet stopped shuffling but his eyes darted even more so and his head shook vigorously as he hastily agreed with the woman.

"But Betty, he's still our boy! He ain't any less just because there's another!"

"Oh but it is less!" wailed his wife, "Don't you see that somehow it is so? He was our everything and our ONLY thing!"

Floyd's brain tried to out-logic her claim, but deep down he knew that somehow she was right. Somehow this odd truth rung true.

"It's alright, I'll fix it!" he assured after a moment. "I'll get it straight, you'll see! Yes, I've got it! He said each piece o'matter could only be copied one time! That's it!"

The hysterical woman gave pause to her outbursts and her eyes shown bright with the light of hope.

"You mean Abel can't make a third?!" she questioned. "If he touches it again?"

"Yes, that's what… Flowgun said," said Floyd. "I'm sure of it, he did!"

"But what about the imposter?" said the woman, "Can he make a copy? That would be the only way we would know for sure. But then we'd have… two to deal with." Something about the way she said this twisted Floyd's guts up with a shiver. "Abel, you be a good boy and wait here." She alternated looking at one of them, and then the other. "Floyd go get the axe."

Floyd's heart skipped a beat and he looked over at his seated wife. He knew what she had in mind and he turned and ran off for the shed. When he returned she seemed to be consoling both of the boys.

"Betty, this is a lot for me to swallow," said Floyd. "We'll run the test but I can't guarantee that I can follow through. That is to say, I just don't know if a can commit."

"It's got to be this way," she said. "Just have faith in the Lord, and then after, you'll use you axe on that dreadful machine! Alright now Abel," she said and stared at the boy on the left. "You be a good boy and lay your hand again on that thing."

"Remember Betty," said Floyd, "We don't know for sure if the copy can copy. This might not tell us a thing!"

"Dad, you aren't going to hurt me are you?" questioned Abel on the left.

"We're just going to see what happens," said Floyd. "That fella told me we can only copy things once. If you don't copy again, and he does, then I think we'll know where we stand."

To this assurance the boy on the left, very hesitantly, raised his hand toward the sensor on the arm of the RahgKanMayLem. You could have heard a pin drop as the tense boy set his hand upon it. And as he did, absolutely no reaction occurred.

"Good boy," said the woman. "Alright son, now it's you turn," she said to the other, with utmost sincerity of a mother. She would love her boy, whichever he was, until she knew with certainty.

The second boy then drew a breath and began to raise his hand toward the device. Floyd gripped the axe handle with sweating hands, thoroughly uncertain of what he would do. Not a bit of breeze seemed to stir as the lad's hand approached the sensor, and then as contact was about to be made, the hand became transparent. The dissemination of the molecules then flowed up the arm as the Sunday-best church clothes disappeared, along with all structure of the imposter.

Floyd drew a breath of relief, dropped the axe and hugged his boy. It was the most wonderful of sensations that he could recall. Not long afterward he smashed the RahgKanMayLem, using caution so as not to strike the sensors. Without delay he dug a deep hole right there in front of the porch, and buried the pieces where they fell. As he threw the dirt on top it occurred to him that it wouldn't have made a darn bit of difference if he had copied his whole life savings from down at the bank. It would'a just disappeared…

26. The Knockout Game

More than anything, I think it was my wife's fault. Things were bad and had been for a long time, but I could deal with sexual frustration. The thing that I couldn't deal with was knowing that she yearned so badly to be somewhere else – anywhere else, and most certainly, with someone else entirely. Literally, emotionally, and physically. She made this very clear with the emotionless looks she gave me, and the sadness in her eyes. The false small talk, and avoiding eye contact – it all got to be a bit much after awhile.

I had kept up my end of the vows after all. I worked, made a good living, stayed in relatively good shape, and never strayed. That last one I couldn't take much credit for though – it isn't so easy for a man to fall into infidelity, not like it is for a woman. If it weren't for the kids I'd be gone in a heartbeat, but then, so would she.

The kids. That's the real source of the problem. She wanted them and I gave them to her. I guess it turned out to be more work than she anticipated. And the toll it took on her body, Jesus Christ, what wear and tear… Young guys always joke about the stretching of the vagina from child birth, and that does happen, but what they don't understand is that it's actually a lot more complex than that. It's all the hormones from growing the baby that do the real damage. They change a woman like you wouldn't believe. Like my wife. She used to have tiny, cute pink nipples with tiny little areolas. Same with her asshole - but all this changed from the damn hormones. All the skin around the areolas turned into more areola. All the skin around her asshole turned into, well, you guessed it. And the hue, that changed too. No more of the bright pink, cute coloration. No sir. Brown and big. That's the best way to describe all of it now. And yes, the stretching from the physics of birthing three kids also...

The irony was that it should have been me who was unhappy with the marriage. After all I wasn't the one who had changed. But it didn't work out that way. Somehow because we didn't "fit" as well together anymore, I was to blame. Now because she couldn't cum and feel pleasure the way she used to, I was deemed to be inadequate. Never mind that she used to cum just fine, that she was happy to get married and wanted the kids, but now, even though I kept up all my ends of the deal, it was me who was perceived as having caused the of the marital failure. It was enough to make me physically sick, but like I said, there weren't many options.

And so as such was my life, and my mood in general, as I walked back to my car after dinner and some beers with my friends. We didn't get together much anymore – every one of us had kids now, and stressful jobs, and probably some form of the same problems of which I've just explained. But I'll be Goddamned if it didn't seem a lot worse in my marriage. But regardless, there I was walking back to my car alone after darkness had fallen, and more than anything I think it was her that led to it all.

Well her and those dirt-bag punks of course. I saw them coming. Two young guys, not of my ethnicity, walking toward me on the sidewalk. They were just a bit too aware of me perhaps. I saw it. It's damn hard to fool me. I might not make six figures but that doesn't mean that I'm not fuckin' smart and perceptive. I saw them change their walk just a bit and get down to business as I approached. Inconspicuousness. It's a hard thing to pull off. I'm no good at it, but I don't try to be. These guys were fuckin' trying, and I saw it a mile away.

I felt my muscles get tense and I consciously forced them to loosen. Soon I'd surely pass them and be back to being alone and miserable on that dark street. As they neared me I held my gaze, head up and eyes pointed forward. I relaxed my eyes and went peripheral as we reached one another, pretending not to be watching every move they made. And then it happened. One of those numb-nuts drew up on me as I was about to pass, his left hand throwing an overhand punch – the one punch that ninety-nine percent of all men possess inherently.

But I saw it and what that little fuck-stain didn't know was that I've been in the ring. Hundreds of minutes during hundreds of rounds, offense, defense, and the muscle memory of years past did not forsake me. I did what all boxers learn during their first spar: get your fuckin' hands up to your chin. He clipped me a little, but as my hands came up I

also ducked and rolled with it – into the opponent and not away –
brushing his belly with the top of my head as I did so, and his intended
punch glanced off my shoulder and not off of my mouth like he'd
wanted.

It was a funny thing then. All of the frustration of the past years
came over me and I think I must have shown the eagerness for fighting
in my eyes. They saw it. I know they did because I saw their eyes
change. No more cockiness and anticipation of bullying an unsuspecting
victim, because I immediately saw their eyes widen with fear and
surprise.

Most people would have frozen, or screamed, or run. But I didn't do
any of these things. Instead I felt the rage come over me and these two
fuckin' numb-nuts were Goddamn well going to feel it to.

The first punk, the one who swung on me, I dropped him with a
single straight right. It beats the hell out of any amateur-overhand punch,
and if he didn't know it, his chin sure as hell did. He crumpled like a
sack of potatoes being dropped on the ground. I'd always been known
for hitting hard, and I guess the instantaneous adrenaline made up for all
those years of atrophy, because he fuckin' dropped.

The reaction of the second guy was priceless. His eyes got as big as
dinner plates and now he had to make the run/fight/scream choice of his
own. Much to his discredit, he didn't really do any of these. He sort of
flailed at the air in front of me twice and I faked another big right but
didn't throw it. Instead I threw what used to be my second best punch; a
crushing left hook that curved around his feminine flailing motions and
caught his mouth from the side. It was a clean punch and it dropped him,
but he didn't go out. His legs were jelly but his torso jerked around like
nothing I'd ever seen. I didn't know quite what to do so I drew up my
heel and brought it down on his nose and something in his head let out a
sound like an apple being cored. He didn't move after that.

The first punk started to revive and without thinking I stayed with
what was working and kicked him in the temple with the point of my
shoe until he went limp again. That was all I thought to do, and then as
quickly as it all started I just walked away – as I'd originally intended. I

turned right at the first road and never looked back. The air was dead silent and I don't think a single soul saw what I had done.

I didn't tell my wife, or coworkers or anyone. There was nothing to gain by running my mouth. The whole thing started to seem like a wild and pleasant dream that I'd only imagined. Then two days later I saw a news bite online and it all came back into focus. Apparently it started in New Jersey by some urban kids looking for kicks. From there it spread to Chicago, and now apparently Kansas City. They called it the knockout game and the objective was to strike an oblivious pedestrian and knock them out with the single blow. They even had video footage of a couple of incidents. Repulsive. Those pukes don't deserve to live, and I truthfully don't care if my two assailants did.

That Friday I went out walking in the dilapidated old part of downtown. The anticipation was tremendous. My guts churned and bubbled with an excitement that I hadn't felt for years. Not since I'd stepped in the ring probably or fucked a woman who came and actually wanted to fuck me. Jesus Christ, what a long time I'd been gone. But not now. I was back again, and alive.

I'd strolled by hundreds of young inner city punks and not a one swung on me. I walked from sundown until after the bars closed and not a damn one drew up on me. I walked until my feet blistered and then returned disappointedly to my car.

The next night was more of the same except I had put on brown loafers and khakis, and tried to make myself look as much as possible like an unwilling victim. Still nothing. I whistled and hummed, sometimes turning and walking by the most ornery of thugs twice or more, daring them – pleading even with my body language – that they should please assault me. It never worked, something was wrong. Perhaps they could sense my malevolence, my inner strength, I don't know, but something was askew. Maybe a scarf next time will do it, I thought, one of those silky, feminine ones…

***

It was a long drive to St. Joseph, but not nearly as far as to Wichita. I had to mix it up now, for safety. They were out looking. This knockout game was under the microscope now. There was lots of national outrage.

192

Playing the victim angle was too slow. I'd proved that out for sure. The only way was to hit them first. They had it coming – they were the dregs of society, the lowliest form of man, to be sure...

Standing there at the edge of the alley I watched and waited. It had to be the right person. I had rules now: they must be under fifty, male, and in some way appearing flawed, so that a punch in the face might be just what they needed. I was helping them, you see. Sometimes it was like that; you could help someone by punching them in the face. Goddamn right.

There he was. A yuppie douchebag, young, toned. Too many hours at both the gym and the salon, most certainly. Yes, he was in need of aid. And I had the medicine. Not yet, closer, closer… He never saw it coming and walked right into one of my left hooks. I thought of that bitch at home, that human zombie that was my fake marriage, as my fist connected with his nose... I thought of that bitch a lot nowadays…

27. Pieces of God

"I thought this only happened in movies," said Dan.

"Not today," replied the dark-suited man behind him.

Dan turned from the closed and powerless elevator doors and looked toward the fellow trapped with him: a stranger approximately his own age. "No offense, but after the day I've had, this is hell."

Dan looked at his watch: 6:50 p.m. Not good. The building would be nearly empty at this hour on a Friday.

"I was looking forward to a martini, not this." He gazed at the stranger, looking for shared frustration at their improbable circumstance.

"No, Hell is different than this." The stranger paused to chuckle. "Have you ever wondered why the powers of both good and evil traffic in human souls? Doesn't it seem like an odd modus operandi to you?"

Dan was in no mood for ridiculous conversations, but did not feel he could ignore this man trapped with him. "I suppose," said Dan. "I've never really thought about it. I just went to catechism like they told me to. Can't say as though I found it particularly stimulating."

"I have a theory," said the stranger. "Would you like to hear it?"

Dan grew slightly uncomfortable at the man's stare. A kook, surely, but what was the harm in talking to a kook while trapped in an elevator?

"Yes, I suppose. But hadn't we better try to call for help or find an alarm button?" Dan ran his hands over the panel, pushing and pulling at corners. "No, there's nothing. We'll have to use our cells."

The dark man neither moved nor spoke. Dan dug out his phone, then paused. "911 do you think? This is an emergency, right?"

"I've seen worse," said the peculiar man, his smug tone suggesting a stifled chuckle.

~ ~ * * ~ ~

"There," said Dan, triumphantly returning the phone to his pocket. "They're going to phone building management and maintenance. I predict twenty-five minutes."

"Phoning your wife?" asked the stranger.

"Not married," said Dan, but his companion barely let him speak before starting in again.

"It is peculiar, don't you think? That God should want the souls just as badly as Satan? Perhaps it's all a ruse."

"I wouldn't know," said Dan, not hiding exhaustion.

"I'm totally fucking serious," said the peculiar man, and the new emphasis in his tone seized Dan's attention. He looked upon the stranger fully for the first time. They were approximately the same height, both dark haired, with similar body types and dress. The odd doppelganger leered back at him with that same smug stare.

"Souls. It's all so logical if you think about it. They are pieces of God. Each one of them. Every person walking the earth carries a miniscule fragment within them of the strongest power in the universe. That is why they are desirable."

Discomfort filled the air between them. "That's an interesting theory," said Dan, staring at the stranger and forcing a smile as the hairs on his arms and neck stood on end.

"Oh, it's more than a theory. There is an occasional empty vessel launched. There have been births in which the fragment of God was inexplicably absent from the tissue. True sociopaths—some of the worst rapists and serial killers to ever walk the earth. But why does God want them returned to his possession? I'll tell you. With each soul he obtains, his strength is reinvigorated. Perhaps launching them in the first place was out of his control. Some sort of rule of nature … "

Dan stared, his exhaustion forgotten. "And Satan?"

"What of him?" replied the man with that peculiar smile.

"What, then, is his motivation?"

"Why, the same as God's of course: the attainment of power." The smug face altered a bit, the gleam in the man's eyes brightening. "With each soul he too becomes more than he was. And perhaps one day his power will exceed that of the creator."

Dan swallowed, sensing an unseen abhorrence churning beneath the skin of this handsome stranger.

"Like your ex-wife, Linda. She might be coming my way. In fact, she's working on cumming right now." The Evil leaning against the elevator wall looked upon Dan with intense satisfaction. "And do you know what she's thinking at this very moment, as she's penetrated by new cock? She's feeling joy from the fact that it isn't you."

Intensity lingered in the closed elevator, hanging thickly in the air.

"What are you?" asked Dan. The question was little more than a whisper.

"You know." The stranger smiled, his teeth repugnantly dry and white. "And what about you, Dan? Would you like to make the bitch feel regret like she has never known? You could experience such pleasure and attain such power that she would yearn for nothing but your return. Would that suit your desires?"

"Lies," whispered Dan through his confusion and fear. "I can't believe anything that you say."

"Not true—in fact, I'm not allowed to lie. Not while bartering for souls. Do you know what heaven is like? It's like being emasculated. Like swallowing four Valium and lying around feeling neither pleasure nor pain. Heaven lacks all semblance of true joy."

"And Hell?"

"It's where the fun people are," remarked the devious being leaning against the wall.

"And the serial killers and rapists too I suppose," said Dan.

"They are the vast minority."

"But they are there."

"You're on the path there anyhow," said the stranger. "Why not commit yourself ahead of time, and feed all of your deepest desires before you go? Linda's pretty, but she's an aging brunette. When is the last time you had blond pussy?"

The thing across the elevator peered at him with interest, awaiting reply. Perhaps he was not omniscient, thought Dan. Perhaps he truly did not know.

"Seventeen years, at least, but then some I suppose …" Dan's gaze meandered to the floor in thought. "… It seems like such a distant dream, like something I imagined."

"You can do much more than imagine it tonight," said the stranger with that familiar tone of enticement.

"This is all so overwhelming," said Dan, and he heard the note of pleading in his own voice.

"I cannot lie," said the embodiment of evil. "Not while I barter. Here …"

It reached out its hand, palm facing the silver ceiling. Dan stared, heart pounding in horror and anticipation, as the skin between that thumb and forefinger bulged, then protruded; the mass of flesh elongating and darkening in color. Soon a thin black disc seemed to hover over the hand. The stranger plucked it, detaching the disk from the skin where it had emerged, and held it aloft.

"Communion," said the strange and handsome thing. "Partake of my flesh and every thirst you have now will be quenched."

Dan hesitated. It was all so much to absorb … and then he thought of Linda, feeling joy from a touch that was not his own. Heat suffused his face as his heart beat faster and faster—and suddenly he relented, extending his right hand to take the dark communion. The smug face leered at him as his thoughts extended beyond his ex-wife, to new pleasures soon to be had. With uncertainty Dan placed the disc upon his tongue …

The elevator suddenly shook with restored power and Dan turned numbly to the doors. He chewed the sinuous material and realized a question he had not yet asked.

"When does my soul transfer ownership?" he said, then swallowed the unholy offering.

A chill came upon him, as though a great breeze blew right through his skin and left him chilled to the bone. His exhaustion was gone … along with something else he could not place. It seemed to him as though he now perceived … the imitation of something he had once known. Some sensation he had once felt.

The silver doors parted, revealing the beautiful blond hair of Beckie from Marketing.

"Oh, hi," she said, and then smiled. He did not remember her ever smiling at him before, and it seemed to him this should have made him feel … something.

"Hello," he said with newfound confidence and charisma. "We were stuck for a bit, but it seems to be fine now."

"We?" she said, then looked at him, slightly puzzled.

Dan turned and saw, without surprise, the three vertical walls of an empty silver box.

"A figure of speech. Come on, it's Friday. I've got a martini to get … can you join me for a round?" He said this with the imitation of a smile, and pushed the button for the lobby once she had entered.

28. Messiah of Evil

INT. A SMALL VILLAGE, VERY POOR, NEAR THE MEXICAN
BORDER

Three boys are kneeling and sitting in an open dirt field of the Mexican
desert. Two of the boys are age fourteen, and they are handsome young
men. They appear to be healthy and happy young men.

The third boy is younger, at the age twelve, and he is not handsome like
the older boys. He has a plain face displaying old burn scars from
injuries received long ago. He does not smile or emit happiness like the
older boys.

They all play with a scorpion that is in the sand between them.
Guillermo, the disfigured boy sits close to it and pokes methodically at
the scorpion with a stick.

> HECTOR (THE OLDER BROTHER OF THE DISFIGUED
> GUILLERMO)
> Be careful Guillermo.

Hector's tone shows genuine concern for his little brother. The other
older boy Pedro watches and sits in a relaxed pose with his legs crossed.
The sun isn't high in the sky. Morning has come not long ago.

> PEDRO
> It's getting riled up now.

Pedro watches the angry scorpion, and young Guillermo's focused
prodding of the animal, with fascination. We see that their friend Pedro
is a close friend to these brothers.

Hector and Guillermo's father Victor then approaches, carrying a sun hat for the work that is to begin. He is a stern and impatient man, and we sense that there is difficult work ahead.

VICTOR
Hector, Pedro, let's go.

The older boys Hector and Pedro rise without delay but do not immediately step away. They seem to want to see what happens with the scorpion.

The father Victor walks up to stand behind Guillermo who still pokes gently at the scorpion, possibly endangering himself, seemingly ignoring his father. The father shows no concern for his disfigured boy. Guillermo doesn't look at him but instead continues his concentrated and intent game with the creature. Both Hector and Pedro look respectfully to the elder man.

VICTOR
Get your tools boys (To his son Hector and friend Pedro).

Hector and Pedro walk quickly back in the direction from which Victor had come. Guillermo still does not react.

His father, Victor, stands silently a moment watching the game his younger son play's with the scorpion, watching as the creature's agitation builds and it prepares to strike down at Guillermo's hand with its tail.

We see on Victor's face some repulsion and we realize that in many ways this father wishes that his peculiar, ugly boy will be struck by the poisonous tale of the scorpion. Quick camera shots between all three (scorpion, Guillermo, and Victor) as the agitation of all three quietly boils and tension builds, and at last the scorpion strikes and Guillermo safely withdraws his hand and lets the small stick fall to the ground.

GUILLERMO

It cannot get me (Aloud but to himself as we see the oddness of his personality in his eyes. He is still staring at the creature).

VICTOR

Get your tools (Behind him over his shoulder. Quietly, angrily – disappointed?).

Victor turns and walks away leaving his disfigured son in the dirt (overhead angle, Victor walks to the bottom left of the screen). We sense that he is indifferent to the welfare of his non-favored, imperfect son.

INT. WORKING WITHIN THE CROPS – LATER IN THE MORNING

All three boys are shown working, but only Hector and Pedro have protective sun hats like the men. Guillermo has none and the sun beats down upon him. They all work peacefully but continually, pruning and spraying pesticide.

They labor in many scenes: Pulling pruned waste into piles, and then filling wheelbarrows, and carrying it away. But with each new row they begin by pruning and spraying.

Hector takes a chocolate bar from his pocket and breaks it, and places a small piece into his mouth.

Victor walks by, inspecting their work as they prune, and then departs back to another row. Hector watches him until he is gone and then walks to his brother Guillermo and secretly hands him a small cube of chocolate.

                              HECTOR
                          Here Guillermo.

Guillermo's unusual face shows a quick broad smile of love and
appreciation as he takes the chocolate.

                            GUILLERMO
                          Gracias Hector.

He breaks out from his aloof oddness only when in comfortably private
situation with his older brother.

Both boys return to working. Another grown man then walks into view
behind the boys as they continue their difficult work. This new man has
just missed by a few moments, seeing their brief rest and exchange of
chocolate. We sense that it is a ritual practiced often between these three
boys as they work, and there is a lightness of comrade among them.
There is a sense of pleasant indifference if they were to be caught not
working.

INT. WASHING UP

Hector and Guillermo wash their hands from a crude outdoor faucet
behind their house. When their father who washes before them finishes
and walks away, they step in and take their turn from the lightly-
pressured water.

As the older brother Hector washes the dirt from his hands and cleans
his face, he looks over through the window of a neighboring house.
Within it one of the young wives of the village is dressing and stands
with her chest bare for a moment. Her breasts are displayed briefly for
the adolescent to see, before she pulls a light shirt over her head. She
then walks out of view of both Hector and the audience.

Hector smiles and turns off the water.

HECTOR
Come on (to Guillermo).

Guillermo had seen the neighbor also.

INT. DINNER WITHIN THE KITCHEN/ DINING ROOM AT
HECTOR AND GUILLERMO's HOME - NIGHT

Victor, his wife, Hector, and Guillermo all sit at the humble table. The
two boys are across from one another and all eat heartily, although there
is an unspoken sadness present in the air between the parents.

MOTHER
How was the day today? (to Victor her husband)
VICTOR
No problems.

MOTHER
Are the crops as you would like them?

VICTOR

They are of a reasonable height for the date – pests are under control.
(Pause – he looks at the clock on the wall as though her question has
brought him out of a deep ponder). Friday night bouts come on in half-
hour. (Pause – then he turns to Hector). I want you to train tomorrow. If
Pedro won't spar with you, then I can.

HECTOR

Sure Papa (still chewing). Pedro will spar. But we have a project we're
working on. We're building a fort out by the hills. We found some
pallets by the road for wood. Can we use your shovel and hammer?

203

VICTOR
(He does not answer the question his oldest son asked) You can train for
an hour in the morning.

HECTOR
Alright Papa.

The father stands and takes his plate and beer out of the room,
presumably to the television. The camera remains of the boys and the
boy's mother as they continue to eat.

Hector looks to his left to ensure his father is gone, and then takes a pea
from his plate, sets it on the table, and then finger-flicks it toward
Guillermo. Both boys smile and Guillermo laughs gleefully.

The mother says nothing when the favored older boy acts out with his
food.

Guillermo then takes a pea from his plate and finger-flicks it at his older
brother.

MOTHER
Boys… no…

INT. IN BED

Hector lies within his small bed, within his small bedroom, and
Guillermo lies in his small bed within the same room. The lights are out
but the boys are awake and speaking before bed. They are like two
normal brothers within the darkness of that room, and it is during these
moments that they are always truly happy.

HECTOR
You tired brother?

GUILLERMO
Hector do you think we will live together when we are men?

Hector is tossing a small ball straight upwards as he lies on his back. He is not worried but we feel that his is energetically restless and cannot sleep.

HECTOR
I don't know. (pause). I won't be in this village though, I can tell you that.

GUILLERMO
You can go anywhere soon can't you brother?

HECTOR
Maybe I could go anywhere but that doesn't mean I could do anything.

GUILLERMO
Papa seems to think you can.

HECTOR
I guess. (Pause). I'd like to open a small restaurant maybe. Far away from here, in a much bigger city. And I want to marry a beautiful girl, but not right away. I want to travel around and try out different ones – blonds maybe.

GUILLERMO
Could I come work for you at your restaurant?

HECTOR
Sure G.

GUILLERMO
(Pause…) I will never get married will I Hector?

HECTOR

Maybe not, but you'll be working for me and we'll be together. (Pause) And I'll help find you some girls from time to time. (Pause, and then a different more serious, worldly-wise tone) There are ways for men like you to have girls too Guillermo…

GUILLERMO

Our Papa will never want me, but Mama can come to visit.

HECTOR

It will be fine. Now go to sleep.

Hector sets down his ball and turns out his table light.

GUILLERMO

Would he like me more if I hadn't been burned by that oil lamp? If I were not ugly would he like me as much as he likes you?

HECTOR

I don't know. He isn't like you and me. You're not missing out on much of anything. Papa's father died when he was very young. He never learned how a father is to be with his sons. His life is not as he hoped it would be, and someone has to take the blame. Now go to sleep – goodnight.

GUILLERMO

I burned my own face in the accident Hector. Not his…

The camera withdraws from the room, out through the open bedroom window, and the boys room shows then as dark as the surrounding darkness of the Mexican night.

INT. BOXING PRACTICE OUTDOORS – MORNING

Pedro is wearing protective headgear and spars Hector who is not wearing protective headgear. It seems clear that Hector's skills are far superior to Pedro's.

Hector dominates the spar but also takes mercy on his friend. The sun is bright overhead and his father Victor sits in a rickety chair, watching nearby. Guillermo sits somewhat behind him playing in the dirt.

VICTOR
Jab, jab – lots of jabs!

Victor looks at his watch, holds it and waits until a few more seconds elapse, and then blows a whistle.

The boys' spar continues, punches, footwork, outside upon the dirt.

VICTOR
Jab, straight right! Everything off the jab!

Hector steps up his effort, and hits Pedro with force as time runs out.

VICTOR
Stop!

Victor stands and puts on a pair of old boxing gloves and steps to the boys.

Victor
You just made him miss with his right hand, and you did nothing afterward except circle him. From now on this is what you do. Pedro, do it again, slowly.

Victor takes a boxing stance and circles slowly to his right as Pedro does the same and prepares to throw his punches at the older Victor.

Pedro throws a straight right and Victor dodges to his left, making him miss, and then throws a soft cross with his left hand onto Pedro's exposed cheek.

VICTOR

Like that. When you make him miss, you come across your body and tag him with a left cross. Do you understand?

HECTOR
Yes Papa.

Hector squeezes a water bottle and it is empty.

HECTOR
Water's gone.

VICTOR
Guillermo, fill the bottle.

We see Guillermo rise from the dirt where he was sitting. He is eager to please his father and do as he is told. He is pleased simply to not be ignored.

INT. STOMACH TRAINING

Cut to both boys lying on their backs with their legs extended at an angle into the air, with straightened legs. Their hands are beneath them, under their buttocks.

Victor paces around them, over them. He looks to his watch and then steps over Pedro so that he straddles the lying boy. He then beds and punches the boy rhythmically in the abdomen as Pedro rhythmically tightens his stomach. After five strikes he steps away, points and yells…

VICTOR
Rest!

He steps over his son Hector and does the same routine, only he uses more force on his boy.

The fifth strike is the last.

VICTOR
Jump rope. Three rounds. Let's go.

Hector and Pedro walk to the edge of the dirt area and pick up a jump rope. They walk back to the open dirt area where they had been training and prepare for Victor to start the round.

HECTOR (to Pedro)
After these rounds we build.

PEDRO
Si.

Victor does not once break his seriousness as he raises his watch to begin the timing of the two minute round.

VICTOR
Go!

The older boys begin fast jump roping. Pedro does only traditional jumping but Hector alternates feet forward, switches quickly back and forth, and all the while maintains a speed that is faster than his friend's.

INT. LATER THAT DAY – SATURDAY

We see a shot of the wilderness nearby and then from a distance all three boys walk into the picture. Hector carries a shovel over his shoulder and Pedro carries a hammer and a bow saw.

The smaller Guillermo walks along next to them. He is pleased to be along, free from his father's reproachful, disappointed gaze.

PEDRO
Once we get the tunnel deep enough we can line the sides with wooden supports. Above the side-supports we'll wedge in the horizontal boards to hold up the ceiling dirt. Those should be done every 12" to 14". That's how the miners used to do it. I read it in my father's miner's guide.

HECTOR
We'll see what seems right.

PEDRO
Our three pallets won't go very far. We could always dig straight down and make an underground fort, and cover it up with the boards and then a layer of dirt for camouflage, but I like the idea of a secret tunnel.

GUILLERMO
If we had trees here we could build a tree fort.

HECTOR
Sure G.

PEDRO
If we had trees here we could cut them down and build anything…

They continue walking with the tools and talking.

HECTOR

I like the tunnel idea. We have the wood. We just have to use it properly
and be careful of a cave-in.

PEDRO

We're short on nails

HECTOR

We'll re-use all of them as we take the pallets apart. Guillermo, that will
be one of your jobs.

GUILLERMO

OK no problem. I can do it.

The camera goes back to the original angle as when the boys walked
into the frame. It stops moving along with them, and they now walk out
of the frame.

They arrive at the site of the tunnel in progress. We see an angle from
inside with the dirt hole that has already been started at the side of a hill.
The sides of the hole frame the shot menacingly and the three boys
approach with their tools.

When they walk up to the hole we see that there is a large hill which the
boys have dug a hole into the side. We see the wooden pallets lying
about, apparently having already been carried by the boys to the site.
Some are partially disassembled.

Hector begins carefully but forcefully using his hammer to remove
boards from one of the pallets.

HECTOR

Nails Guillermo. Straighten some out.

He points to the boards already removed, now lying upon the ground. There are bent nails protruding from them.

Pedro hears this and hands Guillermo the hammer so that he can straighten them.

PEDRO
Here Guillermo.

Guillermo eagerly takes the hammer and proudly sits by the wood pile where some of the bent nails have been piled near a large rock.

We see various close-ups of Guillermo grabbing a nail, holding it against the rock, and then pounding the bend out of it, so that it can be used again.

Hector steps away from his pallet and walks to the hole in the hill. Cautiously he examines the dirt ceiling of the tunnel while he crouches safely outside of it. He touches the dirt of the hole suspiciously.

HECTOR
It's drying out. (Pause) We start today by lining the walls and ceiling with supports. I want them sturdy.

Pedro brings him various boards to choose from and drops them at his feet. Hector gently kneels down and scoots into the hole, then grabs a board and holds it up to the wall.

HECTOR
I'll need that hammer Guillermo. Give him a rock to use for those nails, Pedro.

We see some shots of the sun overhead high in the sky. When the boys are shown again the wood pile is much smaller and Pedro is now fully inside of the tunnel which extends well into the base of the tall hill.

Hector is deep within the tunnel beyond Pedro. Wall and ceiling supports are now lining the tunnel back to where Hector is working.

There is a creaking sound from one of the boards and a very small amount of dirt falls down upon them. We see perhaps a bit of fear upon the face of Pedro.

PEDRO

I'm getting hungry. My Mom will have dinner soon.

HECTOR

We'll finish these and be done. Hand me a ceiling board.

Hector scoots back further back into the tunnel and we see that he now sits where there are no wooden supports above him (camera pans up to show us). Pedro scoots further inward also, lying upon his belly.

The camera cuts to close ups of Guillermo still pounding nails straight with a rock out in the sun, close-ups of the nails and the impact, intermittently with shots within the tunnel, back and forth, and after tension is built we see dirt beginning to fall, followed by boards, and then the horror of a full cave in beginning.

Cut to back inside the tunnel with Hector and Pedro as it all falls.

PEDRO

Hector!

The entire tunnel except a few feet of the entryway has collapsed and all that we can see of Pedro are his feet. The feet shake and twitch a bit and then go still. There is simply too many pounds of dirt pressing down upon him under the large hill.

GUILLERMO

Hector! Hector!

Guillermo rises and runs to the mouth of the tunnel. He pulls at the feet of Pedro but it is futile. He cannot be pulled free. Guillermo scrambles about and yells to both boys.

Realizing this he turns and runs back toward the village, toward his father.

INT. HIS FATHER IS WORKING OUTSIDE NEAR A SHED

GUILLERMO
Papa! Papa! Hector and Pedro are buried! Help them! Please!

Guillermo points in the direction of the hills, and Victor runs a few feet, stares and drops his tool. He then yells to Andres who is working not far away and has heard as well. A look of panic adorns his face.

VICTOR
Andres! Our boys! Come now!

Both men run off to the location of the boys as Guillermo runs behind them.

ANDRES
Where Guillermo?!

GUILLERMO
That way! To the hill!

Both men run off frantically with Guillermo trying to keep up behind them.

Fade…

We see handheld jumpy shots of the ground and then the feet of the fathers as they step into view. We see horrifically that they both carry the limp bodies of their beloved sons. We see this as though we are looking through binoculars. Behind them Guillermo walks dejectedly.

> MOTHER (Guillermo's & Hector)
> Oh dear God! (She draws the back of her hand to her mouth).

Again we see the long shot of the fathers carrying their boys. Other menfolk of the village walk behind them.

INT. INSIDE GUILLERMO'S HOUSE

The bodies of both boys are laid out on cots. The parents sit beside them, and no doctor is present. Guillermo is the only other person in the room, and he stands silently against a far wall.

As the women weep and are consoled Guillermo leaves the wall and subtly walks to the body of his dead brother and stands near him. We see the hurt and loss in his eyes, for the only person who had loved him is now dead.

Hector's limp hand hangs off of the side of the cot, and we view it in the foreground of an upward shot of Guillermo's face. He turns and looks from his dead brother's face to the hand, and then reaches his own to clasp it.

We see Andres, the father of Pedro, somberly watching Guillermo's actions. He displays a sense of empathy for Guillermo.

We see Guillermo's face, who has closed his eyes in either grief or prayer or both, near his deceased brother. The camera is close upon his face, and holds there.

A vision then comes to Guillermo in flashes and flickers, and we are transported into the vision that is within his mind. Flames abound everywhere, and the face of a man with eyes of complete blackness appears within Guillermo's consciousness.

The strange man looks to us (Guillermo) as the overwhelming flames crackles about within this vision. The man's countenance shows an oddly foreboding and emotionless vacant stare, with those unblinking large black eyes. The face is handsome, too handsome, something about the vision of this dark man being false, and all the while flames flicker everywhere about his image.

DARK ANGEL

Call him back to you Guillermo. You have been chosen. Call back your dead brother from the coldness of death. You have the power to revive him if you choose to take it. But there is a price.

The image of this evil man, leans then and clasps around the head of the boy. He lowers his evil face to Guillermo's ear and whispers then something that only he can hear. The noise of the flames is too loud. The man then stands upright.

GUILLERMO

I choose it.

The man of evil smiles and bursts then into flames, melting before us.

Then this image within Guillermo's mind is gone and we return to the room and the upward shot of Guillermo's face with Hector's hand in the foreground as it is clasped by Guillermo's. Guillermo's eyes snap open as the vision ends.

Guillermo returns to concentration, and squeezes forcefully the hand of his dead brother. Suddenly there is a flicker of life as the muscles of hector's hand and arm contract once, and then again. He squeezes Guillermo's hand, perhaps involuntarily. We see the muscles of his athletic arm tense repeatedly.

Guillermo opens his eyes and there is great joy and light upon his face. It is the first true joy upon his face that the audience has seen. He did not display this joy when seeing the topless neighbor or when playing with his brother, but he displays it now.

We see Andres looking upon him, comprehending.

                    MOTHER
              Hector! Hector!

She runs to the body of her oldest son and holds his chest to her chest as he blinks into consciousness.

                    HECTOR
              Mama…

Victor runs to the side of his eldest son and knocks Guillermo from his position.

                    VICTOR
        Hector, my boy! He lives! He lives!

Andres rises and steps up behind them.

                    ANDRES
   It was Guillermo (in disbelief). It was your boy Guillermo. (Pause).
          Victor, it was your boy, Guillermo! Victor!

                    VICTOR
   It was Guillermo what? (With annoyance through his joy)

ANDRES

Guillermo, here boy… (Speaking to Guillermo imploringly)

The other grief stricken father bends to the disfigured boy and seizes his hand, pulling him toward his own dead boy.

ANDRES

Here boy, do as you had done, just as you did to your brother!

PEDRO'S MOTHER (MARIA)

(With great despair and without belief) Oh Andres!

She covers her face with the cloth which she had been crying into. She believes that he is delusional.

ANDRES

Do it boy (imploringly), lay *your hands upon him…*

Guillermo does so as instructed, closes his eyes and again concentrates, pouring all of the negativity from his life out into some form of intense prayer, and feeling an odd joy at this attention that he now receives.

We do not see the vision of the flames and the dark angel again, but we hear the crackling of the flames which we cannot see, and we know that he sees them. Moments pass with no change in Pedro, as anticipation builds.

Then, just as with Hector, Pedro's muscles finally begin to contract with spasms. At this point Pedro's mother begins to shriek and leaps from her seat. The shrieking does not cease as she creeps quickly with arms outstretched, to the spastic and blinking face of her boy.

ANDRES

You've done it boy!

MARIA
(Shrieking with joy) Pedro! My boy! Pedro!

Behind them Victor and his wife hold and rock their boy Hector back to full consciousness.

VICTOR
Hector! Hector! Look at me! Speak!

ANDRES
It is Guillermo! He is blessed! He has returned our boys to life!

Andres runs to Guillermo and hugs him lifting him into the air, hollering with joy and spinning him about.

ANDRES
You beautiful, beautiful burned boy!

We cut then to the still ill looking Hector and Pedro lying upon their cots, as they have now been allowed to revive and recover their senses. Neither of them speak further and they do not smile. There is an appearance of both illness and concern upon both of them.

About them, around the room, everyone is oblivious as they celebrate with joy.

INT. A GREAT CELEBRATION WITHIN THE VILLAGE – NIGHT

The village is having a party to celebrate that the two boys were spared from death. Two tables have been placed outdoors with streamers and decorations as best as the poor village can afford.

The boys including Guillermo, and their mothers sit at the front while other people of the village dance to Mexican music, eat, and walk about.

Victor drinks mightily from a bottle as he stands with a group to the side of celebration. He and the men express great joy. They laugh and speak as though they have no concerns at all. They are the embodiment of the sensation of contentedness.

UNKNOWN MAN (to two unknown women)
They were dead. They were beneath that dirt for half an hour. It's ungodly.

The women do not reply, but look from him warily to the table where the boys are seated.

At the table we see Guillermo sitting in the middle eating happily from a plate of food. He is like a new young-man. On either side of him, Pedro and Hector sit in a daze, with full plates untouched in front of them, pristine.

Guillermo looks sideways to Hector, while holding his corn.

GUILLERMO
(To Hector) Don't be sad brother.

Hector turns and looks at Guillermo somewhat laboriously. First the head turns and then the eyes follow. Something with the movement of his neck muscles seems weak and unnatural. He is more listless than when he revived.

Pedro's mother kisses him from behind. Pedro does not react to his mother's affection.

INT. VARIOUS SHOTS OF CELEBRATION
Dancing, dancing, and dancing. Fireworks, and more meat cooking.

UNKNOWN WOMAN (to a new unknown man)
It isn't right. There is the Devil in this place.

The music stops…

VICTOR
Listen to me everyone, please listen up. Today I am the luckiest man
alive because I have received not one, but two gifts.

He looks back to his wife for encouragement, and then back to the
people.

VICTOR
One moment I had lost everything, and the next, a second chance.

Victor gestures to the table where his boys both sit.

VICTOR
My oldest son is returned to me through the grace of God, against all
odds. But God does not stop there. He shows me also that I have acted
badly with regard to my other son. I will never make this mistake again.
May God bless this village as he has blessed my entire family!

Fireworks explode noisily about the ground.

VICTOR
Now let the celebration continue!

The music and dancing resume.

We now see alternating shots of the celebration and the two sick boys.
Their faces begin to display more and more illness as the celebration
rages on, louder and louder, back and forth.

Hector begins to grab and hold his stomach as his mother begins to panic and grabs for him.

She shouts for help but the noise of the celebration drowns her out.

Hector stands and falls forward leaning against the top of the table. The celebration continues as he begins to retch and a torrent of thick dark blood is ejected from his mouth. It fills the air and then both splatters and lands with a thud upon the dirt of the ground as people scatter backward.

We see the giant chunk of clotted blood that lies repulsively upon the ground.

VICTOR
Hector! Hector! My boy! No! No!

He runs to his boy and holds him with both concern and horror. One of the other men squats down to examine the oddly dark and lumpy blood. It is clearing clotting and non-fluid. It is, to everyone that looks upon it, once living tissue now bound with death.

UNKNOWN MAN
This blood is already drying! Drive for the doctor!

Cut to an overhead angle of the blood and the chaos as people continue to backup, and the camera pulls back (upward) to display the chaos… The horror that something is horribly wrong is now known with certainty to everyone in the village.

Mothers are grabbing their children and running away, into the safety of their homes.

INT. INSIDE HECTOR'S HOME – PRE-DAWN

Hector lies upon his small bed, lethargic and pale. His mother sits on his bed and strokes his head lightly. Hector only lies and stares vacantly. Victor sits on a chair tiredly.

Outside a shabby looking truck pulls in and parks.

The mother rises to greet the doctor.

An older bearded man steps out holding a doctor's bag. He appears unkempt and as though he has been drinking. He closes the car door, then pauses and stares toward the home. He shows hesitation… then walks.

The doctor enters and removes a jacket which he hands to the mother. He waits for Victor to finish moving the chair to the side of the bed, and then for Victor to approach him so that they can have a word between them privately.

Victor and the doctor exchange a few words quietly. The doctor then walks and sits in the chair near the bed.

DOCTOR
How do you feel son?

Hector does not answer.

He reaches and feels the boy's forehead and hands, then removes some instruments from his bag.

DOCTOR
Boy, how do you feel?

HECTOR

...Tired...

DOCTOR
Cold? (He listens to his heart)

HECTOR
No...

DOCTOR
In pain?

HECTOR
...no, not really...

The doctor listens and listens and listens, moving the stethoscope around. He then takes a thermometer from his bag and places it within Hector's mouth.

While he waits he turns and looks around the room until he sees Guillermo sitting on the floor near the back wall of the room, observing. The camera follows his vision and we see him as the focus changes to show a formerly blurry Guillermo.

The doctor looks back to hector and pulls the thermometer and reads it patiently for a few seconds, looks to Hector, then cleans it and returns it to the bag. He then stands and places his hand upon the side of Hector's face, and reassuringly pats him.

DOCTOR
See me to my truck (to Victor).

The doctor removes a cigarette from his jacket pocket once the boy's Mother has returned it to him. Once outside, he lights it, and walks with Victor toward his truck.

VICTOR
Why do you not help him?

DOCTOR
He cannot be helped.

VICTOR
Of course he can. If not you, then the hospital!

VICTOR
No one can help that boy.

VICTOR
You did not see what came out of him! (Grabbing the doctor's arm,
forcing him to halt. We feel as though Victor may push or strike this old,
drunken medical doctor)

The doctor looks at him.

DOCTOR
I was told everything by those who came to get me from my home. I
know of the dirt and the smothering death of the boys, and then their
miraculous return followed by illness. And I know of the other boy. *Both
of the other boys…*

VICTOR
Help my son! I can pay you! If not now, when the crop comes in…

DOCTOR
They told me very much when they came to me. I must go now and see
the other boy before I depart. It will only be a formality…

VICTOR
Depart?

DOCTOR

Yes depart. There is no work for a doctor here. Now listen (The doctor is more assertive now). If you involve outsiders or take your boy to the city, you will regret it. Men will come here and burn your village to the ground, and your family along with it. Then they will consecrate the scorched earth and try to forget that you ever existed. I cannot say it any clearer – they will kill you all to prevent any chance of a spreading of the evil.

VICTOR

Kill us!? Evil? What are you talking about?

DOCTOR

Yes, it is better that you deal with your boy here. Give him what he asks for, and send your wife away when she needs a reprieve. I repeat my warning – bring no outsiders into this matter.

VICTOR

My wife!?

DOCTOR

I have seen this before…very long ago… (Pause. There is a distant look on his face as he remembers something horrible from long ago. Then he returns to the present). Stay in your village and tell no one – not until this is done. And pray to *God* (he emphasizes the word emphatically as he looks at Victor for comprehension).

He gets into his truck and drives further on down the lane until Pedro's family signals him.

Victor is confounded and stands awash in concern and confusion. He holds his head. It is too much for him to deal with.

The doctor closes the door of his truck and drives down the dirt road, to the home of Pedro. Andres waits for him anxiously outside.

INT. INSIDE AGAIN.

Victor enters.

                         VICTOR
     He will be fine (to his wife). We are to keep him drinking water, and
                    food when we will take it.

Nervously Victor removes a cigarette and lights it.

                         MOTHER
             He needs a hospital! He needs…

                         VICTOR
     No! The doctor was certain. (Pause…). They were… gone. And now
          they are not. But you know as well as I that they were gone.

He looks away from her to Guillermo (the camera follows his gaze).

Guillermo, who feels shame and looks down to the ground… Fade…

INT. – DAYTIME

Hector lies listlessly in his bed. There is a knock on his door, and
Guillermo enters. He says nothing but walks in with his usual unkempt
appearance. He walks until he stands right next to his brother's bed.
After a moment of silence…

                        GUILLERMO
                  Hector? (silence) Brother?

Hector turns his head and then the eyes follow.

HECTOR
Yes

GUILLERMO
Are you mad at me Hector?

HECTOR
I was having a wonderful dream until you brought me back Guillermo.
(silence…) There is a God brother. He does love you, just as I love you.
(silence…) But I think there is some reason that bad things have to
happen. I think that there is some sort of universal balance that must be
kept in all of the world.

GUILLERMO
What are you talking about brother?

HECTOR
(Silence…) Guillermo I think that you are going to have to leave this
place. (Pause) But don't be scared. For some reason we have been
chosen to bear the burden of this balance that I'm speaking of.

GUILLERMO
What are you talking about brother?

HECTOR
Leave me now brother, I am tired.

Hector turns his head a bit and stares motionless and emotionless back to
the window. Guillermo does not seem to be alarmed by this and simply
turns and leaves.

INT. OUTSIDE

Guillermo is playing outside near his home when a terrible shriek erupts from the house. We know that it is Hector's mother.

Guillermo runs into his house. Inside his mother is sitting upon a chair a few feet away from the bed. She is crying and sobbing, covering her face with her hands.

Victor runs into the room also.

                    VICTOR
               What is it?

                    MOTHER
               His back!

Victor moves to the bed and kneels upon one knee. Hector's eyes are surrounded by dark patches and he looks very ill, although he is not uneasy and does not wince.

                    VICTOR
               Roll onto your side.

Hector does not really comply but neither does he resist when his father gently rolls him and pulls up his pajamas. Dark patches of pooled blood can be seen where gravity has caused it to collect.

                    VICTOR
               No!...

His face displays horror. He then rolls his son back over, and hesitantly reaches to feel his heartbeat by placing his flat palm against hector's chest. His face goes stone cold with terror when he feels no heartbeat.

MOTHER
We are taking him to a hospital!

VICTOR
We cannot!

MOTHER
You are taking him now!

Victor violently grabs his wife's mouth and squeezes as he yells at her.

VICTOR
They will kill us all! They will kill him! And they will burn our houses
to the ground and try to forget that any of this abomination ever existed!

He pushes her away. Victor turns to Guillermo and is filled with rage.
He walks heavily toward him, pauses before the terrified boy, and hits
him across the face.

MOTHER
Victor!

Victor pulls his belt violently from the belt loops of his trousers with a
load snap, and chases Guillermo from the house while whipping and
beating him.

Outside Hector falls to the ground and continues crawling and
scrambling away as he is beaten.

GUILLERMO
Papa, no! Papa!

A female scream comes then from the house of Pedro, and everyone
stops to look.

We see the strong image of Victor stop and look toward the scream.

Moments later Andres storms out of his home. He walks angrily to Guillermo and then stops ten feet away from him. We know that he too has realized the morbid facts regarding his own boy.

ANDRES
You! (pause) You are the devil! What have you done! What have you done to my boy!

He bends and grabs a rock from the ground, then hurls it with all of his strength at Guillermo, then again, and again.

ANDRES
AHHH! AHHH! Devil! (As he throws rocks – emotion is spewing from him uncontrollably).

The wife of Andres has now joined him and throws rocks also, and they are then joined by all of the adults in the village.

There are various shots of hostile, raging men and women, and Guillermo being struck with rocks.

MANY
Be gone! Leave us you Devil!

Guillermo is crying and scrambles backward to his feet and runs away into the desert and the hills as the villagers run behind him for several yards still cursing and throwing rocks.

Guillermo runs and cries, and runs…

INT. WALKING THROUGH THE DESSERT - DUSK

Guillermo is bleeding and wet with tears. He walks along seemingly aimlessly. He hears water and steps up upon a river bank.

We see that he stands before a great river, with lights across it in the distance. He pauses as though admiring the beauty, and then wades out into the river. He begins to cross to the other side.

We see him make it and climb the opposite bank. He walks toward the horizon of buildings, and the hope that they may bring. It is the border to the United States.

INT. WALKING ALONG THE STREETS

Guillermo walks in the now mostly darkened evening. He is entering a modern, moderately sized city. He walks into the slums and is watched by corner dwellers and hoodlums, but no one speaks to him.

He begins to pass by a dark alley and stops to look into it. When he determines that it appears quiet and empty he turns and walks into its darkness. He looks along the walls for somewhere to lie safely down. Once he is thirty feet in he hears the sounds of shouting and looks back to the street.

There are sounds of fighting and a man is then apparently struck and falls into view of Guillermo. As the man tries to rise a larger man runs to him and strikes him again.

Guillermo, now frightened, runs behind some crates and boxes and covers his ears as he lies down to hide. He cries and whimpers and eventually begins to drift off into sleep.

Fade…

MORNING – AWAKENING

We see Guillermo asleep, blood still dried upon his face, and a cane comes into view and begins nudging his shoulder. When he does not awake he is nudged again. He stirs to waking.

We see a middle aged black man with a beard. He appears somewhat unkempt, but not dirty. He is tall and lean, with a trustworthy face.

WALTER
You are not my usual neighbor, young man.

Guillermo sits up and looks upward at the man. He blinks in the morning light. Walter looks at him patiently and kindly, as though there is a puzzle here to solve.

WALTER
Are you aware young man that you are bleeding about the head?

Guillermo reaches up and feels his head.

GUILLERMO
It feels mostly ok.

WALTER
I'm Walter Anderson. You can call me Walt. Here allow me…

Walter takes a napkin from his pocket and hands it to Guillermo. Silently Guillermo takes it.

Walter then extends his large right hand. There is a calmness about him. He seems to be a conflict of opposite – peace versus angst or inner turmoil. But he looks upon Guillermo without swift judgment. It is almost as though Walt does not even notice Guillermo's disfigurement.

Guillermo takes Walter's hand and is pulled gently to stand.

GUILLERMO

My name's Guillermo.

Walter smiles broadly, a very patient, trustworthy smile and extends his giant hand to shake. Guillermo takes the hand after a momentary hesitation.

WALTER

There. We need to get you back to your parents young Guillermo. They'll be worried sick about you right about now. Did you runaway, young man?

GUILLERMO

(Thinks a moment) My parents are dead. They were killed a few weeks ago. I came here during the night. I crossed last night over the river.

He speaks quickly as he is unaccustomed to lying. He then motions by pointing to the south.

Walt looks in the direction, and then seems to understand. (Pause).

WALTER

Well I suppose you live here now. I was just going to check if there is work today. Would you like to come and see if there's any work?

GUILLERMO

Paid?

WALTER

We'll be paid today. Cash – if there's work. Have you ever had a job before?

GUILLERMO

I was a farm helper back home, but I didn't get to keep the money. It went to my parents.

Walter nods and smiles. He seems to understand.

WALTER
Well nobody is going to take your money from you here. Not when you're with me anyway.

GUILLERMO
OK, I'll go work.

Walt turns gently to walk from the alley, and extend one of his long arms down to pat the shoulder of the boy. They walk out to the street together.

As they walk…

WALTER
The work, if there is any work, isn't half bad. It's agriculture.

GUILLERMO
Agriculture?

WALTER
Farming-which I know you know from back home. You'll do fine.

GUILLERMO
We grew soybean and corn…

They continue walking at a leisurely pace and there is a feeling of great peace between these two. The camera pulls back as they walk on and we see their backs.

Their great height difference is notable, but there seems to be a similarity between them despite their ages. We are not worried about Guillermo for the moment.

INT. A MORE RURAL ROAD – CITY IN BACKGROUND

They still walk but at a quicker pace. Guillermo makes certain to keep up.

> WALTER
> There isn't much work that I haven't done. Farm labor, mechanic, factories, truck loader – you name it, I've tried it. (Pause). But truly, vast money doesn't really interest me. If I found a huge pile of it, I suppose I would keep it, but I'd just buy a big plot of land in the wooded hills of Colorado, and let the rest sit in a buried hole. (Pause).

Guillermo listens, walks, and smiles.

> WALTER
> Me, I've got things mostly figured out. Last night you slept outside of my current home, which is to say, an abandoned tool and die shop that I've converted into a multi-functional dwelling. I eat mostly what I please. There isn't much that leaves me wanting. If we are a bit lucky today, we'll earn some money and we can buy some food. But I've got some stored regardless. We won't go hungry.

> GUILLERMO
> I'm thirsty. (Looks up to Walter).

Walter removes a large metallic thermos from a pocket and pours water into the cap. He hands this to Guillermo as they stop a moment. Guillermo drinks.

> GUILLERMO

More please Mr. Walter.

Another is poured, and Guillermo then hands the lid back to him. They continue on without another word.

INT. FARM

We see both the tall man and young Guillermo walking up the long dirt driveway of a farm.

                              WALTER
                You see little man, it wasn't so far.

INT. BEHIND THE FARMHOUSE

Walt walks to where the day workers assemble. Guillermo is cautious and looks up at Walt repeatedly, but follows along.

                              WALTER
Ask me whenever you need water – I have enough (looking at Guillermo
                very sincerely to ensure that he will do so).

There are six other migrant workers standing near one of the barns. Walter and Guillermo join them, but do not speak to the others. One worker is a strong young man, age nineteen or so, fully muscled and fully grown with an air of hostility about him (Anthony).

The other young man is handsome in a rugged, blue collar sense, but has the unusual characteristic of one brown eye and one blue eye. One gets the sense from his gaze and nervous air, that this physical flaw causes the young man (Anthony) great anxiety.

He looks to Guillermo's face once, then away (this is subtle).

A man and a woman age fifty walk from the house toward the workers. When they are close, the woman sees Guillermo as she walks (a mobile shot from her perspective). There is compassion in her gaze.

The farmer stops a moment, oblivious to what his wife sees, and she walks up to her husband to have a quiet word with him.

FARMER's WIFE
That young boy isn't with his parents. (Pause) He's with Walter.

The farmer leisurely looks and spots him, then replies.

THE FARMER
OK, he can work. We'll keep an eye on him.

The farmer walks to Guillermo and stands before him looking, but not with hostility.

THE FARMER
Have you done pickin' before son?

When he does not answer Walt reaches down and pats his shoulder for support and comfort.

Guillermo
Yes, I farmed back home.

The farmer hesitates and then nods his head. He seems to accept this and walks onward to speak to the other workers.

THE FARMER
OK then (to everyone), same work as Tuesday but at the end of the rows. I need the same rate, and I got the same pay.

The workers grab their pales and begin to walk off. Walt hands one to Guillermo and then they too walk out.

WALTER
(Quietly, only to Guillermo) It's like picking money off the vine. Just have some fun with it.

GUILLERMO
OK Mr. Walter.

INT. PICKING

They all pick in a row, several feet between each. Walt looks to Guillermo, who sees his glance and smiles back to his tall friend. Guillermo feels pride that he is good at something.

The hostile man Anthony, who picks next to Walter, sees this exchange between them and leans backward to see behind Walt's back to Guillermo. His look is not pleasant.

INT. FINISHING THE WORK FOR THE DAY

The workers wait in line and pour their buckets of produce into a bin when it's their turn.

The farmer's wife waits to the side and pays each as they step toward her.

INT. HITTING THE ROAD HOME

They walk home with Guillermo safely farther away from the road and the cars.

WALTER

See Guillermo, an honest day's pay for an honest day's work (He holds his day's money thankfully up into the air). And now back to total freedom.

Walt raises his hands and laughs a bit in mock victory. Guillermo laughs and raises his hands broadly also.

INT. RETURNING TO THE ALLEY

They arrive at the alley and Guillermo hesitates. Walt stops and turns to look back at him.

WALTER
Yes Guillermo?

GUILLERMO
I'm hungry.

WALTER
Yes, me too. Come on, I have plenty of food for now. We don't need to stop at the store tonight.

Guillermo walks immediately with him and Walt leads them back beyond where Guillermo slept the previous night, to a ground level barred window which has been pried away.

WALTER
This here is the only vandalism I've done to the place (he points at the broken concrete where the bars have been removed). But it doesn't really matter. Nobody is going to complain.

Walt couches and steps in, disappearing from view. Inside a light is lit by Walter within the darkness. Walt's head emerges with a smile.

WALTER

Home sweet home (smiles).

He tucks his head back in, and Guillermo follows using the same method of entry.

Inside, the room is vast and relatively clean. We see that Walt has lit an oil lamp, and there are lawn chairs with blankets upon them. The floor is swept and tidy.

WALTER

This is my living room. It is an abandoned tool and die shop – here one day, and gone to China the next. But it is now my home. There is a second floor – the stairs are right there (points) – and there we'll find the kitchen.

Walt lifts the oil lamp and carries it to the stairway, and Guillermo follows only mildly apprehensively behind. The audience does not feel that there is any real possibility of threat from Walter.

WALTER

And the best part, as you will see for yourself, is the warmth of God's light shining upon us.

Walt rolls his free hand upward in a gesture toward a sky light on the second floor. It illuminates the second floor quite well, and the room is cheerful.

We can see an open charcoal grill placed upon the floor with a clean rack placed upon it, ready for cooking.

WALTER

The kitchen as I promised. I do my cooking here so that the smoke and fumes can rise out of the vents above (gesturing upward again, and we see multiple vents). I think all the ventilation is because of the welding they formerly did here. But anyhow, it serves me well now. Well, what do you think? Do you like it?

GUILLERMO
I think it's a nice place to live.

WALTER
And now young man, it is time for two hard workers to relax and to eat. I'll start the fire while you fetch our water supply. There's a gray bucket near the wall where we first came in. Take it across the street to the diner and tell them that you are getting water for Walter. Be sure to say my name.

Guillermo hesitates.

WALTER
Don't be scared – they know me. I eat there sometimes.

This fact somehow reassured him and Guillermo begins to descend the stairs back to the floor on which they had first entered. He finds the clean gray bucket outside, after having exited the building just as he had entered.

Outside he carries it awkwardly. Now that he is alone and exposed outdoors, a mild fear returns to him.

He crosses the road with this same awkwardness, quite certainly a fish out of water, as he starts once, then retreats from a car, then darts safely to the far side.

Once across, the diner is directly before him and he enters and is looked upon by a man behind the counter. Guillermo sees him look down at, and recognize, the gray bucket.

                    DINER MAN
                    For Walter?

He reaches for and takes the bucket out of his hands and does not wait for an answer to his question. The man places the bucket into a deep sink behind the counter and turns on the water. He washes out the bucket once, and then fills it with cold water. He hands it back to Guillermo full with neither hostility nor perceptible kindness.

                    GUILLERMO
                    Gracias.

Guillermo walks away with the now heavy bucket. He feels much more at ease, but he is still certainly a fish out of water.

INT. RE-ENTRY

He places the bucket on the ground-level window entry, then stoops and steps inside around it. Once in he lifts it again and walks it up the stairs to Walter's grilling area.

Walter is still up there preparing. A fire of broken wood snaps and pops in the bottom of the grill. Walter places the grill over the flames as he turns and smiles to Guillermo.

                    WALTER
                    How did it go?

                    GUILLERMO
                    Fine I guess.

WALTER

Did you tell them you were there for me?

Walt sits down in his other lawn chair that he keeps on the second floor.

GUILLERMO

I forgot I guess. They knew from the bucket. A man took it and gave it back to me full.

WALT

Well mission accomplished then. There's something else you can…ARGH!!!

Walter leans forward and holds the left side of his abdomen. He does not cry out again but seems very concentrated on being silent.

GUILLERMO

Mr. Walter! Mr. Walter! Are you ok sir?

Guillermo walks and stands very near him but does not touch him or try to aid him. It is as though he is waiting for him to either recover or tell him what to do.

Walter eventually straightens and sits upright again.

WALTER

I am Ok Guillermo. Just my usual pains that come and go. I might have bent myself a few too many times today is all. But the picking season is almost done and soon I can heal while doing winter work. (Pause) There boy, put that corn and that pepper on the grill (points). We'll eat our grilled vegetables with our canned meat.

Walt lifts a can of sardines out of a box beneath his chair.

WALTER

God speaks to us all and provides what we need, if only we stop and listen. Like for us my little man. You are the best little picker I have ever seen. And I think that we make quite a wonderful team!

Walter smiles broadly and we sense his passion for his free lifetyle, and then Guillermo joins him with a joyous chuckle.

INT. DINNER

Cut to both Walter and Guillermo sitting in the lawn chairs around the dwindling fire. They appear relaxed and wholeheartedly enjoy their meal.

INT. AWAKENING

Daylight shines through the skylight as Guillermo awakes upon the floor of the second floor where they had cooked and eaten. He looks around and sees that Walter is not there.

He removes a blanket he had apparently been given and walks quietly downstairs. He sees Walter sleeping upon a hammock clipped to a support beam and the wall.

Guillermo does not wake him, but sees the gray water pale and takes a drink from it. As he does so we see that Walter begins to stir behind him.

Guillermo turns and sees this, and so, refills the drinking glass and takes it over to his friend. Walter drinks.

Guillermo
Will we walk and pick today?

245

(Pause)

WALTER

Today is a day that I will not work (stoically, sadly).

Guillermo

Your belly hurts still sir?

WALTER

No (Emphatically). (Pause) I'm not angry at you but… I cannot work today. You can work by yourself today if you want to, or you can explore the city if you're not scared. But today I need to be on my own.

Guillermo steps away confused but not distraught. He is no stranger to being shunned. He assumes that it is more of the same. He thinks then of a way that perhaps he can prove himself to his new friend.

GUILLERMO

I will pick today. Can I take your water bottle?

Walter hands him the traveling thermos they had drank from the day prior. Guillermo opens it, checks that it is empty, and then fills it with water from the pale.

He steps toward the window-exit and then turns back.

GUILLERMO

May I come back after picking today, with my money?

WALTER

Yes of course my friend. I am not angry with you. I'm glad you're here. We'll have another great evening when you get back.

(Silence). Guillermo steps again for the exit.

WALTER

Have a wonderful day my young friend. Be safe, and tonight we will have a special dinner. A celebration dinner. Good bye.

This reassures Guillermo somewhat, and he turns and exits holding only his water.

INT. ARRIVES AT FARM ALONE

Guillermo walks up the driveway alone. Once in back we walks to the group of other migrant workers. We see Anthony standing amongst the group. Anthony is not exaggerated by getting his own shot, but his dislike of Guillermo and the hostility he feels toward him can be seen plainly on his face. He hates Guillermo's disfigurement because of his own retinal abnormality.

ONE OF THE WORKERS
Alone today son?

GUILLERMO
Yes sir.

Today the farmer's wife walks out by herself. She addresses the group.

FARMER's WIFE

There will be work for you every day through the end of next Wednesday. But we need to be done by then. That means you need to finish rows 21 and 22 today to keep us on schedule. Rick's illness is back so you'll be dealing with me until then. If anyone wants extra time, just let me know and you can work it.

ANTHONY
How about extra pay for making your deadline?

247

FARMER's WIFE
Rick says you'll each get a $100 bonus if you get the crop in by end of
Wednesday. That's assuming you all do even work until then. If you
miss days or fall behind, you get less. All right, let's go.

She taps the stack of buckets that they pick into.

They each walk up and take one. Guillermo is in the middle. As he takes
his bucket…

FARMER's WIFE
What's your name? (Smiles)

GUILLERMO
Guillermo.

FARMER's WIFE
Have a good day Guillermo (pats his shoulder).

INT. PICKING IN A ROW

Guillermo fills his bucket first and walks quickly back to the motor-cart
where they set their full buckets and take a new one.

Anthony, who is still filling his first bucket, looks at him with disgust.

When Guillermo returns, smiling and feeling proud, Anthony lifts his
own mostly-full bucket and swings it forcefully into Guillermo's face as
he attempted to walk behind Anthony.

GUILLERMO
Ungg!!! (Falls to the ground and holds his head moaning).

ANTHONY

You fuckin' animal! You nearly spilled my bucket! Watch your fucking steps boy. (Pause) Do you think you can do that?

Guillermo humbly rises, and he now bleeds from his nose. He simply wipes the blood away with his hand and picks up his bucket to continue picking.

He walks to a free bush and picks through his pain and humiliation, slowly at first and then faster and faster, and faster (with anger).

GUILLERMO

(Quietly to himself) Hector I miss you brother…

INT. GETTING PAID

The workers stand in line waiting to get paid as they walk out. She hands them their day's pay in cash, and they all walk off silently.

When it is Guillermo's turn she looks at his nose and his black eye and the swelling…

FARMER's WIFE

Wait over there (points off to the side).

When she finishes paying the last worker she walks to him.

FARMER's WIFE

What happened to your face?

GUILLERMO
I fell.

FARMER's WIFE
Was it Anthony?

GUILLERMO
I fell.

FARMER's WIFE
You know Guillermo, I think that you are very smart. Where are your
parents?

GUILLERMO
(Pause…). They are back home.

She looks at his facial scarring and seems to think that she understands.

FARMER'S WIFE
You can stay in the worker's barracks through next week if you want to.
There's running water and a kitchen and a bathroom – but Anthony is
staying there too.

She waits for him to react to this last statement, but he does not.

She then points to the back of the property where two of the workers
walk toward a cabin structure. The other two have apparently departed
for town. Guillermo looks and seems to contemplate it.

GUILLERMO
No, I stay with Mr. Walter. He is my friend.

FARMER'S WIFE
(Pause…) OK. See you tomorrow, and tell Walter about the work
through Wednesday and the bonus.

GUILLERMO
Goodbye.

He walks off…

INT. ARRIVING AT THE DWELLING

Guillermo enters the old tool and die building and sees Walter sweeping and tidying up.

WALTER
Guillermo, how was your day…?

He turns to look at him and sees the bruising and swelling. He sets the broom against the wall and calmly walks toward his young friend, and sits in the chair nearest to Guillermo.

WALTER
Anthony?

GUILLERMO
Si.

WALTER
(Thinking) I shouldn't have let you go alone.

GUILLERMO
I'm ok (he holds out the pay he received for the day and smiles).

He knows that money always improves any situation.

WALTER
You are a fine young man Guillermo, but you don't have to worry about that scoundrel anymore. I promise you he won't be any more trouble.

GUILLERMO
The lady says we have to be done by nighttime next Wednesday. And we get $100 bonus each.

WALTER
Wonderful! Let's go grocery shopping (smiles).

INT. GROCERY STORE

Various shots of the odd pair placing items into their cart and enjoying
each other's company. They do not speak – it is just pure mutual fun and
enjoyment. A small shopping spree to celebrate friendship and
impending money…

INT. DINNER

Close shots of a fire and wood being thrown in. Walter sets the grill over
it and then tops it with cuts of raw beef. He also sets a can atop to warm,
but the label has been removed and we do not know what it is.

INT. EATING

Guillermo and Walter sit in their chairs with their plates upon their laps,
each cutting their beef with good silverware. The fire still smolders in
front of them.

GUILLERMO
Do you feel better tonight Walter?

WALTER
My stomach doesn't hurt. (Takes bite, swallows, pause) I used to have a
son Guillermo. (Pause) His name was Thomas. Me and his mother were
living in Denver and we were very much in love. When my son was
born - I realized many things. (Pause) Some good, some bad … some
great…

He looks to Guillermo to see if the boy understands.

WALTER

Anyhow, Thomas was involved in an accident, and my wife and I were not able to recover… Today would have been Thomas' sixth birthday. That's why I didn't with you this morning to work.

Both of them resume eating to get through the awkwardness of the moment.

GUILLERMO

My brother died…again… and my parents blamed me. I wanted badly to help him.

WALTER

(Pause)… Well sometimes I think that things just happen. The world is a big place Guillermo. God cannot always watch over it all. I'm sorry about your brother.

The fire continues to smolder and both sit in silence as the scene fades.

INT. MORNING

On this morning it is Walter who wakes first, and he shakes Guillermo who has again slept on the upper floor. Walter smiles. He seems psychologically refreshed.

WALTER

Let's have dinner tonight at the diner across the street. We'll order whatever we want. What do you say?

GUILLERMO

(Rubs his eyes) I hope they have pancakes.

WALTER

No problem (smiles). Come on, not much picking for this year now.

Guillermo rises and they both stand at the old work sink and utilize the water left in their pale for washing and preparation.

INT. ANOTHER DAY

We see them walking up the driveway together. In the back the others stand in waiting, and Walter glares at Anthony as he approaches. Anthony does not look away, but rather glares back. Only when they are very near and Walter turns around to stand and look toward the direction of the farm house does Walter look away.

INT. PICKING

We see a shot of the sun, bright and rising high into the sky. It is a hot day, symbolic of the tension that is boiling quietly. Both Walter and Anthony have stripped down to only sleeveless tee shirts on their torsos.

Walter is preoccupied and looks around at the others. He then leans over and speaks to Guillermo when the time is right.

WALTER

Go get a new bucket before that one gets too full.

GUILLERMO

It's OK, I can carry it fuller.

WALTER

No, go dump it now (stares at him).

Guillermo complies and begins to walk away with the bucket ¾ full. When he is near to the motor cart far away, Walter sets down his own bucket and walks to Anthony.

He steps up and stands four feet behind him as he picks.

WALTER

You touch that boy again and you'll have yourself a BIG problem that you've got to deal with.

ANTHONY

I like you man, but I can't see why you take care of that freak? This ain't a fuckin' sideshow.

Anthony glares at the larger Walter with his un-matching, angry eyes. Walter has spoken his mind and could turn and walk away. But something in him forbids it. There is a sense of competitive pride that prevents him from acting cautiously and wisely. He re-asserts himself for further conflict.

WALTER

No you're right fuck-stain, this isn't a sideshow. So why don't you and those mismatched eyes of yours come and convince me I'm wrong.

Anthony now fully turns and drops his bucket. His face and eyes glare with a madness that is eerily genuine. He steps heavily with clenched fists toward Walter.

They each assume a fighting stance and it is clear that both men have fought before. They both assume a right-handed boxing stance and circle naturally to their left, so therefore in unison and in a coordinated circular pattern.

Anthony strikes first but Walter evades the punch, landing a counter punch that hits Anthony in the eye.

Anthony recovers quickly and throws a right hand which Walter mostly blocks, to which Walter again counters and throws a left hook that knocks Anthony to the ground.

Anthony begins to stand and then rushes quickly to Walter, ducking under a right punch that Walter had intended to knock him out with. Instead Walter's punch sails clear over Anthony's head, and Anthony strikes him in the abdomen with a powerful right hook to the body.

WALTER
UGGGHHH!!!

Again Anthony strikes Walter's stomach as Walter steps backward and tries to put some space between them. But after the second body strike lands, Walter can only crumple to the ground and lay clutching his belly.

Guillermo runs up past the crowd which has formed.

ANTHONY
You see old man you get nothing but trouble when you mess with me.

The crowd disperses, including Anthony, and all return to picking except for Guillermo and Walter. When Walter can shakily stand, Guillermo helps him do so, and they then walk slowly to the front of the farm. Neither the farmer or his wife have seen any of this.

The farmer's wife comes out of the house as they near the driveway.

FARMER's WIFE
What happened? What's wrong?

WALTER

256

(Still uneasy) We are done here. You owe us for the morning (Speaking through his pain, trying to deal with business).

FARMER's WIFE
(Pause) OK, wait there.

She goes back in and then emerges with some cash. She hands them their portions. Walter pockets all of it for simplicity and then they walk away. No one speaks.

There are some shots of them walking home, and Walter regains some strength but holds a hand over his spleen.

INT. AT THE DINER

They sit across from one another at a table in the diner.

GUILLERMO
I'm sorry Mr. Walter, it is my fault.

WALTER
No it isn't Guillermo.

GUILLERMO
We don't have to eat here. You don't have to keep your promise. I think you should be lying in your hammock.

WALTER
That fool already spoiled our morning – he doesn't need to spoil our dinner plans too. Here have some bread.

It is subtle but Walter holds his abdomen beneath the table. The waitress brings their food: Pancakes and bacon for Guillermo and steak and eggs

257

for Walter. There is sweat upon Walter's brow and an uneasiness in his eyes.

WAITRESS
Can I get you anything else?

WALTER
No, no thank you.

He motions her away politely.

Guillermo begins to eat and Walter only sits and grimaces while holding his side. He then gets up, apparently to go the bathroom, stumbles sideways and leans awkwardly on the counter, eyes closed, sweating, moaning. Then suppressed moans of agony...

We see quick camera cuts between him clutching his side and grimacing in pain. We know that this strong man is at the limit of what he can endure.

DINER MAN
Walter? Are you alright?

Walter doesn't answer.

GUILLERMO
Walter!

The tall form of Walter crumples and lands on the tiled floor. All at once he seems to come completely apart, and his strength is gone. He can bear no more. Guillermo runs to him and pulls on his rigid arm, and Walter writhes in pain on his side.

INT. THE HOSPITAL

Walter sits in agony in a crowded ER waiting room, bent over with his eyes closed. There are many, many people around them waiting.

GUILLERMO
I will get help.

He goes to the counter to speak to the receptionist.

GUILLERMO
Please help my friend. He needs a doctor.

She looks over to Walter who seems from her angle to be sitting and waiting without a need for emergency.

RECEPTIONIST
The doctor will see him soon. I'll call him as soon as I can.

She closes the sliding window.

We see the clock stop motion to 70 minutes later, and then Walter still sitting. He faints and falls forward upon the floor.

INT. TAKEN TO A ROOM

Walter is wheeled slowly to a bed by a single orderly while Guillermo walks along worriedly behind. The muscular orderly places Walter in a bed and departs without speaking. It is as though the orderly is moving storage items into a warehouse.

A nurse then enters and begins checking his vital signs. Guillermo sits on a chair. The nurse seems somewhat concerned by a reading she gets for his blood pressure and then by his temperature, but she simply makes notes of them on a chart.

NURSE

A doctor will be in soon.

She departs. Guillermo moves his chair over so that he can sit by Walter and hold the hand of the nearly unconscious man.

GUILLERMO

If Hector were here, he would know what to do. None of this would have happened if he were here instead of me. I am cursed by the devil.

As these words are spoken the lighting of the room changes, and the air in front of the closed door of the room becomes translucent in a rectangular shape; a door to another world that is forming.

The shape of a man then steps through it, and translucent flames dance continually just behind his form. He is handsome, dark, foreboding (the dark angel from the earlier vision). His hair is perfectly combed, his complexion a perfection of paleness. And his eyes are entirely black from unblinking lid to lid. He portrays no emotion.

The dark figure steps toward Guillermo and calmly extends his hand toward him, a hand that holds a gift!

Guillermo sees that within its grasp is some object made of course material. When the hand of the dark man is fully extended, Guillermo reaches for what he is being given – for during his life he has seldom been given anything at all!

As he grasps the gift his finger momentarily touches the man's hand and triggers a vision that consumes his consciousness.

About him is hell, stone rocks and bizarre lighting, and masses and masses of tortured souls. They churn and writhe in continual agony in an endless sea of bodies, as though part of a diabolical infinite parade.

260

There are humans being consumed piece by piece by demons, males and females screaming and perpetual agony, as hundreds of mouths pierce their skin, then push further inward and consume the tissue of their inner body.

Guillermo telepathically hears a voice from the dark angel.

DARK ANGEL

Take your revenge. Take your revenge on all of mankind. Your will is their will. You can be their messiah.

Guillermo's consciousness is then returned to sitting upon the chair within that hospital room. He looks to his hands and sees that he still holds the strange, course object. As it dangles from his fingers he sees that it is a course sack which has been shaped to cover his head.

Eye and mouth holes have been perfectly cut and stitched. We see the whiteness of the floor showing through these perfect holes as it hangs from his fingertips.

The dark man is now walking back toward the translucent rectangular portal, then steps effortlessly into it, is consumed, and both man and door then disappear. The light of the room returns to normal.

Beside him Walter is still unconscious and begins to convulse. Whitish bile appears at his mouth and spills out as he shakes. Then just as quickly, he falls motionless and is perhaps finally at peace.

Guillermo slowly stands and then slowly reaches out his hand toward Walter's, and we know that he is about to bring him back. There is a slow motion effort as Guillermo begins to act, uncertain if it is the right thing to do Slowly, slowly he extends he arm…

261

A doctor enters the room suddenly followed by the same nurse. He sees Walter and rushes to him, and they work to revive the dead man. Guillermo is not able to touch him.

The doctor presses a button and soon a team bursts into the room and attempts resuscitation. When they are unsuccessful the doctor calls the time of death, and then looks over to Guillermo as though he is seeing him for the first time.

He walks over and kneels near Guillermo so that their faces are level.

DOCTOR
I'm sorry but your friend is not going to make it. Is there some family that we can call on yours or his behalf?

GUILLERMO
There is nobody.

DOCTOR
Is there someone from your family that we can call?

Guillermo does not answer.

DOCTOR
OK. We'll have a social worker come and speak with you. (To the nurse) Arrange for him to meet with an SW immediately.

NURSE
Yes doctor.

The doctor rises and exits. The nurse exits a minute after and Guillermo watches as the resuscitation team then leaves, all except for one man. This man then brings a transportation table from the hallway and transfers the body of Walter upon it. He then wheels the body from the room, and Guillermo quietly follows.

He watches as the man boards the elevator and the doors close. Guillermo sees that the elevator's numbers descend to three floors below. He then finds the stairs and runs down to that floor.

As he enters the hallway of this lower floor he sees a double doorway where the doors are still swinging to a close. He walks toward them.

When he peaks inside them he sees the man wheeling the body of Walter, speaking to another man in a white coat. The man in the white coat holds this far door open so that Walter's body can be wheeled inside.

Both men remain on the other side. The desk where the man in the white coat sat is now vacant.

 Guillermo enters this now vacant room. He peaks through the narrow glass of the door both men entered and sees that they are pushing Walter's body through another door of shiny metal. The men laugh merrily as some joke is told.

Guillermo then scrambles for a place to hide. He opens a tall cabinet door, sees several white jackets and uniforms, and steps inside and closes the door. He is able to see slightly through the crack in the door.

After a moment he hears the door open and both men apparently enter. He can see the man who moved Walter exit back out the main door, now pushing an empty gurney. He cannot see the man in the white coat but assumes he is sitting at his desk.

Guillermo looks at the mask he had been carrying. It is menacing on the outside but silky and soft on the interior. He does not put it on. Fade…

INT. ASLEEP IN A CLOSET

A noise causes Guillermo to jump awake and we see that he had fallen asleep in the cabinet. He peers through the crack of the door and we see the main door shut. We do not know if the room is empty, but all is quiet.

Guillermo takes a chance and opens the cabinet to peer out, and see that the man in the white coat is gone, his desk sits empty. He closes the cabinet and creeps up to the set of doors which Walter's body had been wheeled through. There is no one in site so he enters.

As he steps up to the metallic doors of the morgue he hears behind him the outer-most doors open and he knows that the man in the white coat now walks toward his desk.

Hastily Guillermo pulls the lever to open the metallic door of the morgue and climbs into the inward half-light of the macabre room. The temperature inside is quite cold, like opening a refrigerator.

He stands there in the dim lighting a moment listening but it seems that he had not been heard. Before him are two rows of tables arranged symmetrically against each wall so that they extend outward forming a sort of aisle between them in the middle of the room.

Guillermo studies them and sees that each body is covered by a white sheet and the feet of most are left exposed, displaying their toe-tag.

He begins to creep away from the wall, in the half-light of that cold room, and pauses just before the aisle of feet begins. He lifts the mask that he still clutched within his hands and slips it calmly over his head. We hear the crackling of the flames from the visions...

He is now a vision of horror himself, standing there like a diminutive criminal. The eyeholes align perfectly to his features. His eyes appear energized with the power of evil.

He steps between the first exposed feet and reaches both hands outward, one to each side, and sets them gently upon the cold flesh. He pauses and the reanimation process takes place, then steps decisively to the next pair and repeats the ritual.

As he steps slowly away from that second pair, the heads of the first corpse begin to sit upward, still covered by the whiteness of the sheets. It is a horrific, terrible scene. The sheet slowly falls partially from the now-animated corpse.

The slow ritual is continued as he reaches for the feet of the next body, pauses, then steps forward to the next pair. The sheet covered heads behind him continue to rise, sitting upward and then slowly swinging their feet sideways so as to stand. The corpses are indifferent to the sheets as they fall from them and land upon the floor, exposing the ashen skin of the recently reanimated (all are at least partially clothed or wearing gowns).

As Guillermo finishes the ritual upon the dead feet of the final pair, he calmly steps to the back of the room and then turns to face the walking dead. Those that he brought back first now walk the aisle toward him, ambling slowing their shuffle of death, as he calmly awaits their macabre arrival.

As the various twelve corpses gather around him, he begins to speak aloud.

GUILLERMO
Come to me. Love me. Kill for me.
(Pause)
Come to me. Love me. Kill for me.
(Pause)
Come to me. Love me. Kill for me!

This last verse is screamed with every bit of torment that is in his soul.
He hear the doors outside open and then the metallic door is opened. The
man in the white coat enters.

MAN
Hey! Who are you? What are you…?

His questioning tappers off as he struggles to realize exactly what it is
that he is witnessing. He views clearly the army of animated dead flesh.

GUILLERMO
Kill him! (His voice is now strong).

As the corpses turn to him and walk to him, we see on his face that he
comprehends that the dead are now alive. He walks backward and hits
the metallic door with his spine, realizing with horror that it has swung
closed. The man spins quickly and pulls at the handle but it is too late.
The walking corpses are upon him and pull him back into the coldness
of the room.

MAN
No! Help! Help me!

He screams as he is forced to the floor.

MAN
No………..!!!!!!

The intense motion of the multiple dead masses are upon him and
quickly extinguish his life-force.

GUILLERMO
Walter?

The tall figure of Walter turns slowly until we (the audience) can see his face of stillness and death. It is a shocking image to behold the once jovial Walter now a mindless mass of dead flesh.

He stands fully upright and walks away from the others, back to where Guillermo still stands. The tissue that was formerly Walter stands before him in obedience.

GUILLERMO
Welcome back Walter (his voice is strong hereafter).

Walter doesn't answer. But he continues to stand emotionlessly. Behind him the others see that the man in the white coat is now dead and motionless, and they straighten slowly and then stand still.

Guillermo walks around the tall form of Walter and prepares to exit the room. The others follow him, like disciples following a miniature prophet.

Walter is last, and he sees the security badge belonging to the man in the white coat, and bends down to grab it before exiting the morgue.

The metal door slams closed with an echoing diabolical sound.

The group walks out through the near doors, then the second set out into the deserted hallway. Guillermo looks for an exit sign and walks confidently toward it. (Guillermo is either shown from a distance or the mask in seen at extreme close ups to prevent him from looking less than terrifying).

There are various shots of the faces of the dead, emotionless except for a stoic sadness. They are simply walking meat without souls.

Guillermo stops at the exit door and contemplates it. He is wary of an alarm.

267

Walter steps forward and slowly, clumsily, swipes the card through the reader. The light turns green and Walter pushes it open, taking the lead.

The exit leads out to a darkened side of the hospital where there are no witnesses. They walk off silently into the darkness of the night; Walter and Guillermo at the front and all of the other eleven behind.

The long angle from above pulls back and we see that empty lots and desert are before them. We know that they will escape unseen.

INT. THE FAMER AND HIS WIFE

We see a shot from outside of the farm house through a window, as the farmer and his wife sit and relax. The audience is unaware if the group of corpses are already there. Cut to inside the home and the male farmer drinks from a tumbler, and she seems to be drinking tea. There a softly bright happiness in the room – tranquility.

The farmer wears glasses and reads from a magazine.

                    FARMER
        I think I need to switch back to the Reader's Digest.

INT. THE FARMHAND's CABIN

Inside Anthony sits at a plain table and plays cards with another migrant worker. He drinks from a beer.

                    ANTHONY
    You need to practice old man. You're lucky we play for change. The
            way you play you should just play for nothin'.

His older opponent says nothing to the young thug.

ANTHONY

You gone deaf old man?

Anthony laughs to himself and drinks heartily from his bottle.

INT. OUTSIDE

Outside we see that the group of the dead now pass by the outside of the farmer's house in the moonlight. It is a slow and patient shot, with the impending horror augmented by repetitive horror sound effect.

INT. INSIDE

The farmer looks up from his magazine as though he has heard a sound. We wait for him to rises and exit, assuming that he will be killed if he does so, but alas, he turns back to his magazine and continues to read.

INT. OUTSIDE

We see the back of the corpse's heads as they walk into the rows of bushes, into the sight of the camera and then passing out the other side of the frame. They are quite literally, death approaching. The dead walk slowly but menacingly through the rows of the field.

Cut to an overhead shot and we see that the distance to the lighted field hand's cabin is forebodingly growing smaller. Silent death approaches… slowly but intently.

INT. THE FARMHAND's CABIN

Anthony and the older man still play cards, but Anthony seems to grow distracted, agitated even. He turns and looks to the window.

MIGRANT WOMAN
Who do you wait for young man?

ANTHONY
I wait for no one. Be quiet and mind your business.

MIGRANT WOMAN
Perhaps you worry because of the tall Negro man who did not return to work.

ANTHONY
No, I'm tired of this place and all of you people. Deal.

The older man begins to deal the cards and a sound comes then from outside. The woman rises to look outward.

We see her view and there is darkness and perhaps the movement of a shadow in the moonlight. The camera then pans to the distant lights of the farmhouse.

She seems calmed by the serene beauty and the thought of the happy couple.

These scenes are a patient, buildup of horror. We know what lurks just outside in the summer night, waiting for revenge.

We see Anthony playing his game and again a sound comes louder, this time from the other side of the cabin.

MIGRANT MAN
Something's come to graze.

Anthony drops his cards face down and stands to investigate.

ANTHONY
We'll see what goes there.

It is a boring shack and a few odd sounds outside are strangely interesting. He walks to look out a window on the other side where the new sound came from. He peers out a few moments but sees nothing.

ANTHONY
Let the animals eat the berries – I don't care.

MIGRANT MAN
(With fright) Anthony…

Anthony steps down from the high screen window and turns around to see the figure of Walter now standing outside of the screen door. His image is macabre, silent, unnerving. And his eyes are white with lifelessness, as though a milky haze has covered the colored portion. This form of Walter does not immediately move.

Anthony stares at him a moment feeling oddly frightened, although he could not say for certain exactly why.

ANTHONY
What do you want? If it's more trouble you seek, then I'll give it to you.

Walter doesn't move or speak. The odd hazy whiteness of his eyes transfixes Anthony, as they peer so strangely at him through the screen.

Anthony steps a bit closer.

ANTHONY
You won't get many warnings from me old man. I think we've made it clear that I can whip your ass.

He steps a bit closer now preparing for another fight.

ANTHONY

All right Walt, we can go again. Step out onto the dirt.

Anthony now walks him down, just a bit quicker, but those dead eyes just keep staring at him through the screen door. They are so oddly milky white…

ANTHONY

I'm not having any damage to this fuckin' shack come out of my pay, now you step out onto the dirt.

Closer and closer Anthony comes, now clenching his fists and feeling unsure of just what he will do. Push him down through the screen of the door?

ANTHONY

(Now angrily) Now I told you…!

Anthony walks quickly the remainder of the distance to the door but Walter comes then suddenly to motion. His dangling arms fly up and burst through the screen door breaking it and charging through. His mouth shows a silent death-scream of ultimate evil unleashed, and he is now determined to kill this man. Somewhere, deep down, he remembers his vendetta and his hatred for the young punk.

ANTHONY

You fuckin' crazy…!

The possessed figure of Walter is now well inside and grabs at the neck of the shorter Anthony. The appearance of absolute evil is still on his face as his long fingers tighten around the man's neck.

Anthony far from done, and begins punching Walter repeatedly with mighty force upon his ribs and abdomen. He hear ribs break as the very muscular and stocky Anthony hammers away at Walter's body. When Walter does not respond to the pain a look of fear and confusion comes over Anthony who is now being pressed backward against the far wall.

The other migrant workers stand in alarm but do nothing, for they realize there is nothing which can be done.

Walter's giant hands are now firmly around Anthony's neck and begin to squeeze the life from him.

Anthony gives up trying to hurt Walter by striking his body and throws a mighty punch upon Walter's face. It lands, and turns Walter's head sideways, and we think that perhaps he will be able to fight off this corpse of animated death.

Walter's head then turns back slowly to Anthony (and the camera) and we see again those terrible white eyes. Walter lets out a deep howl as bile spills from his mouth, and renews his strangulation.

A very frightened and confused Anthony is now overwhelmed and continues to struggle to no avail. Walter collapses upon him to the ground and is now straddled over the body of Anthony, still squeezing the soon to be dead man.

MIGRANT MAN
Enough! Enough!

Walter slowly turns his head and we see again that terrible stare. All of the other workers now flee from the dwelling. Once outside they reach the dirt and turn to see the small army of corpses standing and waiting, with the masked Guillermo to their side.

They can only stare incomprehensibly, pondering momentarily what to do and what it is that they see, and then flee rapidly into the bare land in the other direction.

Guillermo lets them go.

THE FARMER
Hey! What the hell is going on here!

We see him run up behind the army of the dead and push his way unknowingly through them to the cabin. He looks to the image of Guillermo, then moves onward into the cabin.

Inside we hear him.

THE FARMER
Hey! Hey!

Guillermo turns to another man in his army.

GUILLERMO
Go kill him.

The dead man walks into the cabin stiffly and we hear shortly thereafter the farmer's futile screams for help.

THE FARMER
Hey! Who are you?! Get out of here! Hey! Get away from me!

A sound as things break and fall to the ground. Guillermo and the rest of his army stand at attention as they were.

FARMER's WIFE
Edward? (From the middle of the field) Help! Edward!

She runs up from behind just as her husband had done. She too pushes
past the standing dead, unknowingly.

THE FARMER
No! (gurgle)

We see that he too is being strangled to death by the dead hands of the
man. He continues to flail and fight because the corpse who attacks him
is smaller than the taller Walter.

FARMER's WIFE
Get off of him! Get off of him!

She runs inside and pushes the dead man off of her husband who is near
unconsciousness. The corpse falls to the side of her husband. It was the
strength of her adrenaline from her terror that was able to force him off.

She tries to lift her husband but cannot, then looks over and sees Walter
who now stands over his victim.

FARMER's WIFE
Walter? What have you done here?!

She looks then back over to the doorway as she continues to kneel over
her husband, and sees the masked Guillermo now standing just inside of
the doorway. He stares out through the sack on his head like a
diminutive demon (a horrifying sound effect as we see him standing
there, no longer outside).

The corpse that had formerly attacked her husband has now stood and is
between her and Walter on the opposite side.

FARMER's WIFE
Guillermo? Is that you? What's happening? Why? Why don't you all
help us? (Sobs) Guillermo is that you? Is that you?

GUILLERMO
Make her stop looking at me.

The corpse of the man who had attacked her husband now steps toward her and attacks. He throws her head to the ground and as she rises, the man places the palms of his hands upon her cheeks and his thumbs over her eyes. Then as she screams, the corpse pushes his thumbs into the woman's eye sockets and pops her eyeballs into her head as she screams.

She keeps screaming as the corpse drops her to the floor where she lies howling in blind pain.

Beside her the farmer has regained his senses and now sees what has happened.

FARMER
Mary! Mary!

He crawls to her and holds her face but nothing can be done. She screams on and on.

GUILLERMO
Kill him.

The corpse of Walter steps forward and easily finishes the job. When it is done he stands and waits silently like the others.

Guillermo steps to him and places his hand upon the farmer's face.

Moments later the farmer convulses twice, and then opens its eyes. He has become one of the undead, and beside him his wife screams unknowingly that this has happened.

Guillermo then looks to the corpse of Anthony, pauses, then simply stands and walks outside. It seems that his presence, even dead, is unwanted.

As they all file out, the bloody wife still screams upon the floor. She is being left as the helpless witness to a scene which no one will believe.

Outside Guillermo walks between his loyal dead, in the direction that leads him to his first home. Each of the animated dead follow him as they must.

INT. WALKING

They walk through the moonlit fields heading south, until they reach the river. When they reach it, Guillermo kneels by the edge and fills his water flask which formerly belonged to Walter. When he is finished he stands, and as though Guillermo has telepathic control over him, Walter then lifts him and places him upon his shoulders.

The pair enters the flowing water and are followed by the walking dead, one after the other until all have crossed.

INT. CAVE

Cut to bright daylight and the camera pans over the rocks and dirt until we see the opening of a cave. It creeps toward the opening. At first we see nothing but darkness, and then the horrible milky-eyed face of a corpse steps slightly into view for a shock effect (sound / cut away). We now know that they are seeking daytime refuge within a cave.

INT. TRANSITION BACK TO DUSK

Various shots of the wasteland and scorpions in the fading light. As darkness has nearly fallen, Guillermo appears suddenly from the darkness and steps out of the cave.

INT. THE VILLAGE THAT IS HOME

Dusk is now rapidly falling and we see Victor walk to the rear of his home and lean his sickle against the wall. He then turns on the spigot and begins washing his face, apparently after a long day's work. He appears tired and stone faced, and we along with him miss the secondary washing which would normally have been done by his sons.

In front of Victor we see the window where many days prior the young wife was standing topless in her room. The window is now vacant as though perhaps she has fled the melancholy village. Victor is thoroughly lost in his internal agony.

He turns off the water, dries his hands, and then takes a handkerchief out of his pocket. Methodically, he steps toward the shed, knocks, and then pulls open the door (it was propped partially open). Before stepping in, he crumples the handkerchief and holds it against his nose and mouth.

After several moments he steps out again still holding the cover to his nose.

Before the shed door is closed the camera cuts to the inside of the shed and we see the corner of the bed, and in the background we see Victor closing the door. He looks one more time to the bed and a hand is then lowered into the frame (from the bed). It is very discolored with wet holes appearing on the skin atop the forearm, and a moist rotting sagginess underneath.

Victor closes the shed from the outside and walks into his house. We know that it is where they are storing Hector.

INT. INSIDE

Inside his wife is cooking, and although melancholy, things appear oddly normal. Perhaps if we the audience did not know better, we would assume it was just a bad day.

As Victor prepares for dinner she sets a coffee next to him and then silently returns to cooking.

MOTHER
How was he?

VICTOR
How do you think?

He lifts his coffee but does not yet sip it.

MOTHER
Do you think it's time for a fire?

Victor slams his coffee on the table spilling it and walks from the room.

MOTHER
(Sobbing) It worked for Andres and Maria… (Breaks out into outright weeping as her voice trails off)…. I just think that maybe it's time…
(Crying).

There are many moments of her holding her hand to her face with her elbow on the counter.

INT. INSIDE ANDRES AND MARIA's HOUSE

Andres is changing out of his work clothes while Maria smokes a cigarette. There is a great unspoken tension.

MARIA
The crops?

ANDRES
They are fine.

MARIA
I can't stay here anymore.

ANDRES
It is our home. It is my livelihood.

He sits down in his fresh clothes.

ANDRES
If I could be gone, I would be gone already.

MARIA
After the harvest then. We start new. (Pause) Or I leave on my own.

She looks to her husband with wet eyes.

ANDRES
I have given a good deal of thought to walking out into the desert at night and slitting my wrists. I am not sure why I have not done it. (Pause) Alright two weeks, then to market, and then we drive to your sister's.

She nods and looks at the floor, and then walks out of the room to their bed. He remains on the couch.

INT. OUTSIDE AFTER DARK

We see Andres and Maria's house from a low angle outside in the darkness. The unsteady and shambling legs of one of the walking dead then enters the frame and stops to stare at the house.

INT. INSIDE

We see Maria fold down her bed sheets. She is beautiful despite her sadness.

Outside there is a knock, then a creaking as though a shed door has been opened. Maria freezes and looks out to where Andres sits.

Another sound then is heard.

                    MARIA
                    Andres?

He steps up to the doorway.

                    ANDRES
                    Did you hear?

                    ANDRES
                    Hear what?

                    MARIA
                Someone has opened his shed.

                    ANDRES
        (PAUSE) he (Pedro) is gone Maria. You know that…

Another sound comes and this time he hears it. He looks away and then steps to exit the house.

ANDRES
It is only Victor.

But he is now curious as well, feeling perhaps the same desperate hope that his wife feels, that somehow the conscious-dead son that he incinerated in a fire has somehow returned.

He opens the door and steps out into the darkness. We see him pause and look around into the darkness, and then see the shed door which swings gently in the breeze.

Andres reaches back inside of the house to grab a flashlight and then walks with uncertainty to the opened shed. (We see his POV). His face shows a strange apprehension.

He opens the flapping door fully and shines the interior, and we see an empty bed with discolored sheets, and Andres then pauses and we know that he thinks of his son.

At last he closes the door, but before he can latch it three of the corpses encircle him, and his back is to the shed.

ANDRES
What! Who are you?

But this is all he has time to say. One of the dead smashes his head with a rock and his body falls to the dirt.

Inside we see Maria Sitting up in her bed and listening.

Outside we see a low shot of the semi-conscious Andres who is blooding and struggling to speak. The discolored legs of the three dead can be seen encircling him.

Cut to Guillermo standing back in the darkness with the other corpses. All of them appear more rotten, and their eyes more whitish.

GUILLERMO
Finish him!

We see the horrible face of one of the dead, and then the handheld camera pans down and we see that the unsteady corpse hold a bricklaying trowel. The shaky camera shot shows the horror of the corpse's face while it raises the trowel and moves slowly forward to kill Andres.

We see the trowel drive into his belly beneath his ribs. The legs of the other corpses stand dumbly in place.

ANDRES
Arghhh!

The trowel pierces him again and again, intermingled with shots of that horrible dead face. At last he mercifully dies.

GUILLERMO
Bring him.

We see the corpses lift his body and carry into the darkness.

Inside Maria throws her legs over onto the bed.

MARIA
Andres?

There is a bit of fear now in her voice, or perhaps it is only uncertainty. But regardless something new has replaced the awful melancholy which alone had resided.

We see the blood trail and the final images of the dead carrying Andres' body disappear off into the blanket of darkness.

Maria leaves her bedroom and walks into the room which is essentially the rest of their poor house. She wears only night clothing, and steps hesitantly to the door to look out.

MARIA

Andres come in now.

She turns on a bright outdoor light. She sees a wetness in the dirt and footprints, but does not comprehend what they are. She steps outward hesitantly but instinctively knows that she does not want to touch the wetness. Instead she looks around, and is visibly distraught. She senses that something is not right.

The still-open shed door then becomes her focus.

MARIA

Andres? (Pause, creeps closer) Hector? (Pause) Hector if you have come over here please speak to me.

She creeps close to the shed and the open door, growing more and more frightened.

MARIA

Hector I miss Pedro very much too. (Tears well up in her eyes, but the sadness does not outweigh the uneasiness of the fear). He is gone now, but you can stay here as long as wish. Your Papa has said that it must be so.

She is now very close. She reaches out and pulls the door open…. And we see from the bright outdoor light that there is no one inside. Only the remnants of he lost son.

She pauses a moment and then closes the door. We sense that it is symbolic, that she truly needs to close the door and move on in her life.

And as she turns to re-enter her house something in the darkness catches her eye. It was just a white blur and we see it too. She stops and then steps toward the darkness, uncertain what she had seen.

A step closer and we can just begin to see the form of a corpse perhaps, it is nearly too black to tell.

The she steps again closer and now there is no doubt that a body does stand there.

MARIA
Hector?

She stares and inches closer. And then it comes into view and we just as Maria does, see that it is a horrible dead face with rotten eyes, although not the image of Hector, but a different full grown man.

She trips and falls into the dirt, or perhaps her knees gave out as she tried to turn. But the effect is the same and now she is frozen with fear as the dead flesh walk from the shadows and surround her, closing in from above with outstretched hands.

MARIA
No! No!

We see from her POV as all those dead faces and white eyes enclose and reach down to her, smothering out the blackness of the night.

As she is covered she screams a scream that pierces the still of the night and echoes over the desert land.

INT. INSIDE WITH VICTOR AND GUILLERMO's MOTHER

Victor straightens on the couch as he hears the scream. His wife erupts from the bedroom and they look to each other in concern before Victor stands.

Both of them step out of their poor house, into the night. Victor looks about briefly and then takes out his handkerchief.

                         VICTOR
                        Stay back.

He opens the shed just enough and pokes his head inside. He then withdraws immediately and closes it again.
                         VICTOR
     He is there. (He looks toward Andres' house) Go back inside, I'll go
                        check on them.

                         MOTHER
       It is outsiders. They have come to burn this terrible place.

                         VICTOR
                        Go inside.

He leaves her standing as she was and walks off into the darkness between the homes. His movements contain a cautiousness which he is unaware of. It is as though he senses that something is amiss.

He arrives at Andre's and Maria's and steps into the bright outdoor lighting that has been left on. He sees only the wetness of the blood on

the dirt, and then looks to the screen door of the house and the lights that
are on inside.

VICTOR

Andres? (Pause) Maria?

He turns and walks to the blood, squats down and then touches it. When
he holds his fingers up before him we see the redness upon them.

He stands and wipes then on his pants as he looks off into the darkness
about him. He then looks to the house and sees the bloody footprints on
the steps leading inside. Some sense of greater precaution is triggered
within him – he is now fully on guard.

VICTOR

Andres, are you injured?

We see from inside the house and through the screen door as Victor
walks up the steps and looks inward.

The camera pulls back and we see the bloody footprints in a trail upon
the white floor.

Victor is many things but not a coward. He opens the screen door and
walks in.

VICTOR

Andres? (Pause) Maria?

When they do not answer he steps forward and begins to follow the
footprints. We see intermingled shots of his face and then his feet as he
walks along the blood upon the floor. Back and forth, back and forth –
they are somehow intertwined.

He nears the end of the room, about to pass into the bedroom. Tension builds with sound.

The bedroom is now dark, and he steps to the doorframe. He reaches a hand in, and turns on the light.

We see a man standing with his back to Victor, at the far side of the bedroom. He stands motionless and seems to be looking out the window into the dark.

VICTOR
Andres…?

He takes a small, cautious, step closer to this form of a man who will not look at him.

INT. WALKING THE PERIMETER

We cut to a long shot of Maria still standing outdoors in the light outside of her home. She waits for Victor to return.

As we watch her like a peeping Tom from a distance, the images of two of the corpses then pass before the camera. They block our view of the unaware Maria who still stands and waits as they pass.

When the corpses are gone from our field of vision, they have passed to the side that would be *behind* Victor's wife as she stands and waits.

INT. BACK IN MARIA AND ANDRES BEDROOM

The dark haired man still stands motionless with his back to Victor. Victor takes a slow step forward.

VICTOR

Who are you? (With anger)

He steps forward again, and still the figure does not move. He is so
dreadfully still…

We see shots of Victor's feet slowly coming forward, then cut back to
Victor's face, and then to the motionless man. Tension builds further…

VICTOR

(Vocally angry) Who are you!?

More footsteps and cuts – tension builds… They grow close together
now. They are not far apart.

VICTOR

Answer!

This yell seems to awaken the man, and he begins to turn. His body
moves with such a non-coordinated motion… Slowly he comes around.
First the feet, then the torso begins to turn, and then at last the head
swivels…

We see the look of death in the eyes of this macabre figure. Their
whiteness almost shines upon a face that displays only the stillness of
rigor mortis. They do not blink and only stare.

VICTOR

Good God almighty!

The silent corpse continues its stare of death.

INT. THE TRUCK

We see Victor's truck parked in the darkness and the two corpses approach it. One still holds the trowel and the other bends awkwardly and then straightens, now holding a rock.

Both masses of dead flesh approach the vehicle. We see the trowel stab a tire, then a hand with a rock smash a headlight.

Cut to a reactionary shot of Maria as she hears it.

Then a longer shot as another tire is stabbed and the other headlight is smashed.

INT. BACK TO VICTOR AND THE CORPSE

We see the corpse still standing motionless, but still facing Victor.

VICTOR
(Still angry) Where is that boy? I have unfinished business with him. I curse the day his ugly face was birthed!

Upon hearing this, the corpse seems to answer some call which draws motion into its limbs, and purpose into its being. The hands begin to come up and it takes a step forward.

VICTOR
Yes, come dead man. Come for me.

Victor raises his fists and takes a fighting stance. He is an image of a hero that could have been, if only the circumstances of life had been different.

We see his muscles bulge and the strength in his face, and we know that he could have been a war hero or a president or a prince, if only the circumstances had been different…

The corpse then begins to display rage, perhaps telepathically guided by Guillermo. It begins to release a slow hiss-growl from its open mouth and continues its forward motion toward the unyielding Victor.

VICTOR
Can you hear me through this thing Guillermo? Is it your puppet to control?

The groaning corpse moves forward, as Victor steps slowly back, though not out of fear. He is like a fighter in the ring, drawing his opponent onward.

VICTOR
Come Guillermo, give me your best shot puppet-man. Come kill me you cowardly freak of a disappointment!!!

Just as these words are spoken the corpse lunges forward, reminiscent of Walter ascending upon Anthony.

But Victor strikes him squarely on the chin with a powerful punch, then again with the left, then again with a powerful right.

The creature does not flinch or retreat but the jaw breaks and begins to shift sideways with each right hand that lands. We hear it break and then break again, and soon the face does not look like a face, but the creature continues to move forward.

Victor lands one more powerful right handed punch and the jawbone is now below one ear, and the flesh is torn wide open.

Victor breaths heavily. No blood erupts from the massive gash upon the dead man. Victor then suddenly realizes the horror of this fact, and his former berserker rage seems to be suddenly replaced by new fear.

He begins to retreat from the hideous thing that still presses forward toward him. He turns and flees from the house.

INT. VICTOR RETURNS

Victor is seen running quickly back to the exterior of his own house where his wife still waits and worries.

VICTOR
(Breathlessly) They are dead. I fought a walking dead man within their house. (Gasping) We must flee now.

He then realizes that he cannot start his car.

VICTOR
My keys!

Behind them one of the dead steps into view from around the house and it is Maria who sees it first. Victor then turns.

It steps around the house and we see the horror of its milky white eyes. Then they hear another sound in another direction and turn to see that the walking dead are surrounding them, lumbering out in all directions and encircling them from all angles of the darkness.

His wife instinctively clings to Victor, but Victor assumes a fighting stance. He pushes his wife toward the house and grabs his scythe from where he had set it when he had finished working.

The walking dead walk them down from all angles, growing closer and closer.

VICTOR
Guillermo! You little demon! Tonight you die! (We do not see Guillermo, he is presumably hiding in the darkness).

Victor turns rapidly in all directions, holding his scythe before his ready to strike. Around and around and around. This man is a fighter!

He sizes up the dead men and women and then strikes! With one massive blow he slices completely through the neck of the nearest corpse, leaving it standing with the arms still outstretched before it crumples moments later.

He turns again and looks for another to strike. Perhaps we see long angles also to emphasize just how surrounded they are.

Then we see a new angle as the man who put out the eyes of the farmer's wife creeps toward the wife of Victor who still crouches with fear low to the ground. This corpse has her in his sights and we the audience know that he aims to kill her just as he did the farmer's wife.

Cut back to Victor who slices another corpse, and then another. Victor screams with premature victory and is growing more and more confident.

This battle is for him, a greatly cathartic release of the tremendous stress of the past several weeks.

Cut back to the man who stalks Victor's wife and now she sees him.

MOTHER
Arghhhh…!

Victor sees but cannot immediately help. Victor instead continues his vigorous turning and decapitates another corpse and then another. He is nearly victorious!

Only the corpse of Walter, and the corpse with the broken jaw who has now found them, are standing. And Walter is still further back, as though he is first in command under the still hidden Guillermo.

We see the corpse now fully atop Victor's wife and she screams as the palms are set against her cheeks and the rotting thumbs are lain over her eyes.

Victor then slices through the second to last standing corpse with the broken jaw, and then runs to his wife's aid.

We see the thumbs begin to press with force upon her eyes and Maria screams. Cut to the rotting face of the dead man as he straddles her. It is as though we are watching the beginning of some particularly disturbing rape.

Again we see the thumbs press and nearly pierce her eyeballs.

Victor reaches them and slices from the bridge of the dead man's nose clean through the back of his head. The top of the head falls away and the rotten brain can be seen, sitting partially within the open cranium of the man's head. He then falls away to the ground and Maria is momentarily safe, eyes intact we assume.

As Victor then turns one final time, he is immediately grabbed at both the hand that holds his weapon and around his neck. Walter has gotten him. Saving his wife has cost him his own life.

Walter squeezes both Victor's scythe holding hand and his neck, and lifts the shorter Victor from the ground.

His large hand is able to take the weapon from Victor and now Walter lifts it high into the air with his right hand as Victor's limbs flail and grope at Walter's large hand that squeezes the death-hold upon his neck.

Walter hesitates and we are momentarily unsure if he will kill him. Then Walter slices downward and severs the left arm of Victor which had wielded the scythe.

The dismembered limb falls to the ground and now the even more helpless Victor gurgles but continues to struggle.

Walter then slices downward with the scythe again and again, cutting into Victor's torso upon his side above the ribs. Each is deeper and deeper until he cuts completely through and the hips and legs of Victor fall to the ground.

Walter tosses what remains of Victor to the ground, and takes a step to Maria. He is now covered in blood, and a vision of pure horror.

Maria screams with complete and utter terror.

The shed door then creaks open and Hector steps into view. He is badly decomposed, almost unrecognizable.

Walter freezes, perhaps from hypnotic control from the hidden Guillermo who is now shocked by his brother's appearance.

Hector steps slowly down to the earth and walks a few steps outward.

HECTOR

Guillermo… (his voice is distorted from decomposition). Guillermo… where are you?

Guillermo then steps from the darkness and we see his form come into view. He stops and hesitates.

HECTOR

Come here my brother.

Guillermo is struck by the vision of his beloved brother, the only person in the world who had loved him and treated him as an equal. He complies and walks to stand between the frozen figure of Walter and his dead brother.

HECTOR

Let me die Guillermo… And let our mother live….

Behind Guillermo Walter clenches the handle of the scythe and begins to creep up behind his hooded master.

HECTOR

You have had your revenge upon Papa and the others.

Walter creeps forward. Guillermo can be seen contemplating behind the coarseness of the mask.

HECTOR

I want rest… Free my soul…

There is a sound then from Walter's footstep and Guillermo turns abruptly.

Guillermo sees that Walter has raised the weapon and intends to strike him, and we see then a return of ultimate evil rage upon Guillermo's masked face (we see his eyes and mouth, and perhaps, he screams with rage).

Walter then draws the scythe downward with extreme force, slicing audibly through the air, and then cleanly through Guillermo's neck.

His masked head falls to the ground and we see the eyes and mouth through the enchanted and evil mask which was a gift from Satan. His body falls quickly thereafter, landing partially in the frame.

We then see a longer shot of both the standing corpses of Hector and Walter and a wispy, translucent emission from the tops of their bodies. We watch as their souls are freed from their rotting prisons, and dissipate upwards into the air.

Their bodies then crumple to the ground and are mercifully now simply dead tissue as they should have been long ago. The order of nature is restored.

Guillermo and Hector's mother screams with despair and there is a look of insanity within her eyes. She cannot fully comprehend what she has seen, or understand why she has been punished so.

She wails as no human has ever wailed before as she writhes around upon her hands in the dirt, and looks upward into the darkness of night.

The camera pulls back and we see the carnage of more than a dozen bodies.

Their mother screams continually.

Music begins: "Obey me, Love me, kill for me…"

Cut to black, credits begin….

THE END